D0582044

This edition, issued in 1962, is for members of The Companion Book Club, 8 Long Acre, London, W.C.99, from which address particulars of membership may be obtained. The book is issued by arrangement with the original publishers, George G. Harrap & Co. Ltd.

CATTLEMAN

"A blessed companion is a book"—JERROLD

CATTLEMAN

*

R. S. PORTEOUS

THE COMPANION BOOK CLUB
LONDON

Made and printed in Great Britain
for The Companion Book Club (Odhams Press Ltd.)
by Odhams (Watford) Limited
Watford, Herts

S.562.V.RA.

To my daughter SUE
whose boundless enthusiasm severely
retarded the progress of this book

★ I ★

THE plump little nurse said, "Your medicine, Mr McReady."

She said it rather timidly, unsure how her patient would react, unsure of the attitude she should adopt should he refuse to swallow the medicine. This forthright old man did not conform to any of the standards of behaviour she had come to expect from her somewhat limited experience of patients.

"What's that?" Ben McReady's eyelids fluttered, and from beneath shaggy white eyebrows a pair of surprisingly blue and clear eyes glared fiercely. "What do you want to do, girl? Rot me blasted guts! Take the flamin' stuff away."

"It'll do you good." The attempt to sound professionally competent was pathetically weak. "Matron says——"

"Matron says! What the hell do I care what Matron says? If it's so good take it downstairs and tell her to swallow it herself."

The enormity of the suggestion shocked her into temporary silence, and when she spoke again her voice was definitely pleading. "Mr McReady, if you don't drink it I'll get into trouble."

"You will, eh? What *is* this joint anyway? A blasted concentration camp?" Old Ben McReady hoisted himself awkwardly on to one elbow and stretched out an enormous hand. "Here, gimme the stuff. A man can only die once and he might as well finish himself off this way as any other." The medicine went down in one distasteful gulp and he shuddered. "That damned rot-gut do a man good! Do you know what would do me some real good, nurse? A big, stiff nip of overproof rum. That's what I need."

The little nurse took the empty glass and turned away. Being naturally shy she would have escaped in silence, but her short period of training prompted her to have the last word. With the safety of the passage-way only one short step away she half turned her head and said:

"Now, Mr McReady, please don't start that again."

At any other time old Ben would have shouted his defiance after her, but now he was too tired, content to lie back with eyes closed and leave the last word to a girl scarcely as old as his granddaughter. The poor kid wouldn't have any say in the matter anyway. Nor was it any good reopening it with the grim-lipped Matron who looked as though she'd never had a decent drink in her life. No matter. Doc Stuart would put her in her place when he came along shortly. A fine old chap, Doc. One of the old brigade, one who liked his drop of grog and could appreciate the needs of his fellow men.

When he opened his eyes again Doctor Stuart was standing beside him, one hand resting lightly on his wrist. Behind him, stiff in her starched efficiency, stood Matron Parker.

"And how's the big beef baron this morning?" the doctor asked cheerfully. "Still growling?" His hair was as white as his patient's, his cheeks were pink, and there was a perpetual twinkle in his eyes.

"What else d'you expect a man to do?" Ben's white eyebrows came down in a scowl. "Look, Doc, if you want to finish a man off in a hurry you're goin' the right way about it. How would you like to be stuck in this joint, fed on slops, takin' orders from a pack of women, and not a damn thing to drink except water and some foul muck that tastes like rat-poison? Even the blasted bed's about a foot too short. Look at me feet! Stickin' away out over the end."

"He keeps slipping down, Doctor," Matron explained, with well-controlled patience. "It takes two of the nurses to lift him back, and as soon as they leave the room he's down again."

"It's the way he's built, Matron," Dr Stuart told her. "They make beds to accommodate people up to six feet long. The ones like McReady, with a couple of extra inches, just have to lap over. I wouldn't take too much notice of his growls on that score. I imagine he's used to it."

"Well, he's not used to goin' without a drink," old Ben put in. "A man's not a bloody camel, Doc."

"I suppose there *is* a danger of a prolonged drought causing a shock to your system, Ben." Dr Stuart chuckled and turned to Matron. "We'll let him have half an ounce of whisky before lunch and another half ounce before his evening meal."

"For God's sake, Doc!" Horrified indignation showed on the patient's weathered face. "Are you goin' to start weighin' the bloody stuff on scales?"

"A half fluid ounce," Dr Stuart explained, "is about the size of an ordinary nip. That satisfy you, Ben?"

Without hesitation Ben said, "Raise it to one ounce a time and change it to rum and we'll call it a deal." He must have sensed victory because he added quickly, "And chuck in one extra for a nightcap."

"Make a note of it, will you, Matron?" the doctor asked. "He may have one ounce of spirits before lunch and one before the evening meal. I know he has his favourite brand, so his family can get it for him and hand the bottle over to you. The nightcap will be a cup of warm milk." Forestalling further protests he explained, "We've got to try to patch you up and get you on your feet again. See that new colt of yours win a few races, eh?"

In the passage-way, safely out of Ben's hearing, Matron said, "He *is* a difficult patient, doctor. You've no idea how he kicks against hospital routine."

"He can afford to be difficult." Dr Stuart pulled his waistcoat an inch or two lower over a prosperous-looking belly and smiled. "If I had half his money I'd be inclined to make a nuisance of myself, just to remind people who I was. Did you see what he paid for that colt I spoke to him about? Five thousand guineas. It's in this morning's paper. Imagine paying five thousand guineas for a horse, Matron!"

"I can't." She rustled through some papers to bring his mind back to the job. "About visitors? Are you restricting them to his immediate family?"

"Heavens, no! He wouldn't stand for that sort of treatment. Let him see anyone he wants to see. And don't worry about any of them tiring him by staying too long. When he's tired of them he'll very smartly tell them to get out."

Ben's first visitor was Mrs Gregory Arnedale, ushered in

by no less a person that Matron herself. Beyond the fact that he was one of Central Queensland's well-known graziers, Matron knew very little about Ben McReady, but she knew a great deal about Mrs Gregory Arnedale. This tall, elegantly groomed woman figured prominently in the social pages of all the Queensland papers. Here, in Stonehaven, she was the unchallenged leader of society. If she approved of you you were "in", if she disapproved you had no hope of being accepted, no matter how your backers pressed your case. She had well-preserved looks, great charm of manner when she chose to exert it, and a terrifying dignity when she felt the occasion demanded it. Obviously she was wealthy. Her sleek Bentley, her clothes, and the lavish way she entertained all proved that.

"A visitor for you, Mr McReady," Matron announced. Her tone and the smile that softened her usually grim mouth said, a very special visitor. Being a comparative newcomer to Stonehaven she was unaware of the relationship between her patient and his distinguished visitor.

Old Ben opened his eyes and said, "Hello, Anthea. What the devil brings you along?"

"Father!" There was a touch of reproof in Mrs Arnedale's well-modulated voice, and even in that one word the accent was noticeable, an accent fostered in the exclusive school she had attended, and carefully preserved until it was as much a part of her as the slightly hooked nose she had inherited from her father.

"I came as soon as I heard you were in hospital. Really, I do think you might have told me you were ill instead of letting me hear it in round-the-town gossip."

"I thought you didn't listen to gossip."

"I don't. As a matter of fact Gregory heard it at the Club—from your doctor. Rather humiliating for Gregory to learn about his father-in-law's illness from an outsider, particularly as he has always regarded old Dr Stuart as hopelessly incompetent and out of date."

"Now ain't that just too bloody bad for poor Gregory? And what the blazes am I supposed to do about it? Give 'im three days' notice in writin' that I'm feelin' a bit crook?"

"Father, please! Must you talk in that crude way every time you're feeling a bit annoyed?"

"I'll talk how I bloody well like. At least, I don't go bungin' on that la-di-dah accent you cultivate, me girl."

"No, you 'bung-on,' as you term it, the crude vernacular of one of your own stockmen. You love to try to make people think you're the big, uneducated self-made man. It's your favourite pose, particularly when you want to annoy some one, your own special form of vanity."

"All right, Anthea. Let's say it amuses me and leave it at that, eh? You didn't come here to argue with me and find fault, I'm sure." Ben's eyelids drooped wearily, but after a moment he raised one and asked, "Why *did* you come?"

"Don't you think it's natural for a daughter to want to visit her father as soon as she hears he's ill?"

"For some daughters, yes. But you, Anthea, have a habit of only showing up when you want something." The eyelid came down again and Ben sighed. "Ah, well, I daresay you'll work around to telling me before you leave."

Anthea Arnedale prided herself on her self-control. Very few people tried to irritate her, and none of them had had the satisfaction of knowing they had succeeded. Instead of flaring up and denying the charge she smiled sweetly and said, "Actually, my dear, cynical parent, I came to see if there was anything you needed. People do that for relations and friends, you know. I don't think you've ever been in hospital before, but I have and I know how utterly dependent you are on your friends and relatives for all the little extras. There's no slipping out for a packet of cigarettes or notepaper or the shaving things you've forgotten to bring."

"By cripes, that reminds me!" Ben was suddenly wide awake and alert. He even attempted to heave himself into a sitting position, but finding the effort too great he relaxed and concentrated on more important business. "There *is* something I need. As soon as you leave here I want you to slip around to Paton's and get me a bottle of rum. Charge it to my account. They know the brand, but tell them to make sure it's O.P. Don't let 'em foist that wishy-washy, broken-down stuff off on you. And never mind raising your eyebrows.

It's doctor's orders. You can deliver the bottle to Matron when you get back. Save you climbing the stairs again."

"Couldn't Paton's deliver it?"

"They could, but they mightn't get it here till late this afternoon and I want a nip before lunch."

"I see. Anything else you want?"

"No, thanks, Anthea. How's Greg?"

"He's fairly well, Father. He works too hard and worries too much over the business, but otherwise he's reasonably fit."

"Blasted rot!" Ben snapped irritably. "Any man who spends one day a week playin' golf and another playin' bowls ain't workin' too hard. He's not working hard enough."

Anthea's smile was sweetly forgiving as she said, "Don't upset yourself, Father dear. I'm sure it must be bad for you. You know very well that Gregory's golf and bowls are only half-days. And you never seem to appreciate the fact that, apart from the valuable business contacts they make there, men need a little relaxation if they're to keep up with the terrific pressure of modern business. Your money was made so much more easily than a city man's and, apart from an occasional drought, I don't suppose you have ever been faced with serious business problems in your life. Anyway, Gregory is coming along to see you tonight, so please be nice to him."

"Coming to see me! Now what the devil does he want?"

"Must you always be so mercenary in your outlook, Father? Gregory doesn't want anything. When he told me you were in hospital he was most concerned about you. He said, 'I must slip along tonight and try to cheer the poor old chap up a bit.'"

"Like hell he did! More likely he said, 'I'd better go along and see what I can get out of the old cow before he kicks the bucket.'"

Anthea stood up and ran a smoothing hand over her frock. "I think, Father, dear," she said, "I'd better go and get your rum. It might put you in a better frame of mind." She took the morning paper from his bedside table, turned the first few pages, and remarked with apparent casualness, "I haven't had time to read this yet. Some one mentioned that you'd bought a new Sydney-bred colt. Is it true?"

"Quite true, my dear. And the price, in case your 'some one' forgot to mention it, was five thousand guineas." Ben's big shoulders shook as he chuckled quietly. "You know, Anthea, I thought you'd get around to it before you left."

For the first time Anthea allowed her annoyance to show. With just a trace of heat she said, "Well, you must admit it *is* a ridiculous waste of money. Paying all that for a horse you may never see race."

"I'm not quite dead yet, Anthea."

"I'm not suggesting you are. But really, Father, you might show some consideration for your family. You know perfectly well that Gregory and I could have put the money to much better use. And we really need it at the moment."

"I'll bet you do. I've never known the time when you two didn't need more money. I suppose young Ben's still chucking it around like a mad blackfellow?"

"He spends no more than the average student. It's the fees and travelling expenses that run away with the money. You should know that. And fees have more than doubled since you sent us to school."

"All the more reason for you and Greg to make your son understand he's got to settle down to hard study. At the rate he's going it'll be another ten years before he's a doctor—that's if he ever gets through."

"He failed last year, but so did a number of others. The papers were——"

"Never mind how stiff the papers were; that's always the excuse. What if he flops next year, and the year after? Ever ask yourself that, Anthea? What would happen if I kicked the bucket tomorrow and you found I hadn't left you two bob? How long could you and Greg afford to keep him at the university?"

Anthea was far too clever to be drawn into that discussion. Instead of answering the question she said, "Jane sent her love to you. She's coming to see you this afternoon."

"Is she, by crikey?" Ben's deliberately annoying mood vanished and his lined old face reflected his pleasure. "Now there's a fine girl for you, Anthea. Hanged if I know how you and Greg managed to have such a daughter. Throws right back to her grandmother."

"I don't agree with you, Father. No one could have called Mother obstinate. She was too gentle, too thoughtful of others. But Jane is downright pigheaded. She not only takes after you in that way, but you encourage her. I'm doing my best to see that she meets all the right people so that she'll make a suitable marriage, and you are always doing *your* best to ruin her chances by inviting her up to the station where she goes about, mixing with the stockmen, and even dressing like one of them. How would you feel if she ended up marrying some rough bush type?"

"She could do worse."

"I don't agree. And I think I should tell you that Gregory and I both feel you are mainly responsible for the child's outlook."

"I'm glad I've been able to be of some help." The annoying, provocative tone was back again.

"Really, Father, you're quite impossible. I know it's useless to argue with you when you're in one of those moods, but since the child obviously dotes on you I do think it's up to you to use your influence with her and make her see that her mother knows best."

Ben considered the statement for a few moments before saying, "The trouble is, Anthea, that in this case I'm not too sure her mother does know best."

Anthea bent and kissed him lightly on the forehead. Neither arguments nor persuasion could lead anywhere while this mood persisted. "It's after eleven, Father," she said brightly. "If I don't hurry round to Paton's and get your rum you won't have your nip before lunch."

★ 2 ★

LYING there with his eyes closed, Ben wondered whether his suggestion of leaving her out of his will really had thrown a scare into his daughter. You never could tell with Anthea. She believed what she wanted to believe and conveniently shut her eyes to things she might regard as unpleasant. "Humiliating" was her word. It would be humiliating for her to have to admit that he had started from scratch, or actually a few lengths behind scratch. Did she honestly believe she was speaking the truth when she said his money had been made easily and that he'd never been faced with serious business problems? That story she was so fond of telling about him leaving the family property in Victoria—"the Western District McReadys, you know"—with a mob of cattle to start the now famous Wavering Downs! Probably she had told it so often she had convinced herself of its truth.

Ben didn't know. She had never been very close to him, even as a child, but though he had never talked to her of her past she must have heard a great deal of it from her mother. Anne had never tried to conceal their humble start with its hardships and struggles. In fact, in her frank, humour-loving way, she had been fond of recalling the crude toughness of their first years together.

But Anne didn't know everything, thank God. There was one side of his early life he had always kept hidden from her, something that would have hurt her deeply and might even have wrecked their marriage. A woman less loyal and less honest must have suspected, but it was not in her nature to suspect anyone she was fond of. Nothing short of his own confession would have convinced her that her husband was a cattle-duffer, and he saw no reason why he should hurt her by making that confession.

In matters concerning his parents and his early childhood he had been completely honest with her. Quite apart from the fact that she would have seen through the deception immediately, he had never attempted to claim relationship with the wealthy, pastoral McReadys of Victoria.

"Never even 'eard of 'em," he had answered with a wide grin the day she asked him if he were related to the famous grazing family. "I come from Victoria, but me dad never 'ad more than the price of the next feed. Sometimes 'e didn't 'ave that."

Looking back on his childhood now he could not picture either of his parents. He had left home when he was thirteen, a ragged, half-starved kid, scarcely able to read or scrawl a few simple words. Dan Clancy had not been worried about his lack of education. All he had wanted was a spare boy to help him take his droving plant back to Queensland, and the only qualifications he demanded were the ability to ride a quiet horse and the guts to learn to ride a rough one.

Well, he had picked the right boy. Within three years Dan was backing Ben to ride anything with hair on. And backing him with big money, too. Good old Dan! Ben could still see him clearly. Long, lean, and gangling, his white moleskins wrinkled down over the tops of his spurred boots, he always looked sloppy and awkward on foot. But once he swung into the saddle he became part of the horse. No longer awkward, he looked at home there, whether his mount was a quiet old nag cropping its way along behind a mob of feeding cattle, or a wild-eyed colt bucking with an explosive hatred of all horsemen. Dan Clancy, with his sandy hair, enormous freckles, and drooping, tobacco-stained ginger moustache. Dan had taught him all he knew about bushmanship, horses, cattle, and duffing.

And Dan was a master of all of them. He could find his way anywhere, read every sign on trackless ghibber plains, rough mountain ranges, or in the densest brigalow scrub. His memory for places was photographic. It was the same with horses or cattle—once seen never forgotten. When it came to duffing he had few equals. A faint or blotched brand he regarded as a challenge to his artistry, a cleanskin a direct invitation. Squatting on his heels in front of the camp-fire, long, freckled arms hanging loosely over his knees, he used to drawl, "If the owners don't brand 'em it shows they don't want 'em."

Six years he had spent droving with Dan, until he knew every water-hole in every creek on the stock-routes of Queensland. Six hard years, most people would have called them, sleeping each night on the hard ground with only the stars or the weeping clouds above them, turning in on rainy nights with sodden blankets pulled over wet clothes, turning out in drizzling darkness to mount the night horse and ride round and round the restlessly camping herd.

There were nights when the cattle rushed, when he could remember galloping recklessly through the inky blackness of the night, spurring up along the flanks of the unseen, stampeding mob, guided only by the thunder of hooves and unerring instinct of a good horse. Swing those leaders! Head them off and turn them back until you had the mob ringing, churning round and round in a bewildered, bellowing mass. Talk to them, soothe them down until at last you could drive them back to the night camp where, with luck, you might snatch another hour or two of sleep before daylight.

And daylight? A hurried breakfast, a fresh horse, and a count, as the mob struck off camp. If your tally was short it could mean a tiring day following tracks while the others fed the mob along. When the tracks led you to the missing bullocks you hustled them along until you caught up with the mob. If it had been a bad rush you might find yourself fifty or even a hundred head short in the morning. That meant that a couple of hands would have to tail the mob in sight of the night camp while the others searched. At best it could mean a full day's stage lost.

A hard life? Perhaps, but it had been a happy one and a healthy one. He had grown in those years, grown to a lean six foot two, as tough as a greenhide rope and as fit as a corn-fed colt on a fresh spring morning. A tough man to shift from the pigskin, men used to say of him, and a tough man to beat in a fight. Yes, he'd had his full share of outlaw horses and bush brawls. But that was the one sure way to learn. Take on all comers, horses or men, and you finished up at the top.

Looking back on it, it had been a good life, with the occasional wet nights and the still rarer ones when the cattle rushed, serving only to emphasize the peace and companionship of the usual night camps. Those yarns around the campfire, the outrageous lies as one old hand tried to outdo the other in tales of wild cattle or outlaw horses! When it came to bed-time you rolled out your swag, dragged your saddle up for a pillow, and turned in to the distant tinkle of hobble chains and the musical clatter of horse-bells. The ground never seemed hard to a man who could not recall the feeling of a bed.

What a wonderful boss old Dan had been. During those six years on the road together they had, despite the difference in their ages, become inseparable mates and finally partners.

Partners in crime! But somehow Ben could never look on Dan as a criminal, nor himself as a willing accomplice to crime. They lifted a few head of cattle here and a few there and occasionally they picked up a horse that took their fancy. It was easy enough to find buyers among the smaller settlers even though their prices were always ridiculously low.

"We ain't gettin' enough for 'em," Ben used to complain. "These little coves'll never pay a decent price. They're all in the game themselves and they know too much about the risks of gettin' caught with the stuff we pass off."

"It's money for nothin'," was Dan's invariable reply. "Why should we worry when we're gettin' top prices for drovin'? The other's just a handy sideline, and all clear profit."

But already Ben was seeing further ahead. Again and again he pointed out that what they wanted was a small property of their own, an out-of-the-way place where they could breed from the cows they stole, let the steers grow into bullocks, and sell at market prices.

"We can make big money that way," he argued. "Work it right and we'll finish up rich squatters."

Dan would not be convinced. He didn't want to be a squatter, he maintained, rich or otherwise. He was a drover, the best drover in Queensland, with good contracts all over the country. If they took up a selection it would mean settling down in the one place, perhaps even living in a house! No, he couldn't stand that. Besides, they'd have to do fencing and yard-building. Could Ben picture his old mate swinging an axe all day or slogging away with a bar and shovel? No, no, no, he was never any good on foot. Fell over his spurs every time he turned around in a hurry. A man's legs—his legs, anyway—were made forked to fit over a horse.

Even at that age Ben had vision and a stubborn tenacity of purpose. They got their selection, or Ben got it, for beyond helping him settle in Dan would have nothing to do with it. "Once a man puts his signature to any of them land documents," he growled, "he's tied down for life." The thought of losing the mate he'd grown so fond of had put him in a frame of mind where he could see no good in anything.

Young Ben had just turned nineteen and the year was 1891.

There were times during the next two years when he felt strongly tempted to chuck everything and ride off in search of Dan. He hated the dull monotony of fencing and yard-building, but worst of all was the loneliness, the empty nights when he longed for the company and laughter around the camp-fire and the sight of old Dan's face with the drooping ginger moustache and the huge freckles lit by the flickering flames.

Since the day he watched Dan ride away he had rarely seen a white man. There was a blacks' camp down by the river, but, except when he wanted a couple of men, he kept away from it. In acting that way he was only following Dan's excellent example. Dan had always got on well with the blacks, though he only employed them when there were no white men available.

"Don't try gettin' familiar with them and they won't try to put anythin' over you," he used to say. "And keep away from their gins."

The last bit of advice came naturally to Dan because he hated women, white or black.

Ben tried quite a few of his local blacks before he decided on Quartpot and Prince. Both were good horsemen and both enjoyed playing the game his way. Under protest they occasionally helped him with the fencing, but they tired of it quickly and were apt to drift quietly off in the middle of a job. Cattle-work they loved, especially the stealthy game of duffing, and there was plenty of scope for their brand of genius in the latter.

From the huge old gums and shady clumps of ti-tree along its river frontage the selection opened out into coolibah flats. Farther back the coolibah gave way to brigalow, in places open brigalow that made excellent grazing country, and in others brigalow that struggled up through dense vine and turkey-bush scrub—useless, inhospitable country this, fit only for wallabies and scrub turkey. The back boundary needed no fence because there the scrub ended abruptly against a line of steep, apparently unscaleable cliffs known locally as the Jump-up.

But there was, Ben quickly discovered, a certain place where a cattle-pad led a zigzag way to the top, and once over the top the country fell gradually away in a series of rolling, semi-open downs. This was the big pastoral holding of Wavering Downs, rich grazing country with its heavily grassed downs broken by clumps of brigalow and bauhinia. It fascinated Ben with its riches—its rich pastures and the rich harvest of cleanskins waiting to be gathered.

Wavering Downs was held by an Englishman named Delacy, a man who knew very little about running a cattle station and apparently cared even less. The cattle-work was left entirely in the hands of a team of blacks under a half-caste head stockman. Parts of the runs were never mustered, the head stockman being too lazy or too indifferent to see that his men scoured the outlying country. They picked up the cattle along the main watering places and never bothered about the others.

Delacy's main interest was in horse-breeding. He went in for thoroughbreds and there were unbroken colts and fillies on his property that often made Ben sigh with envy. It would be easy enough to lift a few, but the risk of being seen astride one was too great. A Wavering Downs horse, even an unbranded one, would be recognized all over Central Queensland, and though Delacy might have difficulty in telling a steer from a heifer he could tell at a glance the age and breeding of any horse on his property. He bred beautiful horses and he bred a large, unruly tribe of children.

The homestead at Wavering Downs was a big rambling building surrounded by a dozen smaller ones set here and there without any semblance of order or reason. All were solidly built, with slab walls and bark roofs, but the general effect was an untidy jumble. Creepers sprawled over some, trees partially concealed others, and in between, scattered at random in a wilderness of weeds, were beds of flowers.

Mrs Delacy loved flowers, but the planning of a garden was something she had never considered necessary—if she had ever considered the matter at all. She planted seedlings here, there and everywhere, left the watering of them to an ancient gin, and picked the flowers for the house as soon as they opened. She was a small, colourless woman, so vague in manner that she seemed always to be in a trance. She looked, in her enormous straw gardening-hat, as frail as one of her own newly transplanted seedlings, yet she was the mother of the biggest and wildest collection of children in the district.

Had a stranger ridden up, produced an official-looking document, and asked her how many children she had, she would probably have given him the wrong answer. The same would have applied to a question about the number of gins she employed. She herself did no cooking or housework. A varied assortment of gins did everything, and it seemed to Mrs Delacy that they were always coming and going without any apparent reason. She never sacked one and none ever gave notice. Yet every now and again one drifted off and another took her place. Mrs Delacy never asked why. The blacks simply arranged matters among themselves.

Kids and gins! Dan Clancy, who had once called at Wavering Downs to pick up a mob of bullocks, used to say that if you gave the main building a good whack with a stick you'd see kids and gins coming out of every crack and racing like wallabies for the nearest patch of timber.

The year after Ben took up his selection the Delacys installed a governess for the children, though in Dan's opinion they would have done better to start off with an animal trainer. Delacy would never back an attempt at authority by the governess, and Mrs Delacy simply wasn't interested.

Not until his second year on the selection did Ben learn anything of this. He had spent a lot of time on Wavering Downs, but not once had he been in sight of the homestead. His business had been with the outlying parts of the run, and a very profitable business it had proved. He had come to the selection with ninety-seven head of mixed cattle and six horses. By the end of the second year he had over five hundred head of cattle carrying his brand. Put down natural increases at eighty-odd head, and he had a lot to thank Delacy and his head stockman for.

★ 3 ★

"TIME for your medicine again, Mr McReady. Wake up, Mr McReady." The plump little nurse was back on the job again, standing there patiently with the glass in her hand.

He growled quite amiably. "All right, Nurse. No need to wake the whole hospital. I wasn't asleep. Just lying here with my eyes closed, thinking. When you get old you do a lot of thinking. Going over your past sins. What time is it?"

"Nearly three o'clock. And you *were* asleep. You've been sleeping ever since you finished lunch."

"Must have been the rum. Now *there's* a proper medicine for a man, nurse. I don't suppose you brought another one along with you, eh?"

"No, I didn't. Will you drink this now, please? Matron said I was to see that you took it and then give you a message."

He tossed the medicine down in one gulp, shuddered and asked, "What's the message?"

"There's a visitor downstairs wanting to see you. Matron said I was to ask you if you wanted to see her or would she send her away. She's a—er—she's an old black woman."

"Matron said what!" Ben's roar made the little nurse jump. "I'll give that woman a few lessons in manners before I leave here. You go down and bring that visitor up straight away." He levered himself into a half-sitting position. "Wait a minute. Pass me that hairbrush. And straighten this bed up a bit. Make it look respectable." He brushed his snow-white hair carefully, helped the nurse adjust the quilt, and said, "Righto. That's a bit better. Now off you go. And be a good girl and help the old lady up the stairs. She's not too good on her pins these days."

The manner in which the nurse ushered in his visitor made Ben resolve that never again would he make a fuss about medicine or do anything to upset this girl. She kept a helping hand under the old woman's elbow and she assisted her into the chair as though the doing of such things were a pleasure.

"Biddy!" he said sternly. "You good-for-nothing old bag of bones. What the devil are you doing here?"

As though he had not spoken she leaned forward and asked anxiously, "How you doin', Boss? What they got you in this place for?"

"I'm all right, Biddy. Doc Stuart says he'll have me on my feet again in no time. It's you I'm worried about, coming all this way and climbing stairs as if you were a young filly. Did you take a taxi?"

"No, Boss. I bin come alonga that bus."

For a few moments he studied her, shaking his head slowly in reproof. Her skin had the colour and texture of old dried-out leather, not quite black but close enough to it now that age had taken the warm brown glow from it. Her hair was white, as white as his own, and she wore it neatly combed back and rolled into a wisp of a bun at the nape of her neck. The eyes behind the old-fashioned spectacles were bloodshot in the manner of all old aboriginals, but they were still alert. She gets thinner every time I see her, Ben thought, noting the claw-like hands and the frail little body under the neat navy-blue linen frock.

Taking up one of the small black hands, he patted it gently and said, "I dunno what to do about you, Biddy, blowed if I do. I've told you you're to take a taxi when you want to go anywhere, but you walk down to the bus-stop and then walk all the way from the bus-terminal to here. And don't think I don't know why. It's because you've been giving your money to those useless sponging relations of yours and you don't like to ask me for any more." He flung the hand impatiently aside. "But I'll fix you, me girl. I'll hire a taxi to wait outside your door all day and every day, just in case you want to go somewhere."

"No, Boss, you wouldn't do that. It wouldn't look good." The bloodshot old eyes sparkled with mirth, and she chuckled with a rich, infectious aboriginal cackle. "People might start thinkin' things about me."

She hasn't lost her sense of humour, Ben thought. But

then he couldn't imagine her without it. It had always been so much a part of her, just as she had, through all those years, been a part of his adult life. "It's been a long time, Biddy," he said, knowing they were thinking the same thoughts. "We can't expect to last much longer. I'm eighty-two and you must be well over seventy." His big hand smacked down on the quilt. "But I'll last you out, you skinny old black crow. I'll come to your funeral and stand there among all your relations to remind them they're not likely to get another bob out of me."

With obvious sincerity Biddy said, "I hope you do, Boss. I hope you do last me out."

For several minutes they remained silent, each staring at the white quilt without seeing it. Ben was picturing Biddy as he had first seen her, a shy, wide-eyed, comely little gin, wearing a shapeless sack dress and deeply aware of her new maturity. She was not quite full-blooded, for her skin had a soft chocolate tinge and her features were sharper and more even than those of any other gin in the camp.

He could still see her clearly, standing there in the doorway of his hut, smiling shyly as she balanced on one leg like a resting crane on the bank of a lagoon. Only instead of having one leg tucked up out of sight she was scratching with it, using her big toe to scratch nervously at the other bare calf.

"What the hell do you want?" he had growled.

And she had answered simply, "Me Bindarbarie," or some name like that.

Bit by bit it had come out that in return for tucker and maybe a little tobacco she would come up from the camp each morning, tidy up this fine new house for him, and do any odd jobs he might find for her.

And why not? It *was* a fine new house, his first house and one to be proud of. It had two rooms, a fireplace, and a small lean-to at the back. It had the usual slab walls and bark roof, and a floor of antbed, puddled and stamped down until its surface was hard and smooth. There was even a front door that swung on greenhide hinges. The old hatter who had built it for him had been very proud of that door. Surely a house like that deserved a housekeeper? And besides, he was lonely.

"No more all this Bindarbarie business b'longa you now," he had told her. "You Biddy. Savvy?"

Yes, she had savvied, grinning her pleasure. And Biddy she had remained, just as he had always remained Boss to her.

The quilt of the hospital bed took shape and Ben broke the long silence. "Anthea was here this morning."

"Youi." Biddy smiled and shook her head. "She don' know me no that one."

"The stuck-up bitch. Gettin' too big for her boots, that's her trouble. I dunno, Biddy. They reckon you should always send your kids away to the best school you can afford. The Missus always said that. We sent Anthea to the swankiest school in Australia, and look what it's done for her. She'd have been a better woman if she'd stayed in the bush with the Missus and you."

"Flash schoolin' never done young Mister Ken no harm, Boss. He sent his love to old Biddy every letter he wrote when he was winnin' all them medals over at the war."

"Yes, I s'pose you're right there. But school spoilt him for the bush. He never wanted to live there when he finished."

"An' then there's Miss Jane," Biddy went on, ignoring the last remark. "She went to the same school as her ma, but it never made her stuck-up. She don' forget old Biddy. Only last week she come bustin' into the house, singin' out, 'Happy birthday, Biddy. Look, I made you a cake all by myself. I hope it don' give you a bellyache.' "

His face lighting up, Ben said, "She's got the right stuff in her, that kid. Takes after her grandmother, don't you reckon?"

"Yeah, that right, Boss. Like the Missus when she first come alonga that selection. But a little bit like you too, Boss. You wanta watch out you two don' lock horns some day. I dunno who's coming out best then."

"We're not likely to lock horns, you old crow. Did you get my present?"

"Youi, Boss. I bin get 'im. You don' forget, eh?"

No, he didn't forget. How could he forget when Anne had

always made such a point of remembering Biddy's birthday. In her own quiet way she had drilled it into him and into the children. The boys had always remembered, even when they were overseas. Jane, who was Anthea's daughter, remembered, and only Anthea, wrapped up in her social activities, forgot. The first of May, Biddy's birthday. The amusing thing about it was that it was a fictitious birthday, invented by Anne because Biddy did not know the date of her birth. Anne's birthday fell on the thirtieth of April and in order that Biddy should not feel left out she set the following day aside for her. So the first of May had become Biddy's birthday, observed with such regularity that she had come to regard it as the actual date of her birth.

No, he couldn't forget a date that reminded him so strongly of Anne. Nor could he forget a lot of other things about this quietly dignified old aboriginal woman sitting so patiently by his side, things he never wanted to forget. And there were, in the light of later events, things he would have liked to forget. The first year that Biddy came to him could well be wiped off the records of his mind.

She had gone back to the camp at sundown that first day and as soon as she was out of sight he knew he had been a fool to let her go. If she didn't turn up next day, he decided, he'd go down to the camp and fetch her. But she had turned up, standing again in the doorway and smiling as the big toe scratched away at the back of her leg. And she had not returned to the camp at sundown. During the next twelve months she had shared his life, visiting the camp only to distribute his presents of tea, tucker, and tobacco to her various relatives. It had seemed to Ben that he was keeping the entire blacks' camp in tucker, but he had rarely complained. Biddy had quickly proved that at cattle-work she was the equal of any man. Fearless in scrub, she would race through the thickest timber to swing the leaders of a galloping mob, grinning delightedly for the sheer joy of the chase. Cattle-duffing she regarded as a thrilling sport, particularly when she and Ben rode up over the Jump-up by themselves. Those were picnic days when she taught him all the blackfellow tricks of hunting and living off the country. Even now

Ben could recall the delicious flavour of porcupine roasted on the coals, and native bee honey drained from a crack in an old coolibah while the little black native bees crawled like sticky ants all over their hands and faces.

"Biddy," he said. "remember the time we tried to pull that old rock python out of his hole and he let go so suddenly we fell over backward with the damned snake on top of us?"

"My word, yes, Boss." She chuckled until the tears ran down her wrinkled old cheeks. "I nebber see you jump up and run so fast."

"You weren't so slow yourself," he reminded her. "And that python must have broken a few records getting back down his hole."

The incident had taken place at the foot of the Jump-up, and, thinking of the many times the two of them had ridden up and down those cliffs, Ben said, "We certainly pulled a few swift ones when we were young. If we tried that sort of thing nowadays we'd be pinched quick and lively."

"Like the time the Baranda copper pinched Mister Dan. Remember that one, Boss?"

Remember it? For many reasons it was a night he would never forget, the night of the epic ride when he had done something to repay his debt to Dan Clancy and had brought himself very unfavourably under the notice of the police.

In those days the police trooper stationed at Baranda was a man named Ryan, an energetic, conscientious young policeman who had announced his intention of putting an end to the cattle-duffing in his district. There was certainly plenty of scope for him, but it was sheer bad luck for Dan, or a chain of circumstances, that made him Ryan's first victim. He simply happened to be passing through with a mob when the manager of Strathmella station rode in to report the theft of over fifty head of bullocks. Since Dan's mob of travelling cattle was in the vicinity the manager thought it might be a good idea to look up the drover in charge.

Dan got a nasty shock when he saw the police trooper, black tracker, and a stranger ride up. He hadn't a single Strathmella bullock in his mob, but he did have fifteen head he had "lifted" from Wavering Downs. The Strathmella manager spotted them at once. Together he and the trooper knocked holes in every excuse Dan could think up and within an hour the Wavering Downs bullocks were on their way to Baranda police paddock, driven by Ryan and his tracker. Dan was also in the party. Wherever the tracker went he followed, his horse's nose never dropping more than a length behind the police horse's tail. He had no other choice for a stout greenhide rope connected the two animals.

Ben knew nothing of all this until Biddy's urgent whisper roused him that night. "Boss!" she was saying. "Wake up, Boss. Horse bin come, bin gallopin'."

At first he could hear nothing. The night was so still and quiet he would have doubted Biddy had he not known that the blacks never made mistakes like that. And presently he too heard the hoof-beats, faint at first but gradually becoming louder.

He was outside, fully dressed, when the horseman pulled up and hurled himself out of the saddle. It was young Tommy, Dan's blackboy, and he gabbled out his story while his horse stood there with spread-eagled legs, fighting for breath in great, tearing gasps while the sweat dropped from its heaving belly.

"Steady up, Tommy," Ben ordered. "More slow."

Bit by bit, with Biddy helping to translate, he got the whole story—the inspection of the mob, the cutting out of the Wavering Downs bullocks, and finally Dan's whispered instructions to Tommy to get word to Mister Ben.

Good old Dan. Besides Tommy he had five men in his droving team, yet when he found himself in a jam it was to him, Ben McReady, he had turned. Well, he had put his trust in the right man.

"Pull the saddle off your nag and leave 'im, Tommy," he said. "He'll be all right. You can take one of mine and get away in the morning." And to Biddy, "Get the horses in. Make sure you get Moonlight and Warrior."

A wonderful pair of stayers, those two, and they hadn't been worked for a week. And by hell they'd have to stay tonight. Already Ben had it all worked out. Ryan could not hope to make Baranda in one stage. He'd have to camp tonight and the only logical night camp was Bradley's Yard. He could put the bullocks in the yard, camp in the old hut with his tracker and prisoner, and leave for Baranda at daylight.

He talked it over with Biddy while they caught and saddled their horses. By following the old wagon-track along the river and branching off five miles from Baranda they would have good open going all the way. The track would be easy enough to follow in the starlight, but it was by no means a direct route to Bradley's Yard. At a rough estimate Ben made it sixty miles. They would have to punish the horses cruelly to cover the distance and carry out their job before the first streak of dawn aroused Ryan and his tracker.

It was strange that though neither of them had mentioned it each had taken it for granted that Biddy would come. And each had a clear conception of what must be done when they reached the yards.

"Hurry up," Ben snapped as he swung into the saddle. "It's a good sixty miles round by the wagon-track. We'll 'ave to ride like the blazes."

Biddy finished tightening Warrior's girth and said quietly, "More better we go longa Jump-up, Boss."

"What! In the dark! We'd get slewed in the scrub and waste hours tryin' to find the track over the top. Might never find it."

"We find 'im, Boss." She mounted and urged her horse past his, unhesitatingly taking the lead.

White man's measurements meant nothing to her. Had anyone asked her the distance to Bradley's Yard by the Jump-up short-cut she would probably have said, "Twenty mile, thirty; I dunno for sure." Actually it was forty-eight miles.

Examining his big old silver watch in the starlight, Ben saw that the time was already ten-thirty. He doubted whether grass-fed horses could do what he was about to ask of these two tonight; he doubted whether Biddy could strike through the miles of scrub and come out at the one cattle-pad that could take them up the cliffs, but, since Dan had called on him, he must keep the horses going to the limit of their endurance and trust Biddy's aboriginal instinct. There were no alternatives.

There were times during that ride when he gravely doubted Biddy's instinct or whatever it was she was relying on. She led the way, veering sometimes to the left and sometimes to the right, keeping always to the more open brigalow and skirting the pockets of dense vine and turkey-bush that stood barring their progress like solid black walls. When the going was good enough she lifted Warrior to a trot, but in the main she was content to keep him at a brisk walk.

Ben flattered himself that in daylight he could hold his own with any bushman, but in this darkness, with even the stars shut out by the overhanging branches, he found himself incapable of recognizing a single landmark. Scores of wallabies thud, thud, thudded away at their approach, occasional mobs of cattle crashed off through the undergrowth, and once a lone curlew rose from under Warrior's feet, startling both horses with his eerie, piercing cry.

It seemed to Ben that they were hopelessly lost in the middle of the scrub when Biddy forced Warrior into a patch of thick undergrowth and called back softly, "Watch out longa that wait-a-while, Boss."

Following on Warrior's heels, he ducked low to avoid the sharp, clawing hooks of a wait-a-while vine, brushed aside a few low branches, and found himself through. The scrub was behind him and ahead of him towered the grey-white walls of the Jump-up.

Sliding from the saddle Biddy said, "More better we walk up." Already her sure bare feet were on the cattle-pad that led to the top, the pad they had used so often in daylight.

They led their horses to the top, rested them for a few minutes, and pushed on. No longer hemmed in by scrub Ben was now sure of himself, riding knee to knee with Biddy as they struck a line across the open downs, varying their pace from a fast walk to an easy, swinging trot.

Once they pulled up and dismounted. A dingo was howling mournfully and away to their left they could hear the faint, persistent barking of the dogs at Wavering Downs homestead. More than half-way, Ben noted, and the horses were still fresh, scarcely sweating in the chilly night air. They unsaddled and changed horses there. Like all good horsemen Ben was light in the saddle, but there was no escaping the fact that he was six foot two in height and nearly twice Biddy's feather-weight.

At ten minutes to one they opened the Wavering Downs boundary fence and led the horses through. As nearly as Ben could judge, they were seven miles from Bradley's Yard. The horses needed constant urging in the trotting spells now, but the pace had been well judged. Once they neared the yards they would not be asked to extend themselves beyond a walking pace.

At two-thirty Biddy reined Moonlight in and whispered, "Horse-bells."

"Which way?" Ben asked.

She extended a dusky left arm, and instinctively they both swung to the right, putting the yards between them and the distant bell. To ride near the hobbled police horses could be dangerous, for Dan's horse would be with the others and it was quite possible it might scent an old droving mate in Warrior or Moonlight. One sniff of recognition would bring a whinny, low at first but growing louder and louder as the others joined in, until the noise acted like an alarm clock on the sleeping policeman and tracker.

One hundred yards from the sliprails Ben and Biddy halted. This was the critical time when luck could play as big a part as all Biddy's stealth and skill. Holding the two horses while she crept forward Ben found himself scarcely daring to breathe. If the bullocks took fright and raced to one end of the yard as she neared it the noise could rouse the sleepers. The drumming of their hooves if they trotted out through the open sliprails could be an equally effective alarm. It seemed an age before he saw her backing away from the yard, her small figure bent over as she carefully fanned her tracks from the dusty ground near the rails.

She was mounting Moonlight when the bullocks came out, not jamming through the rails in a noisy, hustling bunch as Ben had feared they might, but stringing off quietly, one behind the other. It only remained for the two horsemen to follow them at a safe distance, letting them take their time until they were well away from the yard. Born and bred on Wavering Downs, the bullocks would return to it as a bird returns to its nest.

Back in the hut Dan would be sleeping between policeman and tracker. No need to worry about him now. With the evidence against him gone Ryan could only release his prisoner. In his own mind he might be certain of his guilt, but he could never prove it.

With the yard well behind them, the two horsemen closed on the cattle. The night's work was not yet over, and the sooner the bullocks were through the boundary fence the better.

At dawn Ryan would discover his loss. He might even discover it earlier, but he would not leave the yard until full daylight, for even the best tracker could not follow tracks in the dark. Probably by sunrise Ryan would have satisfied himself that the bullocks had been driven towards the Wavering Downs fence. He then had two courses. He could follow the tracks to the point where the horsemen put them through the fence and then follow the horse-tracks in the hope of catching up with the culprits, or he could hurry after Dan's travelling mob on the logical assumption that a couple of Dan's men had come to the rescue.

Ben, certain he would adopt the latter course, put the bullocks through the fence, retied the wires, and struck out for the Jump-in. Neither he nor Biddy saw any reason for attempting to conceal their tracks. The time was twenty minutes to five and daybreak was not far off.

"We'll ride for a couple of hours and then camp for a while," Ben announced. "Even if Ryan catches up with us he can't prove a thing."

He might suspect, he might even be sure in his own mind, but he could prove nothing.

They camped for over two hours, resting their heads on their saddles in the shade of a bauhinia-tree while their leg-weary horses fed near by. Trained in droving ways, Moonlight and Warrior would never stray far when their reins were left trailing on the ground. Besides, they were too tired and hungry to wander.

Hungry! Ben would never forget how hungry he was when they finally released their horses outside the selection hut. It was after sundown. In twenty hours they had ridden nearly one hundred miles and during that time they had eaten nothing.

Ryan and his tracker turned up late the following afternoon. The policeman was tired, dirty, and extremely irritable. Ben's invitation to let his horses go and spend the night he completely ignored.

"You've had a win this time, McReady," he said. "I suppose you've been telling yourself how well you put it over me. But I'll get you yet. Your herd's increasing far too quickly for my liking and I'll get you if I have to ask to be left at Baranda for ten years."

* 4 *

FOR a long time after Biddy left Ben lay back on the pillows with his eyes closed, half dreaming, half remembering. It was so easy to slip back into the past after a talk with Biddy because there was scarcely a phase of his past that she had not, in some way, shared. Anne had known only one side of his life, but Biddy had known both—the respectable and the lawless. And not once had she betrayed him, not even by a hint or a carelessly dropped word. The most faithful cattle-dog could not have exceeded her loyalty, a loyalty that gradually spread until it embraced his whole family. Yes, he had a lot to thank Biddy for.

And, strangely enough, he had a lot to thank Constable Ryan for. Summing it all up he found it difficult to assess the balance between the good and the bad brought into his life by that vindictively efficient policeman. Ryan had put a stop to the easy profits he had been making from Wavering Downs. Ryan had given him Anne, who had undoubtedly been the greatest single factor for good in his whole life. And finally Ryan had deprived him of his eldest son. Admittedly the policeman had only been the indirect cause of the last two events. Each might have happened without his interference, and again it might not.

Only a fool would have disregarded that warning about the quickly increasing herd, and Ben had never been a fool. During the next three months he did not once scale the Jump-up. Instead of running in the saddle horses each morning, he and Biddy put up a small holding paddock and improved the yards. Twice he took the dray into Baranda to pick up tools, wire, and stores. There were even odd letters to be posted or collected now that he was becoming established and selling small mobs of cattle. Correspondence, indeed, was rapidly becoming a major problem. His spelling was atrocious, he wrote slowly in an awkward childish hand, and he loathed doing it. It required more effort to write a short business letter than it did to ride the thirty miles in to Baranda to post it. And the worst of it was that letters seemed to breed like dingoes. The more you wrote the more you had to answer. It went on and on. Solely because he had to have an address he called the selection "Coolibah." Even that took quite a lot of thinking out though his hut sat on a rise and looked out over the coolibah flats.

It was a lovely spring morning when he decided to take Biddy and once more try his luck on Wavering Downs. Ryan, with a huge district to look after, could not afford to spend all his time trying to trap one man, particularly when that man had behaved like a respectable, law-abiding settler for three solid months.

It had been a good winter and the country over the Jump-up was looking its best. A breeze was ruffling the long grass on the downs, bending it over in a series of running waves. Waves, wavering, Wavering Downs. It was easy to see where the property had got its name. The country stretched before them like a rippling green sea with the clumps of timber standing above the surface like islands, sometimes deep green and sometimes silver when the sun glinted on the leaves of the brigalow.

The Jump-up was about two miles behind them when Biddy said, "Some one bin follow us."

Without even glancing behind him Ben asked, "You sure, Biddy?"

"Youi, Boss. Long way back." She ran a caressing dusky hand along her horse's neck and kept her eyes fixed on its ears. Ben was prepared to swear she had not looked back since they left the Jump-up. "I think might be that one Jumbo, eh?"

"We'll keep straight on," he decided. "Straight for the homestead. We're headin' near enough for it now. When we get there I'll go in and see the boss and you go down to the camp and see some of your mates. Stay there till I come and pick you up."

Already he had worked out a reasonable excuse for calling on Delacy. Not only was it a reasonable excuse, it was a very sound idea. The mail coach from Baranda called at

Wavering Downs every Saturday and returned each Monday, and by having his mail sent via Wavering Downs he could almost halve the distance he would have to ride for it. Delacy, of course, might raise objections, but it wouldn't hurt to ask him.

The owner of Wavering Downs was not easy to locate. As he hitched his horse to the saddle rail Ben caught sight of several children, but each time he approached one the youngster vanished behind one of the numerous buildings. Eventually he found Mrs Delacy standing waist-deep in weeds, her face almost hidden beneath an enormous, mushroom-shaped straw sun-hat. In one hand she held a bunch of seedlings and in the other a rusty trowel. She seemed neither surprised nor interested at finding a strange young man confronting her, and she was vague about her husband's whereabouts. He might be down at the horse-yard, she said, or he might be in his office. She indicated a small building with a disinterested wave of the trowel.

Delacy, surrounded by an untidy clutter of English sporting magazines, was in his office. He was a short, thick-set man with a pronounced paunch. Faint traces of grey showed in his stiff, dark hair and a large bushy moustache completely hid his mouth. From beneath the moustache an enormous curved pipe hung. Prominent eyeballs stood out like eggs against florid cheeks, and the general impression was one of belligerence or intolerance.

"Well?" he barked, removing the pipe and pointing the stem at Ben's slim waist. "What is it?"

As briefly as possible Ben stated his business.

Delacy listened impatiently and asked, "What did you say your name was?"

"McReady. Ben McReady."

"Oh, yes. Heard about you. You're the fella on that selection over by the river. How the devil do you expect to make a living out of a little place like that, eh? Starve to death, and serve you right for being such a damned fool. There isn't even a decent living in a place the size of Wavering Downs. The whole damned country's only fit for the blacks."

He was stand-offish and arrogant, inclined to be contemptuous of all colonials, but he admitted that he saw no reason why Ben should not collect his mail at Wavering Downs.

Riding back to the selection, Ben took careful stock of the number of cleanskins he saw. He was wondering whether it would be safe to drive a few head back with them when Biddy reined in and pointed to the ground.

"That one Jumbo all right, Boss," she announced positively.

Ben dismounted, but even by bending over them he could see nothing unusual about the tracks in the long grass. Certainly they were horse tracks, but the rider, if the horse had been ridden, could have been one of Delacy's stockmen. Because he was proud of his tracking ability it irritated him that Biddy, without dismounting, had been so sure. Could it be that she was only bluffing, or perhaps going on a hunch?

Still bending over them, he followed the tracks for more than fifty yards before he came to a small patch of bare ground. And there, plainly visible, was the imprint of a horseshoe. As usual Biddy had been right. In this district only the police horses were shod.

Ben had no means of telling whether Ryan's tracker had been ordered to keep a watch over his movements or whether he had simply come on them that morning by accident. He only knew that he could not afford to take any risks. Not once did he think of cursing Dan for bringing this unwelcome police attention on his activities. Had he been in a fix Dan would have come to his aid without counting the cost. It was as simple as that.

Three weeks later Ben called at Wavering Downs for his mail and met Anne. He did not know her name and he only spoke a few words to her, but the change she was to make in his life started that day. The mail coach had gone when he arrived, and the only person in sight was a young woman sitting on the step of the main building. She was reading a letter, but as Ben walked towards her she stood up and smiled. She was small and slender, he noted. Her eyes were soft and brown and her hair was as black as a crow's wing. A certain nervousness prevented him from making any other observations. He had spoken to few women in his life and this one so obviously belonged to a class he had never made contact with. She must be the new governess, he concluded. Probably she was laughing inwardly at his rough untidiness.

Still smiling, she said, "I suppose you are Mr McReady?" Her voice was soft and slightly husky, and there was a warmth in it that ignored the trivialities of class and clothes.

Self-consciously he removed his hat, exposing a mop of untidy fair hair. "Yes, miss," he said. "That's right." He was acutely aware of the rip in his faded blue shirt, the horsehair and sweat on the insides of the legs of his wrinkled moleskins, and the dust on the battered old hat he was twisting so nervously.

"There was a letter for you in the mail." She held it out. "Mr Delacy asked me to give it to you if you came."

He took the letter, said, "Thanks, miss. Much obliged," and strode back to the saddle rail. Not until he was preparing to mount did he realize that he still had his hat in his hand.

"Musta thought she'd met a white blackfella," he told his horse as he rode away. He would never have believed that she had scarcely noticed his clothes.

She had, in fact, noticed the rip in his shirt because she wished she could have mended it for him. Young ladies, she was aware, should not wish such things about strange young men, but this one was so pathetically shy. Apart from the rip the things she had noticed were that he was tall, broad-shouldered, and slim-waisted. The face beneath the rumpled fair hair was clean-shaven and deeply tanned. A strong face, she thought; even a handsome face, in spite of the hooked nose.

But it was a long time before Ben learned what she had been thinking that day.

He saw her almost every Saturday after that because he made a point of being at the homestead when the coach pulled in.

The arrival of the mail coach was quite an event in the lives of the people on Wavering Downs. Every one turned out for it. Delacy, looking like an English country squire, took up a position by the saddle rail while his wife and Anne stood on the front verandah. The children came out of their hiding places and in the background the station blacks waited to see the four-in-hand come swinging up the rise. Big Mick O'Brien always whipped his team up to a last-minute spurt when he came in sight of the homestead. He changed horses here, and the appearance of his blackboy cantering ahead to run in the fresh team was the first warning of the approach of the mail. Ten, or perhaps fifteen, minutes later Mick, his magnificent black beard fanned out over his chest, reined in opposite the saddle rail with a flourish of rein-pulling and a ringing shout of "Whoa there! Whoa!" It was pure showmanship on his part. His leaders knew the exact limit of their stage and even Mick's whip could not have urged them beyond it.

If there were passengers they alighted and sorted themselves out, neighbouring squatters and their wives going to the verandah for a cup of tea with Mrs Delacy while the less fortunate working men and Ben helped Mick unharness the horses. Occasionally Delacy would bellow, "Letter here for you, McReady." More often he would hand the letter to the governess and say, "Give this to McReady."

"I'm Anne Croxley," she said to him one morning. "I teach the Delacy children."

"I guessed that, miss." He managed a shy grin. "Must be quite a job. Reckon you'd need a couple of good stockmen to round 'em all up."

It was a long speech for him, the longest he had made to her in six meetings, and he was rewarded by hearing her laugh. He wondered whether she found much to laugh at on Wavering Downs. Delacy treated her as a servant, and Mrs Delacy always seemed unaware of her presence. With no other company except the blacks it must be a very lonely life for a young girl.

Two weeks later he plucked up his courage and said, "Miss, I wonder if you could 'elp me with a letter. I gotta tell the Lands Department some things they been askin' me about and there's a few words that's too good for me." He took a deep breath and decided to make a full confession. "You see, miss, I never really 'ad no proper schoolin' and it ain't easy to catch up on things you missed when you was a kid."

"I suppose it isn't." She considered his request for a few moments, and afterwards he realized what a difficult decision he had asked her to make. Apart from her own feelings there was her employer to be considered. Delacy, with his air of arrogant superiority, might well object to his employee devoting time to an outsider, particularly an uncouth outsider, one he regarded as unfit to be offered the simple bush hospitality of a cup of tea.

"There's no time now, Mr McReady." Anne had made her decision. "The lunch bell will be going soon and Mr Delacy hates to be kept waiting."

Trying to conceal his disappointment, Ben said, "Oh, it don't matter miss."

"But it *does* matter. I'd like to help you. Look, Mr McReady, when you leave here do you ride straight home?"

"No, I boil up and 'ave a bit of tucker down along the creek."

"I thought you did. I've seen the ashes of your fires, near the big bottlebrush. If you wait there I'll come along as soon as lunch is over."

"Miss, I wouldn't like to get you into trouble with your boss."

"You wouldn't be getting me into trouble. I'm free on Saturday afternoons and I usually go for a walk along the creek. Sometimes I sit under the big bottlebrush and read, or watch the birds or the little fish in the shallow end of the pool." She glanced towards the main building. "I think that's the lunch bell. I must go now."

Their conversation that afternoon was confined strictly to business. Sitting together on the short grass under the bottlebrush while Ben's horse fed close by, they straightened out the problem of the Lands Department letter. Anne had brought writing materials and she wrote while Ben explained what he wanted to say. He learned, among other things, that "bullock" was spelt with an "o" and pronounced that way, although he had never heard the animal called anything but "bullick." As he had trusted Biddy's bushcraft he now trusted Anne's superior education. In all things he was an excellent pupil.

If Anne was amazed at his ignorance she did not show it. The easy, natural charm of manner that was so much a part of her made it seem a perfectly normal thing for a young woman to sit on the bank of a creek and teach a grown man how to spell and pronounce simple words.

Thanking her before he rode off, Ben said, "If you could manage to gimme a few more lessons some time, miss, I—er—I wouldn't mind payin' you for your time."

"Please, Mr McReady!" She flushed uncomfortably. "I couldn't possibly accept money. I'd like to help you, if I can, but please don't offer me money again."

It was Ben's turn to flush. "I only meant, miss," he stammered, twisting the reins awkwardly around his hand, "I only meant it didn't seem fair to expect you to teach kids all the week and then teach me on your day off."

"It's a pleasure to find some one who really wants to learn," she told him. "Good-bye, Mr McReady."

He waited for her again under the bottlebrush next Saturday and was delighted when she at last appeared, carrying some school books.

"This *does* seem rather silly," she said as they sat down. "I'm sure you don't want to go through all these." She indicated the books in her lap.

But he did want to go through them. As a lad he had wanted to learn all Dan could teach him about stock work, and now as a man he wanted to learn all this girl could teach him about writing and speaking correctly. There was something ruthless about his ambitions. He was determined to forge ahead, and the thought that other people might suffer for his advancement never worried him in the least. Give him time and he would become a wealthy landowner. Give him enough education and he would be able to hold his own in any company. At present Delacy looked down on him as an uncouth lout, but one day he would be looking down on Delacy.

The Saturday afternoon lessons became regular features in their lives, but Ben rarely looked on Anne as anything but his teacher. Ruthlessly ambitious in material things, he still could not picture himself as Anne's equal. Her very niceness was so far above him. Although she had told him her name was Anne he never thought of addressing her as anything but "Miss" until she herself forced the issue.

"I wish you wouldn't keep calling me 'miss,'" she complained one afternoon. "It makes me feel such an old school ma'am."

He grinned and said, "All right, miss. I'll try not to."

But it was another two weeks before her name slipped out. He was frowning and chewing the end of his pencil as he puzzled over a grammatical problem she had set him when he suddenly burst out, "Look here, Anne. This don't make sense."

"Doesn't," she corrected calmly.

"All right. It doesn't make sense."

She explained it carefully and when she was sure he had grasped it she said, "Ben, it's time I promoted you to another class. You've really made wonderful progress, but you can only learn to speak correctly by talking freely while I listen and correct you when you go wrong."

"I'm not much of a hand at talkin'."

" 'Talking.' Remember there's a 'G' on the end of it. Tell me about your selection, about your neighbours, and your house."

"There ain't—aren't—any near neighbours. And the house, it's only a hut, and a pretty rough sort of hut at that. Only an antbed floor and nothin'——"

" 'Nothing.' "

"Nothing much in it. Not even a bed." It struck him that she must be thinking him a little above the level of a blackfellow, so he finished lamely, "You don't get much time when you're starting off on your own. There's fences and yards to be put up. All sorts of jobs to be done before you can start making the house nice. And anyway, I've got used to sleeping on the ground."

"But don't you feel terribly lonely, living by yourself like that?"

The question made him flush deeply under his tan. He could not tell this innocent girl the truth and say, "No, I'm living with a black gin," yet he must give her a reasonable answer. "I'm too busy," he told her lamely.

Poor Biddy! She felt the sting of his contempt that night, and though she felt it regularly during the next few months she bravely concealed her hurt.

* 5 *

OLD Ben was dozing. He had slipped easily from memories to disjointed dreams when he became aware that he was no longer alone. Without raising one eyelid he knew that some one was watching him. A man could not live as he had lived without developing such an instinct. He did not have to hear a stealthy movement or even catch a faint sniff of some strange smell as a dog might have done. He simply knew he was being observed.

"Well?" he snapped. "What is it?"

"You old fox. I just knew you were bluffing."

The young feminine charm of the tone sent a glow right through him. The slight huskiness, the lovely rich warmth of the voice were Anne's. But Anne was dead and this voice was vividly alive. Strange how a likeness could skip a generation and appear with startling clarity in the next. If he opened his eyes he would see Anne as he had been seeing her in his dreams, standing there under the bottlebrush with her schoolbooks tucked under her arm. Only Anne's hair had been long, neatly parted down the centre and drawn back into the bun Biddy had so faithfully copied. But all the rest would be there—the slim little figure, the soft brown eyes, and the smile that came from away down inside, embracing you with its single-hearted generosity.

Opening first one eye and then the other and grinning his delight, Ben said, "Can't fool an old cattle-duffer, eh, Jane? Come on in and sit down, you young hussy."

She pulled the chair close to the bed, sat down, and took his big hand between her two small ones. Nice little hands, Ben thought, brown from the outdoors, and capable.

"Bossy," she said anxiously, "is it serious? I mean, are you dangerously sick?"

"Lord, no, child. I'll be out of here in no time. Between you and me I'm wondering why I let Doc Stuart talk me into coming near the blasted place."

"Truly, Bossy?"

"Fair dinkum, Jane."

"I brought something for you." She placed her shopping basket on the bed beside him and he saw it was filled with flowers.

"They're beautiful, Jane," he said gallantly. "My favourite flowers."

"What a horrible old liar you are, Bossy. You know you can never tell one flower from the other." She moved the blooms aside and pulled out a bottle of beer. "Feel that," she invited, resting it againt his cheek. "Straight out of the 'fridge. Interested?"

"Jane! I've always thought there must be *some* good in you. The trouble was to find it. Here, don't let's mess around. If the Matron comes in she'll beat us to the punch. Tip the water out of that glass. There's another above the wash-basin. What a girl! You even thought to bring an opener."

He watched her carefully fill his glass. "Now pour one for yourself. You don't think I'm going to drink with the flies, do you?"

She filled the other glass, raised it and said, "Mud in your eye, old-timer."

He drank deeply and watched her refill his glass. "Your mother was here this morning."

"Yes, I know."

"She practically accused me of corrupting your morals, putting silly ideas into your head, and turning you into a rough bushwhacker. Said I undid all the good she was trying to do for you."

"What blasted rot, Bossy!" Jane managed to put all his own intolerance into the words. "I know Mother's tactics. She's dying to marry me off to what she calls 'one of the town's eligible young bachelors.' And honestly I haven't a single thing in common with any of them. Just at the moment I'm sure she and Daddy are trying to stir up a little counter-attraction."

"What to?"

"Well." She bit her lip and looked down at her glass.

"They've—er—they've got some wild idea into their heads that I'm falling for some one they don't approve of."

"And are you?"

She raised her eyes, meeting his squarely. "Yes. It's no use trying to fool you, is it, Bossy? I'm afraid I am."

"Young Reid Calder?"

She nodded. "I s'pose it does seem silly, doesn't it?"

He pondered over the question for a long time before answering. Reid Calder was his overseer, a good lad and a first-class horseman, with the makings of a really good cattleman. Ben liked him otherwise he would not have kept him on. Reid was a tireless worker and he was genuinely fond of Wavering Downs. But weighing against all his good points was the inescapable fact that he had no money. Like so many bush lads, he spent his wages lavishly when he went to town and invariably returned from a holiday flat broke.

"And how does Reid feel about it?" Ben asked at last.

"He wants me to marry him."

"Does he? Now look, Janie. I don't want to preach a sermon; we can safely leave that to your mother and father. But has Reid ever got around to explaining how he's going to support you?"

"No, Bossy. We've never discussed it."

"You should. It's important. Point is, Janie, I've known Reid longer than you have, and I've noticed he's flat out supporting himself. I reckon you ought to remind him that you cost a bit to keep, too."

She put her head down on his hand as it lay on the sheet and her hair spread out over it in a black wavy mass. "Oh, Bossy," she sobbed. "Everybody's against us and if I can't have him I'll be miserable all my life."

"I'm not against you, honey." He withdrew his hand and ran his fingers gently through her hair. "I only want to make sure you'll be happy when I'm not around to keep an eye on you any more."

"I'd be happy in an old bark humpy in the bush if I had horses and dogs, and Reid. I hate the town and I——"

"Take it easy, honey," Ben soothed. "Don't go rushin'

your fences. Just canter along steady for a bit and we'll see how things work out, eh?"

"Bossy, you are an old darling." She sat up, shook her hair into place, and dug frantically into her handbag for handkerchief and comb. "Oh, my gosh! What would Matron think if she walked in? An empty beer-bottle on the table, two half-empty glasses, and me with my hair all mussed up and maudlin tears streaming down my cheeks! She'd say we'd been indulging in a drunken orgy!"

When Matron did eventually look in she saw her patient lying quietly back on his pillows while his granddaughter sat beside him, primly holding a basket of flowers. All evidence of the orgy had been carefully removed.

"Could I take those flowers and have them put in water for you, Miss Arnedale?" she asked.

"Oh, no, thank you, Matron." Jane hugged the basket tightly to her. "They're not—they're for a friend. Grandfather doesn't like flowers in his room. And I must be going now."

As Matron withdrew and Jane bent over and kissed Ben on the cheek he whispered, "I'd have given a fiver to see her lift those flowers out and find the dead marine."

"Live in a humpy in the bush," he muttered when Jane had gone. "I wonder if the kid realizes what it would mean."

He wondered again whether Anne had realized what she was in for when she said she didn't care how rough the hut was. But though she must have been appalled at its stark bareness, she smiled bravely and made the best of it.

How vividly he could picture the scene that had made him ask her to share it with him. He had Delacy to thank for that—the arrogant, bigoted Delacy with his suspicion and contempt for all colonials. Come to think of it, he had a lot of people to thank for his progress in life. Had it not been for Delacy he would never have dared to ask Anne to live in a bare hut without floor or furniture, without even a bed!

They were lying facing each other in the shade of the bottlebrush. A few feet of grass and a scattering of schoolbooks separated them, and they were laughing over a droving story he had just told. They were talking freely together by then, often spending a whole afternoon without opening a book.

In the middle of Anne's laugh he looked up and saw the owner of Wavering Downs standing on the creek bank above them. Delacy's complexion had turned from red to purple, and as he strode down the bank Ben had the fleeting impression that his protruding eyeballs were about to burst right out of their sockets.

"So this is the sort of thing that's been going on!" he bellowed. "I've a damned good mind to horsewhip you off the property, you dirty mongrel." He swung on Anne, now scrambling hastily to her feet. "And you! To think I've been employing you to teach my children, you shameless slut!"

Ben came to his feet in one lithe, effortless movement. Until then he had been too dazed at the unexpectedness of it all to do anything but stare. His long arm shot out and his open hand smacked loudly across Delacy's cheek. White and shaking with rage he still could not bring himself to use his fists on some one he regarded as an old man.

"Tell her you're sorry you said that," he roared, "or by hell I'll chuck you in the bloody creek."

"Please, Ben! Please!" Anne was pleading with him, tears streaming down her face as she grasped his arm. "Please don't make it any worse."

"I'll make it worse for you, my girl," Delacy raved. "Get back to the house and pack your baggage while I deal with this lout." Whatever his faults he did not lack courage.

Ben took a firm grip on himself. Freeing his arm from Anne's grasp he said quietly, "Look, Delacy. I've belted bigger and better men than you with one hand tied behind me back. Now *you* get back to the house before I lose me temper again and start on you. And by Gawd, if I *do* start I'll chuck you in the creek and hold you under till you bloody well drown."

He proved himself a master of strategy then because, instead of standing there and forcing the issue, he turned his back on Delacy, put an arm round Anne's shoulder, and said, "Come for a walk down the creek."

The move left Delacy flat. Wrath, indignation, and even

the courage to challenge a vastly superior adversary could do nothing against two retreating backs—nothing, that is, except shout a threat to toss Anne's belongings out on to the road.

Around the first bend Ben stopped and said awkwardly, "Don't cry, Anne."

"The horrible beast of a man!" she sobbed. "I hate him. I've always hated him for the way he treated you, like one of the blacks, not fit to be asked in for a meal. And now—and now this!"

He comforted her as best he could, keeping his arm around her shoulder and assuring her that everything would be all right. His words, he realized, lacked conviction. He knew that Anne had taken the job on Wavering Downs because her parents were hard up. Weeks ago she had told him all about herself, not complainingly, but as a return of confidences when he had told her about his childhood.

"Don't worry, Anne," he soothed. "He can't throw you out like that. He's got to pay you what wages you got comin' and he'll have to keep you until the coach comes back on Monday."

"I don't care if he does throw me out. I never want to go inside his wretched house again. I'd rather camp out on the road until Monday. I hate him and his horrible children and everything about the place." It was one of the rare outbursts of temper he was to see in her through all the years.

To get her mind temporarily away from Delacy he asked, "What will you do when you leave here?"

"I suppose I'll have to look for another job. There must be others. But I don't know yet what I'll do. How *can* I know? Please, Ben, don't keep asking me, please."

Instead of pointing out that he had only asked her once, he tightened his grip on her shoulder, took a deep breath, and made a quick decision. In his later life he was to become famous for his quick decisions on important matters, but this was to prove the quickest and most important of them all. He was not in love with Anne. He had never considered asking her or any other girl to share his life. For one thing, he had nothing except the crudest of living conditions to offer a wife, and Anne, in spite of her poverty, had obviously been used to much better things. Yet with his ruthless ambition and her help they could go a long way. She could do worse and it wouldn't hurt to test her reactions.

Without even looking down at her he said, "You could marry me. Things is pretty rough over on the selection, but they won't always be that way."

He never could recall what else he had said that day, but because it was so typical of the way she later faced up to every adversity he could still remember her answer.

"I don't mind how rough they are, Ben."

He was waiting for her when the mail coach pulled in to Baranda on Monday, but they had to wait five days there for the parson, she boarding with the storekeeper's wife and he camping down on the creek-flat. The storekeeper had willingly acted for the father of the bride, since the wedding was providing a thrill for his wife and handsome profits for him. He had even got rid of a double bed, an ancient monstrosity he had long written off as a dead loss.

Baranda in those days existed mainly because it was the terminal for the mail coach from the port of Stonehaven, and the starting point for the lesser service that passed through Wavering Downs and other station properties. Set on an almost treeless rise, it consisted of an hotel, a police-station, store, and about a dozen other buildings. The hotel was a crude shanty, built to cater for the thirsts of teamsters and drovers, the store was a barn-like structure, and few of the other houses were more pretentious than Ben's hut. It was an unlovely township and even the prospect of a thirty-mile day trip could not dampen Anne's pleasure at leaving it.

The journey home was slow and rough. Sometimes they rode on the springless dray piled high with their purchases and Anne's luggage, and sometimes they walked beside it. As Anne said, they got down and walked for a rest, a rest from the incessant jarring as the wheels crashed over ruts, logs, and hidden stumps.

It was sundown when they arrived at the hut. A fire was burning in the open fireplace, and on the home-made bush table stood a tin filled with sprays of bottlebrush, the crimson blooms making a splash of colour in the twilight.

Anne, always a lover of flowers, cried delightedly, "Oh, Ben! How lovely! Some one must have known we were coming."

"Must've been one of the blacks," he answered, doing his best to hide his annoyance. "There's a camp down the river and I use two of the boys to help me with the cattle sometimes."

He was wondering how Biddy could have known they were arriving that day and he was inwardly raging at her disregard for his orders. "Clear out, and don't come back here any more," he had told her when he returned from that last visit to Wavering Downs. "I'm bringing a proper white missus home and I don't want any gins hanging around the place."

She had answered with her invariable, passive, "Youi, Boss," and faded quietly off—right out of his life, he hoped. He certainly did not want her coming back to tell tales to Anne. At that time his knowledge of the blacks was superficial and he knew nothing of the intense loyalty they could show to anyone they were fond of.

"Is it worse than you thought it would be?" he asked Anne the morning after their arrival.

"I don't think it's nearly as bad as you made out," she answered sincerely. "And we can make it quite nice." She moved to the doorway. "And, Ben, you didn't tell me how lovely the view was. Some day, if we could build a verandah with ferns and creepers along it, it would be perfect."

It was the first time Ben had really noticed the view from his front door. He had chosen the site for practical reasons, because it was close to permanent water, yet above flood level. Now that Anne drew his attention to it he found himself looking out over a lagoon studded with water-lilies. Gum saplings lined the lagoon banks and in between their white trunks he could see over the rich coolibah flat to the river with its tall gums and graceful ti-trees. A fine sweep of cattle country in his eyes. A lovely landscape in Anne's.

He had to ride the boundary fence that day and when he

returned at sundown Anne said, "Ben, I've had the dearest little black girl here all day. Biddy, she said her name was. She's been helping me with the unpacking and she's coming back to help me hang curtains tomorrow if we'll let her. I offered to pay her out of my own money, but she said she didn't want money, only tucker and a bit of tobacco sometimes. Would you mind if I let her come? She's such a help and she'd be company for me when you are away all day."

Ben minded very much. Had it not been for the fact that he was already finding it difficult to refuse Anne anything he would have told her to chase Biddy with a stick if she came near the place. As it was, he said, "Let her come if you want her, Anne."

After all, he reasoned, if Biddy wanted to damn him in Anne's eyes she could easily find ways of doing it even if he refused to let her inside the hut. To put it bluntly, his future happiness was in Biddy's dusky hands.

It could not have been in safer ones. Within a year Biddy was installed in a little lean-to at the rear of the hut, willing housemaid and assistant gardener to Anne and devoted nursemaid to her son.

All Anne's modest dreams had come true. They had a verandah with ferns and young creeping vines that would soon give an illusion of coolness on the hottest day, they had flower-beds and a small vegetable garden, and there were gay curtains and furniture to hide the bareness of the slab walls. Ben, with an assured income from cattle sales, would have bought the hideous furniture on sale in the Stonehaven stores, but Anne would have none of it. She had taste, a natural flair for recognizing or inventing the right thing, so that almost everything in the hut was home-made. There were kangaroo and calf-skin mats scattered about the floors. The chairs, designed by her and built by Ben, had cowhide seats with the hair uppermost. Years later such furnishings were to become ultra-fashionable, but Anne had instinctively recognized them as the only fitting decoration for such a setting.

She was a born gardener, and during her pregnancy she was constantly planting things. "I can't help it, Ben," she said once when he told her she was doing too much for a girl in her condition. "I want to feel the earth in my hands all the time. It's a sort of craving. I can't get enough of it."

Beyond insisting that Biddy do all the water carrying, he left her alone after that. She and Biddy went for long, rambling walks, always coming home with some new seedling shrub or creeper. The relationship between them had changed from mistress and maid to one of mutual friendship. Indeed it was quite often Biddy who gave the orders. When she said firmly, "More better you don't do that one, missus," Anne knew she meant "That's no job for a woman expecting a baby. Sit down at once and let me do it."

Usually Anne gave in, though occasionally she said with an unexpected show of authority, "Nonsense, Biddy. It won't hurt me a bit."

When Anne arrived home with the new baby Biddy took charge immediately. Her motherly attitude amused Anne, but Ben once growled, "You'd think he was her son instead of ours."

They named the baby Daniel after the only real friend Ben had ever known.

★ 6 ★

How proud old Dan Clancy had been of his small namesake. Whenever he passed through the district he called at Coolibah, though it had been difficult to persuade him to step inside the hut at first. With his deep-rooted dislike of all women he would have preferred to yarn with Ben over at the horse-yard, where the two of them could squat on their heels and talk the free and easy language of the droving camps. It was hard to convince him that Anne would feel deeply hurt if her husband's best friend refused to share a meal with them.

"The tucker's on the table, waiting for you," Ben informed him. "You'll have to come in, old-timer. And for Gawd's sake don't say a word about cattle-duffing. She doesn't know about the things we used to get up to."

"She's changed you, Ben." Dan shook his head sorrowfully. "I dunno; you're different. You talk like a toff and you'll be tryin' to tell me next you'd ride right past a big cleanskin and never think of shovin' your brand on 'im. I always warned you about wimmin. I never yet knew no good come of a man gettin' himself mixed up with one."

Yet by the time the baby was walking Dan had lost his shyness with Anne, and by the following year he had obviously become fond of her. It would have been strange indeed if he had not fallen under the spell she cast over every one she met. Her easy naturalness, the all-embracing warmth of her smile, and the friendliness in her brown eyes captivated them all, men and women, young and old. Her manner never changed, whether she were speaking to a ragged, rascally old black, a visiting cattle-buyer, or the Anglican bishop. It would not, could not have changed for a member of the Royal family. The amazing thing was that it took him, her husband, so long to appreciate it all.

Her innocence amazed him. Once she temporarily stumped

him by asking, "Ben dear, there aren't any cattle-thieves around here, are there?"

When he recovered sufficiently he answered as casually as he could, "I've never heard of any. They certainly don't worry me."

"I thought not." She dismissed the unworthy thought with a toss of her neat dark head. "Mr Delacy used to say the country was full of them, but he thought the worst of every one."

How could he tell such a woman that the greater part of his income came from cattle-duffing?

Dan had only been partially right when he said that Anne had changed him. She had taught him to speak correctly and she had improved his manners, but she had not changed his outlook towards other people's cattle because it was a side of his nature she knew nothing about. Constable Ryan had put only a temporary stop to his activities, and once the policeman tired of watching him he'd be making up for lost time.

Two years after Anne came to Coolibah Constable Ryan was transferred. He left the district without carrying out his threat to get Ben, and his place was taken by a man with a grudge against the police officials responsible for sending him to the dead outback of Baranda. He hated the bush and he soon made it known that if anyone wanted him he could be found at the police-station.

Scarcely a week after Ryan's departure, Ben, followed by his two blackboys, was heading for the Jump-up. There were rich pickings waiting for him up there.

During the next two years the Coolibah herd increased at an amazing pace. An astute owner would have noticed the rapid decline in the Wavering Downs brandings, but Ben knew he had nothing to fear from Delacy.

Anne, of course, suspected nothing, and though Biddy must have known or guessed what was going on she never once mentioned the subject. She was devoting a lot of time to young Danny then, taking him for long walks and pointing out everything, so that by the time he was ten he was a shrewd bushman, well able to live off the land. He was also, Ben pointed out proudly, a fearless horseman.

Anne was the only one dissatisfied with his progress. "I simply can't get him to take any interest in his school lessons," she complained to Ben. "He's just itching to get outdoors all the time." A smile replaced her worried frown. "He's not nearly as good a pupil as you were, my sweet."

Those endearing terms of hers! In another woman they would have sounded trite, but coming from Anne they carried an unforgettable ring of sincerity. "But in every other way he's like you all over again."

The likeness, remarkable enough then, was to become more and more pronounced as the youngster grew up. He had his father's fair hair, he was tall for his age, and it was obvious that he would inherit Ben's broad shoulders and hooked nose. He even walked like his father, with the short, somewhat awkward steps of the man who spends most of his life in the saddle.

When he was ten Anthea was born. She made her arrival at an unfortunate time, and while grudgingly admitting that she could scarcely be held responsible Ben found himself unable to develop any affection for his only daughter. She was to have been born in the security of Stonehaven hospital. All arrangements had been made when the Big Flood intervened.

It started raining three nights before Anne was due to board the mail coach at Baranda, and for a full week it never let up. In the vain, almost desperate hope that it would ease off after daylight Ben ran the horses in as soon as the first dreary light of dawn struggled through the downpour. He had a fine buggy and pair now, and given a short break in the weather the road to Baranda would be trafficable for them. But the break never came. For five days and nights it rained steadily and daylight on the sixth day revealed a raging river overlapping its banks and spreading out over the low-lying areas.

"That settles it," Ben announced gloomily. "We'll be cut off for a week or more."

It was typical of her that she took the situation much more calmly than he did. She said, "Don't worry, dear. The river might go down in a day or two and the baby isn't due for two weeks."

Too worried to even discuss it with her, Ben only grunted. At the best of times he was a poor conversationalist and when anything was worrying him he became positively inarticulate, jerking his words out as though he begrudged each one.

He gulped down a quick breakfast, buckled on his spurs, and said gruffly, "Goin' down to the camp for a couple of boys. Have to shift the cattle back off the river flats."

"You'll be careful, won't you, dear?" Anne reached up and put an arm across his shoulder. "And don't worry about me. Even if the river stays up and the worst happens I'll be all right. I've got Biddy."

"Her!" Impatiently he pushed her arm away and strode to the door. "A lot o' good she'd be! An ignorant, bloody black gin!"

Fortunately, there were few cattle on the flats for the two black boys were almost useless. They accompanied Ben reluctantly and in spite of his threats and curses they kept glancing anxiously back at the rapidly rising river.

"Get 'em together and keep 'em moving," Ben roared. "What the hell have you got to be worried about? The camp's on high ground and there'll be plenty tucker comin' down the river soon."

"Youi, Boss. Altogether too much." Quartpot rolled his bloodshot eyes, glancing upstream through the rain. "Might be this one altogether ole man flood."

Might be! Might be! And might not be. What the hell would they know about it anyhow? A pair of ignorant savages. Yet despite his sneers Ben could not help feeling uneasy. In matters of this sort the blacks had a kind of instinct a white man could not even begin to understand. They had always maintained that their camp had never been flooded yet they were obviously uneasy about it this morning.

"Righto, righto. Clear out and let yer horses go." Impatiently Ben dismissed them. With the cattle now stringing off towards the high ground it was easy enough for one man to keep them moving.

It was nearly noon when he turned back for home, satisfied that his cattle were safe from anything the river could do. And judging from the leaden sky and the way the rain was pelting down this could well be a record flood. The melon holes in the scrub were overflowing, joining up in a series of small lagoons that made it difficult for his horse to pick its way without stumbling belly-deep into a hole that might be thirty or forty yards across. Ben made no attempt to guide it. Water cascading from the brim of his hat and streaming down his face made it virtually impossible to pick out landmarks that were at best only vague grey blurs in the grey downpour. But with its unerring instinct the horse would take him home despite the fact that it was moving crabwise with hanging head and flattened ears in a vain effort to minimize the sting of the driving rain.

Once it stopped abruptly, threw up its head, and neighed loudly. Shading his eyes, Ben saw that they were only a few yards from the horse-paddock fence. Beyond the fence, huddled together in a miserable mob, the horses stood. Their tightly tucked-down tails were turned to the rain, their backs were humped and their heads hung dejectedly. They were fetlock-deep in water. Yellow water, Ben noted in alarm.

River water! Impossible! How could the river get right back here, nearly two miles from its channel and on a rise the blacks had told him was above the highest flood? Why, their camp was on the far end of this ridge!

But it *was* river water. Yellow, dotted with an endless procession of lesser debris, it was moving slowly but surely across the horse-paddock.

Hurriedly Ben dismounted, opened the fence, and swung back into his sodden saddle. The horses would find their own way out to the higher ground, but he must get back to his family before the floodwaters cut him off. Between here and the house were hollows that would soon be a swim.

With visions of a distracted and badly scared Anne trying to pacify a panic-stricken Danny and Biddy, he spurred his horse savagely. The time for relying on its homing instinct was past, for now it would try to swing back after its mates rather than flounder forward through the rising flood.

The water was swirling around the horse's shoulders when they came in sight of the homestead. And a terrifying sight it was. House, horse-yard, and buggy shed stood on an island roughly two hundred yards long and less than one hundred across, and away to the left rows of post-tops marked the position of the main stockyard. Except for tree-tops showing above water nothing else was visible. A lull in the rain would reveal mile on mile of swirling, muddied water with not one other speck of land standing above its surface.

As he removed saddle and bridle and shut the horse in the yard Ben made a quick estimate of the situation. The water would have to rise another three feet or more before it reached the floor of the house. And since this flood had already risen higher than any in the memory of the blacks, it was fairly reasonable to suppose that it was now almost at its peak. True the rain was still pouring down, but purely local rain would have little influence on the river height. It was what was happening up around the headwaters that would count.

In any case he could do nothing now but wait and sweat it out. With only one horse between four of them, and Anne in her condition, they were all marooned on this island until the flood subsided.

Anne was waiting for him in the doorway and she was obviously relieved to see him. "My poor darling," she greeted him. "What a dreadful time you must have had. Come in and take your wet things off. Never mind the mess; just drop everything there. Here's a towel. When you've dried yourself you'll find dry clothes on the back of the chair." How like her! Not a word of complaint about her own fears, just concern over him. "Are the cattle all safe?"

"Eh?" He stopped towelling his dripping hair and wondered if he'd heard her aright. "The cattle, did you say? Of course. Damned sight safer than we are here." For a moment or two he studied her as she stood there, calm, almost serene in her conviction that all would be well now that he was back. "You know we're in a bad way, don't you? Stranded on a bit of an island, cut off from anywhere. And the river's still rising."

"Yes, I know. I've been watching it. Hurry up and get dressed. I've got a hot meal waiting for you." She moved to the fireplace and lifted up a steaming pot of stew. "I watched it rising all the morning. The river, I mean. But in the last hour or so it has hardly moved. It can't get much higher, can it, Ben? The blacks always said this ridge never got flooded."

"They said that about their camp, but it's under water now." He finished drying himself and pulled on the fresh shirt and trousers. "Look, Anne, we might as well face up to it. If it's still raining like this up the head of the river anything could happen."

"You mean—you mean the house could be swept away?"

"I said *anything*, didn't I?" He snapped the words at her, his anxiety making him irritable. "And we're stuck here. I've let the horses out bush, but even if I had them all in the yard they wouldn't be any help. You couldn't ride the way you are, even on dry ground."

"No." She looked down at her swollen body and smiled ruefully. "I'm afraid I couldn't, so there's no use thinking about it, is there? We'll just have to stay here and pray for the rain to stop. Sit down and eat your dinner while it's hot."

She's game, Ben thought as he sat down and started to eat. Most women would be screaming their heads off at a man to do something. And what *could* he do? Go out and order the river to stop rising? Yell to the skies to send down a boat? No, he couldn't do a dam' thing. Except hope. Pity he didn't believe in praying like Anne did.

"Hey!" he said, suddenly realizing that no small boy had come rushing to greet him. "Where's young Danny?"

Anne walked to the foot of the table and sat facing him. Her anxiety now showing plainly, she said, "Darling, you're going to be terribly cross with me for being so stupid. I let him go with Biddy."

"When? Where to?" The questions came out with the explosive force of rifle shots.

"Down to the camp. Soon after you left. I didn't want to let him go with her, but he kept pleading with me. And Biddy backed him up. She kept saying, 'More better you let 'im come, missus.' And as they were leaving she said, 'Missus, might be this one altogether big flood, but I don't forget you, and I bring 'im Danny back to you safe. True.' She made me promise not to worry. I tried so hard to keep my promise, but the morning dragged on and on and the flood got higher and higher, and I just couldn't help worrying." A solitary tear trickled unheeded down her cheek. "Oh, Ben, what can have happened to them?"

Struggling to shut out a vision of his small son being swept away in the swirling flood Ben snarled, "Bloody rotten gin! You shouldn't have trusted her. All the damn' blacks are the same. Never trust any of 'em."

"But Biddy adored Danny. She'd never let him out of her sight if she thought he was in any danger."

"How do you know what she'd do when she found her own black hide in danger? Those two useless bucks cleared out and left me in the lurch this morning. They're all the same underneath, every black-hided, black-hearted one of 'em." In his anxiety for his son he was deliberately hurting her.

Anne's head went down on her arms and she cried miserably. "It's all my fault," she sobbed. "All my wretched fault. I shouldn't have listened to Biddy. I shouldn't have let Danny out of my sight."

In later years Ben sometimes wondered when he had first fallen in love with his wife, and the only conclusion he ever reached was that it must have been a very gradual process, creeping on him so steadily and consistently that he was not even aware of its progress. The final, full awareness leaped upon him at the sight of her sitting there sobbing. Only once before had he seen her cry and on that occasion he had asked her to marry him. He wasn't in love with her then, but by Heaven he was now.

He knelt beside her, pulled her head down on to his shoulder, and ran awkward fingers through her neatly combed hair.

"Don't, sweetheart. Don't cry," he soothed. For the first time an endearment slipped out naturally and easily. "You mustn't blame yourself for anything. The youngster'll be all right. When the flood goes down he'll come back safe and sound as ever."

"But how *can* he be safe if the camp is under water? And you said yourself that you couldn't trust the blacks."

"I dunno, darling. I dunno what made me say it." His fingers were making an untidy tangle of her hair. "But it's not true. In some things you can't trust 'em, but when it comes to looking after kids you can. Look at the way they spoil their own. And they all think the world of Danny."

"What if they were all trapped in the flood?"

"The blacks! Not them. They had a sort of feeling this was coming and my guess is that they cleared out early, back to the high ground. Most likely they were on their way when Biddy and Danny got there and they took them with them. Just what they would do."

"Will they have any food?"

"They'll get it. It mightn't be your idea of good tucker, but you can bet they won't starve." He gave her an affectionate shake. "Now will you stop worrying?"

"Yes, Ben." She heaved herself awkwardly up and ran a hand over her rumpled hair. "Your dinner's getting cold. Finish it while I go and comb out this mess."

* 7 *

MOST of that afternoon they spent on the verandah, watching the flood. The rain had eased off to a series of showers, but still the water-level rose. Ben estimated the rise as little more than an inch an hour even though their island was shrinking alarmingly.

"It looks worse than it is," he assured Anne when she pointed out that the water had crept right through the horse-yard and was now only a few yards from the buggy shed. "The ground rises pretty steeply from there. We must be nearly three feet above that yard and that's a long way for a river to rise when it's spread out like this."

Spread out! During the breaks in the rain they could see for miles in every direction, and nowhere beyond the narrow limits of their little island could they see one speck of solid land. The river, Ben declared, could be anything from ten to fifteen miles wide.

Between the house and the Jump-up it was more or less a backwater, carrying little debris and moving only slowly. But from the strip of ground in front of the house to its normal channel it surged in a swift, undulating, muddy torrent. Logs, branches, and whole trees swirled past, their twisting progress giving the impression of life—living things writhing in agony, occasionally throwing appealing arms skyward in mute appeal. Scores of cattle swept by, some swimming feebly with the current, but most of them bloated in death.

Once Anne called excitedly, "Look, Ben! Look! We've got a visitor. Over near the buggy shed."

Ben looked out and saw the cow, a pitifully exhausted wreck of a cow that was to become all too familiar to him before the flood subsided. She was standing belly-deep in water, head hanging, and ears drooped in misery.

For perhaps thirty minutes she stood there, and at last, step by painful step, she dragged herself clear of the water. Then, placing each foot carefully she turned until she was facing upstream and started to bellow. At first she could only manage a feeble, high-pitched squeak, but as her strength came back the sound grew in volume and deepened in tone until it resembled the raucous blaring of a ship's foghorn. And like the foghorn's warning it came at regular intervals, blaring out over the swirling waters with a monotonous repetition.

"What on earth is the matter with her?" Anne asked. "Is she hurt or just lonely?"

"She's lost her calf. Must have been only a few days old. Look at the size of her udder."

"The poor pet." Anne leaned heavily against him. "The poor darling. I know exactly how she feels about her baby."

Slipping a supporting arm around her Ben led her back into the kitchen. "Try not to listen to her. She'll keep that up all night and probably all tomorrow too. And don't worry about Danny. I tell you he's safer than we are."

They went to bed early that night and fell asleep with the sound of rain drumming on the roof and the rumbling growl of the flood waters shattered at regular intervals by the bellow of the cow calling for her drowned calf. There was a hopeless note in the bellowings now as if the poor animal realized the futility of calling any longer, yet felt impelled to keep it up while her breath lasted.

At ten o'clock Ben felt a hand pressing his arm and heard Anne say, "Ben. Ben dear. I'm terribly sorry, my poor darling, but I'm afraid the baby is starting to arrive."

He was out of bed in a second, clumsily turning up the lamp Anne had insisted they keep burning. The warm light flooded over the room and he turned to her in a helpless, panic-stricken daze.

"It can't be! It's much too soon! You must be making a mistake!" Stupid words. Thoughtless, meaningless words jerked out to hide his own horrible fear. "It can't be, I tell yer." Why couldn't he keep his damfool mouth shut? Of course it could be. Of course she wouldn't make a mistake about such a thing. Why couldn't he face up to it calmly instead of cringing behind a string of unconvincing denials?

"I'm afraid it *is* true, my poor pet. The pains started quite a long while ago and I waited until I was quite sure before I woke you."

There she was, calm and unafraid, thinking, as she always did, more of him than of herself. As though he, and not she, would be racked by these cruel pains!

"But what are we going to do, Anne? There's nobody here to help you. Nobody but me." Her unselfishness had steadied him a little, but he was still a long way from attaining her calmness.

"We'll just have to manage. I got everything ready in case this happened. Biddy and I did. But we both thought she'd be here to help me."

"That damn' useless bloody gin!" He was trying to work off his fears by raging against Biddy. "I told you you couldn't trust one of 'em. When she comes sneaking back here after this is over I'll flay her black hide and chase her off the selection."

"Please, Ben! Please don't talk like that. You know you don't really mean it and you know Biddy would have come back here if it had been humanly possible. I don't believe she'd ever desert me."

"You've got a hell of a lot more faith in her than I have."

"I don't think so, really. You're just upset, you poor dear."

She writhed as a fresh spasm of pain gripped her. Turning her head to hide the contortions she could not control she dug her fingers fiercely into the bed clothes.

Outside the cow bellowed mournfully.

The spasm passed and Anne gasped, "The poor wretched cow! Every time the pain comes on she bellows. You'd think she was having the baby instead of me." She smiled, a weak, not very convincing smile. "Look, dearest, will you stoke the fire up and put the big kettle on? When you've done that open my big trunk and give me the bundle wrapped in a sheet."

He had the kitchen fire burning well and was opening the trunk when the cow bellowed again. Unable to help himself, he turned to see the fingers clutching frantically at the bed clothes, digging like talons into their unresisting softness.

"What do I do next?" The racking pain had eased, leaving

Anne pale and panting. The neatly wrapped bundle was beside her on the bed, and Ben had himself more or less under control.

"Nothing just yet, dear. You'd better go into the kitchen and leave me alone for a while." She reached for his hand and squeezed it tightly. "Try not to worry, and don't take any notice if I start to bellow like that poor old cow. When the time comes I'll call you. You'll know what to do, won't you?"

"I think so. I hope so. I hope to God I will, Anne." He bent over and kissed her gently, running his hand over her forehead and feeling the wetness of the sweat clinging to it. "You know I love you and couldn't get along without you, don't you?"

"I hoped you'd say that. I did so hope you'd say it before you left me. I know it's true now, and knowing it will make things so much easier."

Standing in front of the kitchen fire Ben fought hard to achieve some of Anne's calm self-control. Birth was no stranger to him; he had seen it scores of times during his cattle-work. He'd acted as midwife to many difficult births—in animals. But now that only made him feel worse. What if there were complications such as he'd seen in stock? He'd had to be brutal on some of those occasions. And he hadn't always been successful. What if he killed Anne by his clumsiness?

The cow bellowed again and, like a faint echo, a low moaning came from the bedroom. Time and again the noises were repeated until he felt an almost uncontrollable urge to take his old rifle from the corner and go out and shoot the cow, as though by silencing her he could put an end to Anne's sufferings.

She was whimpering now, whimpering like a frightened pup as she fought to stifle the louder moans, and he was thinking he *must* go to her when he heard the back door rattle. It couldn't be some one knocking! Couldn't possibly be. He and Anne were cut off from the entire outside world, cut off by miles of floodwaters. Yet the rattling persisted, growing more insistent as he hesitated.

Still unbelieving he unlatched the door, jerked it open, and saw Biddy standing there.

At any other time he would have noted that she was on the verge of extreme physical exhaustion. Her wet hair hung in straggling rats' tails around her face, a gaunt, haggard face with dark eyes sunk far back above ridge-like cheekbones. She was supporting herself against the door frame and she was completely naked.

But now, as the lamplight shone on her gleaming body, Ben only saw that it *was* Biddy.

"Biddy!" he gasped. "Thank God you've come. Can you help her?" No word of explanation that Anne was in labour. Just the bare question.

But Biddy understood. With a fixity of purpose and an endurance beyond belief she had waded and swum through miles of flood-waters, much of it in the dark, in order to get back to her mistress, yet instead of mentioning it she slipped quietly past him and said:

"Youi, Boss. I bin fix 'im orright now."

And, strangely, he believed her.

Feeling relief flow through him he stepped outside. He needed air, clean fresh air and exercise. He wanted to go for a long brisk walk but that was impossible. The rain, he noticed, had eased to a light drizzle and a pale moon was struggling to shed its light through the clouds.

A long, pleading whinny from the horse-yard reminded him that the horse was standing knee-deep in water. No need to leave the poor animal shut in any longer. It certainly wouldn't try to swim away now and it could get a bit of picking around the house.

As he passed the buggy shed Ben almost collided with the cow. Obviously she hadn't seen him because her head was turned away and she chose that particular moment to shatter the silence with another full-throated bellow. The noise, coming so unexpectedly out of the darkness less than an arm's length away, both startled and infuriated Ben, causing him to do a very stupid thing.

He yelled, "Shut yer bloody mouth, yer bellowin' sod," and kicked her hard in the ribs.

Since he was barefooted the kick hurt his foot more than it hurt the cow. But it certainly startled her and she reacted just as, had he been in a normal state of mind, he would have expected any half-wild station cow to react. She spun sharply around and hooked. It was a vicious, slashing hook of upswept horns, the kind of attack any alert cattleman expects from an infuriated cow. But Ben was far from alert; he'd been through too much during the last few hours. Moreover he was too close to elude the attack. He heard the rip of his tearing shirt and felt the searing burn as one horn skidded along his ribs.

Trembling all over with rage the cow snorted and hooked again. She was too late. In a split second the shock of her first slash had transformed Ben from a distracted husband to an agile cattleman, well used to dealing with this type of situation. He might not be a competent midwife but, by hell, no bad-tempered old bitch of a cow was going to take a second swing at him and get away with it. Before the cow realized what was happening he had shot up along her flank and grasped her firmly by the tail.

Now *he* was master of the situation. Let her try another hook! She did. She swung around, intending to put an end to this nonsense, and felt her rump being dragged forward to meet her head. Caught completely off-balance, she crashed heavily on to her side.

"Try it again," Ben taunted, holding her uppermost hind leg clear of the ground.

She struggled feebly for a moment and then lay still. Still weak from her long swim she had put all her remaining energy into the attack. Now she needed time to recover.

Ben cleared his throat, spat on her, and said disgustedly, "A man oughta drag yer back into the water and let yer drown."

He hadn't the slightest intention of doing it. His disgust was directed at his own stupidity rather than at her act of self-defence. He did not even feel like kicking her again as she lay there. Instead he released his hold and slipped quietly away.

He found the horse pawing nervously at the water and as

he opened the gate it almost knocked him down in its anxiety to get to the higher ground.

Time I was getting back up there too, Ben told himself. Getting back for what? With Biddy in charge there was nothing for him to do but wait. It might be all over now. Anne would be weak and exhausted. And Biddy! For the first time he realized what Biddy must have endured to get back here. He remembered now that she had been naked, remembered too how she had clung to the door frame for support. She must have been on the point of collapse. There *was* something he could do.

When Biddy, wearing one of Anne's frocks, at last came out of the bedroom he had a cup of tea ready for her, the strong sweet tea he knew she liked. He had also set out bread and beef, remembering that she must have been without food all day.

"You go longa Missus now," Biddy said. "Little one girl this time." And then, catching sight of his torn and slightly bloodstained shirt, "What you bin do, Boss?"

"An old cow out there hooked me. It's nothin'. Only a bit of a scratch. Just grazed me ribs with the side of her horn. Served me right too. Me own damn' fault."

"More better you wait here." She slipped into the next room and came back with a clean shirt. "Put 'im on," she commanded.

He obeyed meekly, but to even the score he led her to the table and sat her down in front of the meal he had prepared. Satisfied that she would eat it, he poured another cup of tea and took it into the bedroom.

Anne, pale as the pillows that supported her, greeted him with a smile. "It's a daughter, darling," she said, indicating the bundle at her side. "Isn't she sweet?"

He glanced down at a red, wrinkled face that failed to arouse the faintest flicker of paternal pride in him. Indeed, at that moment he would not have cared if Biddy had taken the new baby out and tossed it into the flood waters. His only concern was for Anne.

He said, "Was it very bad?" and bent to kiss her damp forehead.

"Not really bad at all. And Biddy was wonderful. Ben, fancy her struggling all that way back to be with me. She must be nearly dead. Do you think you could get her a cup of tea and something to eat and then send her off to bed?"

"She's eating now. I'll send her off as soon as she finishes," he assured her. "I've brought you a cup of tea too. Can you manage it?"

"I'd love it." She took the cup and drank thirstily. "Ben, Danny's safe. They took him right back to the Jump-up. Isn't it wonderful?"

Hell! He must have been in a bad way. He'd been so worried over Anne that he'd clean forgotten all about his son.

He returned to the kitchen to find Biddy fast asleep with her wet black hair sprawled over the remains of her meal. Very gently he picked her up and carried her to her bed. And then, looking down at her as she lay sleeping the deep sleep of utter exhaustion, he said:

"You're whiter than I am, Biddy. I won't forget this."

When he went outside again the moon was shining through a break in the clouds and rain had stopped. He walked to the water's edge and there, an inch or two from it, was a faint line of minor debris.

The river was falling!

His wife was safe, his son was safe, and even his cattle were safe. Any fencing that was swept away could soon be replaced, and to offset that loss he'd be sure to pick up a few head of cattle swept down from the up-river stations. Why, he might even show a nice profit from the flood. He hadn't a worry in the world. He could go inside, stretch out on the floor in front of the kitchen fire, and sleep and sleep.

★ 8 ★

SOME one was addressing him as "Boss" and asking how he felt. The voice was subdued and sympathetic, just a shade too sympathetic. Old Ben kept his eyes closed, unwilling to be dragged away from the old, hard-battling days to the smooth efficiency of this well-run hospital. And his visitor.

Without opening his eyes he could see the man standing at the foot of his bed. Medium height, carefully brushed hair turning grey, especially around the temples, and a face that the owner liked to hear described as handsome and distinguished because the description *had* been true before so many years of steady drinking had left their marks on it. The evening being warm, he would be wearing a well-tailored, light tropical suit. His belly would be straining at the waistband of his trousers, overlapping it if he relaxed the least bit.

Still Ben's eyelids did not flicker. He disliked his son-in-law and the longer he could "play possum" the less time he would have to spend trying to be polite before Gregory had to dash off to the club. With luck his visitor might decide to leave without disturbing him.

But that was only wishful thinking. He was here because he wanted something, money possibly, or perhaps a tip for Saturday's races, and he wouldn't leave without working gradually up to the point. Blast the man! Might as well get it over.

Opening his eyes he said, "Hullo, Gregory. I guessed it would be you. How are you?"

"Oh, I'm fine. Fine, thanks. But how are *you*?"

"Lousy."

The candid answer temporarily stumped Gregory who had been expecting the old man to declare himself perfectly fit. He had his next line all ready to counter such a declaration, but now all he could say was, "Oh."

"D'yer think I'd let myself be yarded up in this joint if I wasn't feeling lousy?" Ben demanded irritably.

"No, no. Of course not. Certainly not. Er—have they any idea what's wrong with you? We asked Doc Stuart at the Club last night, but he covered up with some lengthy Latin description he knew none of us would understand."

"That's what's known as professional etiquette. Pity more blokes wouldn't use it."

Deciding that if the barb were directed at him it might be best to ignore it, Gregory said, "Anthea rang to say she'd been to see you this morning. She told me to ask you if there was anything else you wanted."

"Nothing, except to get out of here, and you can't do anything about that. Now come down to tin-tacks, Gregory. What do *you* want?"

"Always looking for an ulterior motive, aren't you, you old cynic? I don't want anything. I just dropped in to see how you were and to see if there was anything I could do for you."

"Very noble and unselfish of you. And now you've done your duty as a son-in-law, wouldn't you like to shoot off for a grog session with your cobbers?"

"Not at all. Not at all. I'm in no hurry, Boss."

Ben winced slightly, as he always did, at Gregory's use of the title. Still, it was better than "Dad." There had been a time, a very short time, when Gregory considered that his marriage to Anthea gave him the right to address his father-in-law as "Dad," but he had soon been disillusioned. In the end, the relationship calling for a certain amount of familiarity, they had compromised on "Boss," though Ben still considered only Biddy, Charlie Turner, and the station hands had the right to use it. Jane, of course, made an endearment out of it by calling him "Bossy," and he loved to hear her say it.

"As a matter of fact——" Gregory decided to come to the point, or at least lead up to it. "As a matter of fact, I'd appreciate your advice while I'm here."

"Shoot."

"Things have been on the quiet side in real estate lately

and I've been thinking of branching out, expanding really, by starting a stock and station agency. Only as a sideline, of course. I've got a first-class man waiting to take on the outside work, knows the cattle business from start to finish, and I was wondering what you thought of the idea."

"I think it stinks."

"Any special reason for putting it that way?"

"A dozen. And I told 'em all to you when you and Anthea got the idea into your heads about twenty years ago."

"But this is quite different. The man I have in mind is an experienced cattleman."

"So what? You'd still be the boss, the bloke the station owners have to deal with in the end. Don't get the idea that by reading yesterday's market reports and buying beer for graziers when they come to town you'd fool 'em into giving you their business. Because they wouldn't. They'd drink your beer, but if you listened to 'em outside you'd hear 'em asking each other what the hell you know about cattle anyhow."

"I'd scarcely go about it that way." Gregory gave a fair imitation of a hearty laugh. "After all I've been in business for quite a few years. I know how clannish you bushmen are, and I thought if I had one or two good accounts to start off with——"

"Like the Wavering Downs account, eh? I'll say it for you and save you the trouble of workin' up to it bit by bit. And the answer would still be 'no.'" Ben heaved himself up until he was leaning on one elbow. "Look, Gregory, if you had any blasted sense at all you'd know you were wasting your time and mine. Stock and station work is a specialized job. You've got to know cattle, got to like the look of 'em and the smell of 'em. And that's where you fall down. You never did like us bushwhackers; you look down your nose at us. You reckoned you wanted my advice. Well, here it comes. Stick to real estate and leave the cattle business to blokes who can sit on the top rail at a sale and tell you the weight and meatworks price of every bullock in the yard, blokes that feel at home among wet cow-dung. I've heard you say you couldn't stand the smell of a yard of cattle. And you've got the nerve to talk about dealin' in 'em!"

Exhausted by his long speech Ben slumped back on his pillows, but before his son-in-law could think up a suitable answer he went on, "You and Anthea cooked this idea up together. I can hear you sayin' 'The old man won't last much longer, so I think I'll slip round and put it on him for the station business. If I land it I can easily pick up a man to look after the outside work.' And Anthea coming back with, 'Handle him tactfully, won't you, Gregory? If you antagonize him you know we'll get nothing out of him.' "

"Why, Boss, you must have been eavesdropping!" Better, Gregory decided, treat that last bit as a joke. Nothing would be gained by losing his temper. If he humoured the old devil he might get a tip for Saturday's races out of him before he left. The old man was usually pretty cagey about the prospects of any of his horses, but on the rare occasions when he *had* opened up his information had been worth a plunge. Not that Gregory ever plunged on those tips without checking. He was far too shrewd a punter to risk being led astray by what could easily be his father-in-law's idea of a joke. Oh, no; he had his own ways and means of finding out when a horse was ready to go.

Gregory Arnedale was a gambler, and like so many of his kind he fancied himself as a very shrewd punter. He knew all the worthwhile trainers and jockeys intimately, even though he could scarcely tell one horse from the other without the aid of the jockey's colours or the saddle-cloth number. He had had some big wins, wins that all his friends heard about, and since they never heard anything of his losses they could be pardoned for feeling a little envious of his astuteness. The bookmakers knew how much he lost in a year, but even they were not aware that there were times when he was hard-put to pay his gambling debts.

"We'll miss you out at the track on Saturday, Boss," he said jovially. "I don't suppose you'd like me to place any bets for you?"

"I don't bet unless I'm there to see the race run."

"But you're starting a couple of horses, aren't you?"

"Yair. I'm startin' a coupla 'orses." The deliberate lapse in his speech should have warned Gregory. "And you want ter know if it's safe ter back 'em, eh? That's it, ain't it?" With obvious effort Ben hoisted himself up again. "Well, I'm goin' to give you another bit of advice, Gregory. Lay off the 'orses before they break yer, if they haven't done it already. Your trouble is you gamble too much and you drink too much."

"So that makes two of us."

"Like hell it does! You started supportin' the bookies as soon as your old man died and left you the business, and you've been doin' it ever since. I never had a bet until I'd made me pile and was older than you are now. I dunno what racing costs you, but offhand I'd say it was more than you can afford. And d'yer know what it costs me? Nothin'! Not a brass rhazoo. I make money out of it. I spend a bit on booze, but I can afford to because when I was makin' my money I'd often go a whole year without tastin' it."

Very coldly Gregory said, "Supposing, for argument's sake, all the things you've said about me were true, wouldn't that be entirely my affair?"

"So long as you don't come cryin' to me to square up with your bookie."

"Now look here, Dad——"

"Don't call me 'Dad'!" The trumpeting roar of the words could have been heard across a yard full of cows bellowing for their freshly weaned calves, and the effort brought on a flush that made old Ben's white eyebrows stand out like tufts of white feathers on a red billiard ball. It left him weak and panting and it brought a startled nurse to ease him back on to his pillows and hold a glass of water to his lips.

"You mustn't upset the patient like that," she reproved, glancing accusingly at the equally startled visitor. "Are you all right now, Mr McReady?"

Ben growled, "Of course I'm all right. Can't a man let his head go once in a while without every one fussing over him?"

"There are other patients in the hospital," the nurse reminded him.

"Righto, righto. If it'll make 'em feel any better you go round 'em all and tell 'em I'm sorry."

"I'm sorry too, Boss," Gregory said when the nurse left. "I honestly didn't mean to upset you. The name just slipped out in the heat of the moment. I think I'd better clear off now and let you get a bit of rest."

"Good idea. It's not your lucky day, is it, Gregory? You came in here hoping to land a nice bit of business and pick up a sure thing for Saturday's races. And you didn't get either of 'em."

"I must confess I wasn't over optimistic. You aren't exactly noted for your generosity to your family."

"I don't suppose I am." Ben appeared to think the matter over for a moment. "Why shouldn't I help you? After all you *are* my son-in-law. I'll give you a tip, but keep it to yourself because I don't want this information spread around. I've nominated two horses and they're both starting in the second race. Only one of 'em's trying, so if you want to have a mild flutter put your money on the filly Starry Gold. And in return for the tip you can do something for me. Ring Charlie Turner, tell him I'm here, and ask him to drop in and see me tonight."

As he said good-bye Gregory felt relieved to see that his father-in-law had recovered from the effects of his outburst. The old chap was lying there, breathing normally, a contented smile spreading over his face as he raised a hand in farewell.

When he stepped diffidently into the room two hours later Charlie Turner thought his old mate looked too well to be in hospital. Ben's evening nip of rum had been followed by a good meal, after which two competent nurses had propped him up with extra pillows until he was almost sitting.

"Well, Gawd stone the flamin' crows!" Charlie greeted him. "What the hell are *you* doin' in this joint, Boss? You look all right to me."

"I *am* all right," Ben assured him. "The hospital was a bit short of patients so they shanghaied me in to help pay expenses. Drag yourself up a chair, old-timer, and let's hear all your worries."

"I got no worries, Boss." Charlie moved a chair to the bedside, perched himself uncomfortably on the edge of it, and fiddled with his hat until Ben said, "Chuck it on the floor. No one's gunna pinch the damn' thing."

He looked out of place in such austere surroundings, this gnarled, bow-legged, little old man with the faint odour of stables clinging to him in spite of his best suit and polished shoes. He was small and wiry, his skin looked as if it had been made out of an old pack-saddle bag, the maker using too much leather so that it hung in wrinkles around his neck. His sparse grey hair had been soused in water, parted on one side and brushed carefully. Against the weatherbeaten tan of his face his white collar and pale blue tie stood out in jarring contrast. The grey suit was innocuous enough, but beneath the trouser cuffs the dazzle of highly polished shoes again caught the eye. Neat shoes, expensive shoes, obviously made to order, they fitted with glove-like perfection a pair of absurdly small feet. Even more than his bow legs those feet stamped him as a professional horseman.

From stable boy to jockey, from jockey to trainer, Charlie's life had started with and would end with horses. He trained Ben's horses and he regarded Ben as his best human friend. There had been two horses that took precedence.

Now, as he placed his hat carefully under his chair, he said anxiously, "Nothin' serious, I hope."

"Only old age. It catches up with us all, Charlie. You and me, we've had a fair crack of the whip, and I've got a few years on you."

"Not too many."

"Enough to put me in the lead." Ben shrugged his heavy shoulders. "But never mind about our creaking joints. I didn't send for you to talk about them. How's the filly coming on?"

"As fit as she'll ever be. She could win Saturdee. If you want."

"I don't."

"Goin' to give the colt 'is 'ead, eh? He might do all right against that company and you'd get a good price on 'im."

"He's not goin' to win either."

"You're the boss." Charlie had never been one to question orders or waste words. Talking, in his opinion, never got a man anywhere. Except into trouble. If Ben wanted to give his reason for holding a horse back when it was ready to go he'd be glad to listen; if he didn't want to that was his business.

"I can't get out of here," Ben complained. "So you'll have to handle this for me. You've got Spargo booked to ride the filly and you couldn't get a better man for the job. Give him his instructions when he's finished riding work tomorrow morning. Tell him the truth about the filly. You and me both know, and I'll bet he knows, that she won't run well if she's jammed in. Tell him to get her clear of the bunch and put in his run early and tell him if he doesn't win there'll be no more rides coming from this stable. Got it?"

"So far."

"Right. Young Lee still riding the colt?"

"Unless you want to put another boy up."

"I don't. Lee knows how to keep his mouth shut and he'll do what he's told. But don't give him his instructions until just before the race, and then tell him he's only got one job to do. He's got to get outside the filly and keep her jammed in. When Spargo tries to break out for his run Lee heads him off. He'll know how to do it without gettin' hauled up in front of the stipes. By the time they get to the turn of the straight the filly will have packed up anyhow. She never could stand being shut in or cut off for long. All clear?"

"Clear as mud. But if that's the way yer want it that's the way it'll be."

Ben chuckled until the bed shook. "I'll tell you what it's all about, you old clam," he said. "You'll laugh like hell when you hear it. It's rich. I'm givin' me son-in-law a lesson in the racin' game. He was in here fishin' for a tip so I told him to have a mild flutter on Starry Gold. Only a mild one, mind you. But who know Greg Arnedale's form. If he thinks he's on a cert he'll put his shirt on it. And he'll make sure this is a cert by checkin' up on me. Trust his old father-in-law? Not him! He knows Spargo is boozing too much and he knows that for a tenner or even a fiver and a few drinks he'll spill the beans. When Spargo tells him he's got to win this race Gregory'll really plonk the money on. Won't be anything mild about *his* flutter. I'm tipping he'll go broke over it." Old Ben chuckled again. "That'll teach him a lesson, eh?"

Charlie scratched his head thoughtfully. The situation needed a bit of thinking over before venturing an opinion. When he finally did speak all he said was, "Sounds a bit screwy ter me."

"Why?"

"Well, he's your son-in-law, and if he's mug enough to do his dough on your say-so, you're the bloke that'll 'ave to help him out if he can't settle up with the books."

"It'll be worth it."

"So long as you think so. It's your money, not mine."

"You don't reckon it's a good idea?"

Charlie considered the question carefully before answering, "Well, Boss, since you're asking me, I don't. You'll never cure Arnedale of puntin'. Never. And this idea of puttin' 'im on a crook tip and then givin' him the money to pay the bookies! I dunno. It don't make sense to me."

"Who said anything about giving him money? Not me. No bloody fear. When he comes crying for help I'll tell him to send the bookies round to me. *I'll* settle with 'em. And two hours later every racing man in town'll know Greg Arnedale's credit is finished. He won't be able to lay a ten-bob bet without putting up the cash first. That'll really hurt him. And by lunch-time next day the news'll be all over town. What a smack in the eye that'll be! Why, I'll lay you a shade of odds he won't even show up at the club that night."

"Be a bit crook on yer daughter, won't it?"

"Do her good to get taken down a peg. Teach her not to bung on airs, and chuck so much money around on social stuff."

"You're a tough man, Boss."

"I've been through some tough times."

"You and me both."

"That's right, old-timer. A long time ago, wasn't it? A hell of a long time. Do you ever find yourself thinking about those old First War days, Charlie?"

"Not often. Sometimes when some of these flash, know-all youngsters start tellin' me what a horse can do and what he can't I get me back up and tell 'em about one or two of them desert rides. Like that Beersheba stunt! That always sticks in me mind. That and the night your young brother got killed. Gawd, what a night that was! I still dunno how any of us got out of it alive. Funny. I've forgotten the name of that joint. What was it again?"

Ben stared into space and said nothing. He remained silent for so long and was so obviously unconscious of his surroundings that Charlie asked anxiously:

"You all right, Boss?"

"Yes." Ben came slowly back to the present. "I'm all right, Charlie. I was just thinking. I dunno why I haven't told you this before. I often meant to, but somehow I never got around to it. And if anyone has a right to know it's you. The lad who died on that rocky hill in front of El Burj that night wasn't my brother. He was my son."

* 9 *

My son. He was my son. Not only my son, but the best cobber a man could ever wish for. And he died before he was twenty-one, died as he had always lived, fearlessly, the way a man should die.

The lights were out and the hospital had settled down for the night, but Ben was not sleeping. He was not even lying there in his bed; he was drifting back through the past, back to that hellish night on the hillside at El Burj, even further back to the chain of events that, once set in motion, swept them inexorably forward to the bitter, bitter climax.

Like so many major events in his early life it started with a bit of cattle-duffing. In its way it was the biggest and best conceived lift they had ever attempted. "The Big Lift," they called it, and neither he nor young Dan could see any flaws in the plan.

Oh, yes, young Dan was in it. In fact, the idea had been his, vaguely formed when he was on a droving trip with old Dan. The youngster may not have been much of a scholar, but at the age of eighteen he was as keen and capable a cattle-duffer as his father.

What times they had together! How they looked forward to those raids over the Jump-up! Like a pair of kids setting off for a picnic.

Anne had often remarked that the relationship was more that of two brothers than father and son. She did not quite approve of Dan's habit of addressing his father as "Boss," but she was too wise to attempt to break him of it. In their own rather awkward way they both loved her, but their affection for each other was something quite apart. They were two virile, outdoor men, living together in a man's world, a world of horses and cattle. Possibly Anne, with her infinite understanding, sensed that they shared some secret they only discussed when they were away from the house. If she did she would have approved, happy in her belief that some innocent thing connected with their world of stock was welding them together. Never would she have believed that her husband was teaching her son to steal cattle.

Yet, ironically enough, it was Anne who made the Big Lift possible. Had she been home they would not have ridden off and left her for several weeks. But she was down in Sydney visiting her sister. Ben's insistence that she accept her sister's invitation had nothing to do with the Big Lift; he had not even thought of it when he pressed her to go. The change would do her good, he felt, and it was time she had a holiday after all those years in the bush. It would give her a chance to enter Anthea for a good school, something he knew she longed to do. Her efforts at teaching young Dan had not been very successful. Perhaps it was not so important for him, but at least Anthea should have the benefits of a good education. Ben agreed. Unable to feel any real affection for his daughter, he was only too willing to make amends by giving her the best that money could buy.

"Pick a good school," he told Anne. "Never mind what it costs. We're not hard up any longer."

He arranged for Anne to have her own bank account, and paid in a sum that Anne laughingly declared would last her for years and years. Neither of them dreamed that when the mail coach pulled out of Baranda that day it would be years before they saw each other, and that Anne would never see her son again.

A few days after her departure Dan Clancy called in at Coolibah. He was on his way south with a mob of bullocks and he needed no pressing to stay for a meal and a yarn while his men camped the mob down for the night on the river flat. For the three of them it was a happy reunion, because young Dan had already made several droving trips with old Dan.

"As good a man on the road as you used to be," old Dan told Ben. "When I see him on a buckjumper, grinnin' all over his face and beltin' the horse down the shoulder with his hat, I keep thinkin' it's you. And he's the same as you used to be in a brawl. Wades in as if he loved it."

"Not so much of this 'used to be,' " Ben complained. "I'll

still back myself to ride anything you like to bring along. And I've still got to see the day when I'd back out of a fight."

"I wouldn't doubt it, Ben. Not for a minute. You haven't aged much since you was with me. Lookin' at you and young Dan together a man would say you was brothers. He looks older than his age and you look years younger than yours. And you're the spittin' image of each other."

With Anne on her way to Sydney and Biddy away visiting her own people, they talked freely that night. Their conversation was entirely about cattle. They knew that Britain was at war with Germany and that Australia had offered to send troops, but for them the war was little more than a remote incident, something that might boost the price of cattle if it lasted more than a few months.

It was while they were on the always-absorbing topic of duffing that young Dan brought up the subject of Carina, a sizable station property about one hundred miles south of Coolibah. The two Dans had taken a small mob through there some months ago, and both had been impressed by what they saw and heard. The owner was living in Stonehaven, and the head stockman he had left in charge spent a lot of time in the nearest township. An elderly storekeeper's young wife was rumoured to be the attraction, but neither young nor old Dan was interested in the truth or otherwise of the rumour. What did interest them was the fact that he was often away for weeks at a stretch. During their leisurely trip through the property they noted several things. Cleanskins were plentiful, the adult cattle were so badly branded that in many cases it was impossible to read the brand, and lastly, the Carina ear-mark and the Coolibah ear-mark were almost identical.

"It's too good a chance to miss, Boss," young Dan urged. "We could pick up half his herd before anyone woke up to us."

Ben was enthusiastic and old Dan agreed that it should be possible, even though the magnitude of the scheme father and son were discussing so casually was far beyond anything he had ever conceived. He would like to help, he said, but he had to deliver his present mob to a northern New South Wales station before he could undertake anything.

In the end Ben outlined a plan that looked foolproof in its simplicity. From the Baranda policeman he would get a waybill giving him permission to shift three hundred head of cows and calves from Coolibah to the New South Wales border. The waybill would describe the Coolibah brand and ear-mark. All open and above board. Nothing to excite anyone's suspicion in that. With the permit safely in his pocket he, young Dan, and a couple of blackboys would muster thirty or forty head of Coolibah cows and move them down to Carina. The method of filling up his quota could wait until he had ridden ahead and spied out the land. When they eventually got the mob together they would move them along the normal stock-routes to the border, where old Dan would take over. He would be armed with a fresh waybill and he knew at least two men in New South Wales who would pay cash for a good line of cows and ask no questions.

The money, they agreed, as old Dan set off for his camp at midnight, was as good as in the bank.

The job of lifting the Carina cows proved even easier than they had expected. The head stockman was away, so they were able to camp inside the boundary, take their time, and pick only the cows with faint or blotched brands. Within four days they were on the road with three hundred head, not counting the calves.

They moved openly then, without fear of detection. The Carina head stockman would not discover his loss for months, if he ever discovered it, so there was no reason for them to attempt to avoid notice. Theirs was a normal droving trip and if anyone cared to ask for it Ben could produce a waybill showing that he owned the cows and had permission to travel them.

"Start sneakin' off the regular stock-routes," he reasoned, "and some one's sure to get suspicious."

Once they met a policeman and his tracker riding back to their police-station from some routine job. The policeman was bored. He wanted to stop for a yarn with the head drover and he made his request for the waybill an excuse to do so. Ben passed it over willingly and the two of them rode through the mob, yarning as they rode. The inspection was perfunctory, the policeman noting that the ear-marks and such brands as he could read corresponded with those shown on the waybill.

"You blokes up north must brand 'em on the gallop," he laughed as he handed the waybill back. "I suppose you *can* read your own brands even if no one else can."

"Yair," Ben agreed. "I s'pose we are a bit rough and ready."

What did it matter if this policeman, or anyone else, thought his branding slap-dash? It only served to show how sound his scheme was and how well the mob was standing up to the test.

Nearing Warwick he rode on ahead to buy rations for his team. Had he been in the least musical he would have sung or whistled as he hitched his horse to the rail outside the store. This was the last lot of rations he would buy before they started on the homeward trip. His part of the contract was almost over, he hadn't lost a single beast, and no one had looked on his mob with the least suspicion. In a few days he would be meeting old Dan and handing over to him.

He bought generously, adding a few luxuries to the normal drover's rations, and he was waiting for the storekeeper to add up the price of his purchases when he heard some one say:

"Hello, McReady. Bit off your beat, aren't you?"

He turned and saw Constable Ryan.

Although the sight of his old enemy shook Ben severely he was careful not to show it. Ryan was in plain clothes, but that did not necessarily mean he had left the police force. Even without the uniform he looked, and always would look, the efficient policeman.

Pretending not to hear the storekeeper's quiet, "Good morning, Inspector," Ben said casually, "Good day, Ryan. Left the police force now, eh?"

"No. Still very much in it. This is part of my district. And what brings you all the way down to Warwick?"

Ben felt like saying, "I certainly didn't come down here

for the pleasure of *your* company," but he contented himself with, "Just passin' through."

"On your own?"

It could have been an innocent question, asked more to keep the conversation going than for an ulterior motive. On the other hand it could have been a small bit of bait, a lead-in to a trap.

"No. I'm on the road. I don't see what it's got to do with you, but I've got three men and a mob of cattle." The answer came without a moment's hesitation. Why tell a lie when the truth was so obvious? The stack of rations on the counter, the split-bag to carry them in, the horse standing so patiently outside, and his own dusty clothes all told of the drover in town to stock up for his team.

"Got your waybill on you?"

"Yes. You didn't think I'd be mug enough to travel a mob without one, did you?"

That was the stuff to give this nosy copper. Brazen it out and sit him back in his place, as any innocent drover would.

"Mind if I see it?"

"Why should I? That's what they make us carry 'em for, isn't it? To keep you coppers in a job." Ben took the waybill from his pocket and passed it over. Let him see if he could find any fault with that!

Inspector Ryan studied the worn scrap of paper carefully. "Three hundred head of cows with calves at foot," he said. "And all bearing your brand. That's quite a sizable mob to come off that selection of yours, isn't it?"

"Cows breed if you run bulls with 'em. Didn't you know?"

"I had heard of it." Ryan smiled, but there was no mirth in his smile. "And I've seen places where the bulls *and* the cows would need a strain of rabbit in them to account for the increases in the herd." He passed the waybill back to Ben. "Are you selling out up there?"

"I'd have the bullocks and steers in the mob, too, if I was, wouldn't I? I don't suppose you've heard about it, Ryan, but there's a war on and prices should be good while it lasts. I thought of cashin' in before it's all over. Any objections?"

"Me? None at all. It simply struck me that it would be a

better proposition to get your bullocks down to the good market instead of selling out most of your breeders."

"It did, eh?" Any hesitation, any explanation, or even politeness would be interpreted by Ryan as a sign of guilt. That was what he was watching for. "Well, suppose you stick to the police game and leave the cattle business to the cattlemen?"

With another cold smile Ryan said, "I always do, McReady. Always do. Unless the cattleman is silly enough to break the law."

"Better stay till I settle up," Ben sneered as Ryan walked away. "I might try to do the storekeeper out of a couple of bob."

He felt as he rode back to the mob, that he had handled the interview in the only possible way. Throughout he had played the part of a drover who had nothing to fear from the law and disliked the attitude of the policeman who was questioning him. Nevertheless he was worried. There was not the slightest doubt in his mind that Ryan was looking for an opportunity to even that old score. And here was his opportunity, made to order. The cows would pass any casual inspection. That had been proved. But would they pass a searching examination by a man already suspicious, or at any rate anxious to bring a charge against him? The answer was certainly "No." Suppose the cows were put in a crush and the hair clipped away from the blotched brands? Some of them would be readable. The same would apply to the ear-marks. A pair of clippers or even exploring fingers would reveal the slight difference between the Coolibah ear-mark and the one registered for Carina.

All this he told his son when he rejoined the mob. And Dan, as he had known he would, took the news calmly.

"Looks like he's got us, Boss," he said. "That's if he's really out to get us."

"He's out to get *me*," Ben assured him. "He told me that years ago, after I got old Dan out of his hands. And Ryan's not likely to forget."

To both of them it was obvious that it was useless to try to elude a policeman who had made up his mind to inspect the cattle. If they turned back with the mob it would be an admission of their guilt, and a mounted policeman could overtake the slow-moving cattle without lifting his horse faster than a walk. They could, of course, abandon the cattle and make their getaway, but both were reluctant to do that. The hunt for them would be on and they would return home to find the local policeman waiting for them with a warrant. Besides, there was always the chance that Ryan might not bother to come out and inspect the mob. He *could* have been satisfied that everything was as stated on the waybill and that he would only make a fool of himself by trying to prove otherwise.

They discussed the matter from all angles and when Ben finally made his decision young Dan agreed without a moment's hesitation. The spare horses were put together, and father and son each changed over to the best horse in his string. Ben paid the two blackboys off and told them to take the pack-horses and all the spare horses home. He could trust them to do that although he knew they would travel too fast without a white man's supervision.

He and Dan would keep on with the mob. Two good men could easily handle it now, and if they met Ryan they only had themselves to look after. If they passed through the district unchallenged they would scarcely notice the hardship of going without blankets and very little tucker for a few days.

They were stringing the cattle off the dinner camp when the policeman rode up. He was polite, almost friendly in his attitude, but from the start it was obvious that this was to be something more than a normal routine inspection. After copying the particulars into his notebook he handed the waybill back to Ben and rode to the head of the mob.

Dan joined his father then and asked, "That your cobber Ryan?"

"No," Ben growled. "Why should Inspector Bloody Ryan ride all the way out here when he's got understrappers to do the dirty work for him? And this bloke knows his job. Looks like he had plenty experience with cattle."

Quietly and expertly the constable was stringing the

leaders out so that the cattle filed slowly past him, each cow presenting him with a view of the brand area on her near-side rump. And as each group passed he made an entry in his notebook.

"What do you reckon, Boss?" Young Dan's nervousness was starting to show.

"Dunno yet, son. He might be satisfied that everything's on the level."

"And if he isn't?"

"We'll wait and see. He won't find anything to hurt out here, but if he's not satisfied he'll order us to yard 'em somewhere."

"Has he got any right to do that?"

"If he's a stock inspector, yes. And you can bet your boots Ryan wouldn't send out a bloke that wasn't." Ben looked affectionately at his son, this splendid, sturdy young replica of himself, and for the first time in his lawless career he felt a twinge of conscience. "You stay out of this, son," he said kindly. "Keep the mob in between you and this copper so he won't get a good look at you. You and me are too much alike for him to mistake you. If he gets tough I'll handle him. This is my affair and there's no need for you to get mixed up in it."

"Like hell!" Dan's nervousness vanished and all his youthful arrogance came out. "We're in this together, Boss. I started it and I'm stickin' with you."

Proud as he was of that assertion Ben forced himself to be practical. "You do what you're told and keep out of this," he ordered gruffly. "It's your mother I'm thinking of."

"Bit late for that now, isn't it, Boss?"

The logic of the question shook Ben. All these years of flouting the law and not once had he faced up to the question of how Anne would be affected if the law caught up with him. Even now he shied off it.

"Some one'll have to look after her if I'm landed," he said lamely.

It was typical of Dan that before cantering off to turn in a straying cow he said with absolute finality, "If you think I'm going to clear out and leave you to face this by yourself you'd better think again."

The policeman checked the last bunch of stragglers, put his notebook away, and urged his horse forward until he was riding knee to knee with Ben.

"Satisfied?" Ben asked.

"No." There was no malice in the answer. Everything was still on a nice friendly basis. "I've been through your mob very carefully and as near as I can work it out I can only read one brand in every ten. Some of the ear-marks don't quite tally, either."

"So what?"

"It could be careless branding, and it could be something else. My orders were to make a thorough check so I'm afraid I'll have to ask you to yard them."

"Because Ryan's looking for a chance to get squared with me?"

"I don't know anything about that. I've got my orders and I'm only carrying them out."

"What if I refuse to yard 'em?"

"I don't think you'd do that. Especially if you can prove they're all yours."

"Where's the yard?"

"About three miles ahead. Right on the stock-route."

"Righto. We'll yard 'em. And when you and Ryan are satisfied I'm only movin' me own cattle what compensation do I get for the hold-up?"

"We'll apologize."

"That'll be a big help! Any objections to givin' us a hand?"

"None at all. You're a bit short-handed, aren't you?"

"Yair. There's only the two of us. I sent the plant on ahead to the night camp."

"The young chap your brother?"

"Cousin." Ben touched his horse with his spurs. "You keep the tail goin', eh?"

He trotted up along the wing and called across the mob to Dan, "We're yardin' about three miles on. Keep your eyes well peeled."

He could trust Dan to be on the alert for any developments, and in the meantime it was up to him to see that something did develop.

Riding slowly up and down the wing, he thought of several plans and discarded all except one. If the policeman would only dismount for a moment the rest would be simple. But the policeman was diligently keeping the tail going, bustling the slower cows in his anxiety to get them to the yard.

With less than two miles to go Ben dropped back to the tail, passed some remark about the weather, and then said with apparent nonchalance, "Your girth's a bit slack. These cows aren't used to being yarded and if we have any trouble your saddle might roll with you."

Since there was a certain amount of truth in the statement the policeman dismounted, dropped the reins over his horse's head and unbuckled the surcingle. The police horse had been trained to stand when its reins were dropped, but it certainly had *not* been trained to ignore the tactics Ben immediately adopted. Spurring his own mount against its flank he slashed it across the rump with his doubled stockwhip and yelled with all the force of his powerful lungs. The startled horse bolted. Left alone, it might have pulled up in a few hundred yards, but Dan was on its heels before its pace slackened. Scattering cattle left and right, he pursued it through the mob, yelling as he galloped.

"Looks like you've got a bit of a walk ahead of you," Ben called. "Say good-bye to Ryan for me when you get back."

The policeman watched Dan complete the rout of his horse and wheel back to join his father. "You'll be sorry for this," he shouted. "We'll catch up with you. You won't get far."

★ 10 ★

"You won't get far!"

It depended on what he meant by "far." If he had been thinking in terms of miles or even hundreds of miles he was a long, long way short in his estimate. By daylight next morning they were over the border, riding up to old Dan's camp just as he was putting the billy on.

"Better hobble the horses out and sit down to a feed," the old drover said. "Breakfast'll be on in a coupla minutes."

Obviously something had gone wrong with the plan and his mates were in trouble; the jaded state of their horses alone told him that. But explanations could wait until the horses were turned loose and their riders had a bit of tucker under their belts.

After his second helping of damper and steak grilled on the coals Ben explained everything, how Ryan had upset their plans, how they had outwitted his policeman, and then ridden across country and over the ranges all through the night. Before he finished his tale young Dan was stretched out on the dewy grass, fast asleep.

Squatting on his heels in front of the fire, one long freckled arm stretched out as he absent-mindedly stirred the ashes with the forked twig he had used for turning the steak, old Dan said, "She's a bit of a mess. Things is crook all right. What do you reckon on doin' about it?"

"I s'pose you'll reckon I'm mad." Ben shrugged his big shoulders. "You could be right, too, but I'm going off to the war."

"You're what?" old Dan exclaimed in horror. "Jesus, Ben! I didn't think you was *that* mad."

"It's the only thing I can do. I didn't think you'd understand, but I've got to think of the missus."

"Bit late for that now, ain't it?"

"Damn and blast you!" Ben's roar made young Dan stir uneasily in his sleep. "I mightn't be the best husband in the world, but you don't all have to keep rubbing it in by sayin' that."

"The lad say it too?"

"Yes."

Old Dan smoothed the ashes with his twig and studied the effect for a moment before remarking, "I dunno much about women, but I can't see how you goin' off to this here war is goin' to make things any easier for her."

"I didn't think you would." Ben's tone softened as he tried to explain his viewpoint. "If Ryan gets his hands on me I'll do time; he'll see to that if he has to spend a week in the witness-box. How do you think Anne will feel when she hears her husband's in gaol for cattle-stealin'? They wouldn't have any sort of case against the lad, but they'd shove him into the witness-box at the trial, and the whole business would just about finish his mother. So you can see I've got to keep clear of the police."

"They'll be waitin' for you in Brisbane when you go there to join the Army."

"I won't go to Brisbane."

"Well, Sydney. They'll find out your missus is there and that's the very place they'll be on the look-out for you."

"I won't go to Sydney either. I'll head for Melbourne and join up there."

"Down to Victoria, eh? That should be far enough." Old Dan's freckled face twisted into a wry smile. "Why, that's where I picked you up when you was a miserable little bit of a kid! And now you're headin' back." He nodded towards his sleeping young namesake. "Does he know?"

"Yes. He was dead keen on coming with me, but I jumped down on that idea hard. Told him that one fool in the family was enough, that some one had to look after his mother, and that the Army wouldn't take him anyhow because he was too young. 'Besides,' I said, 'if you want me to get pinched the best way to go about it is to stick with me. They don't want you, but the police in Queensland and New South Wales will be on the look-out for the two of us. If we stick together we'll be picked up in the first town we strike.' He saw the sense of that. I wanted him to go straight back home and look after the place; the police haven't got a thing on him. But he says he'd sooner keep out of the way for a while and go back when things quieten down." Ben had been staring into the fire as he talked, but now he looked straight at his old friend. "So it's up to you, old-timer. You'll have to go up there and run the place until the youngster shows up."

Just like that! No asking old Dan if he could or would do it. Simply "You'll have to go."

And old Dan grinned and said, "That'll be all right, Ben. I reckon I'm a bit young to settle down for keeps, but a bit of a spell off the road won't do me no harm."

A bit young! Ben was not sure of his age, but he guessed he would be over sixty.

"That's settled then. You'd better dig me up a bit of paper and a pencil and I'll put it in writing so you won't run into any trouble with the bank or the police."

Old Dan rummaged through his swag until he found the pencil, two old waybills, and a circular letter from a stock and station agency. "You could write on the back of that," he suggested, passing Ben the typed letter.

"It'll do." Ben glanced around for a suitable writing-table. "Chuck over one of those pack-bags to write on and I'll make everything legal."

With only the vaguest idea of what would pass as a legal document he wrote, "Mister McBeath of the Union Bank in Stonehaven. I am writing this to show that my mate Dan Clancy is going to act for me while I am away. He will run my place Coolibah for me, and you can pay out on any cheques he signs." He read it through, signed it, pulled out his cheque-book, and made out an open cheque, payable to Dan Clancy.

"That'll fix him," he declared. "If he reckons this document ain't legal enough for him you just shove this cheque under his nose and tell him you want to draw the lot. Every bloody penny I've got."

Old Dan folded document and cheque and put them in his shirt pocket. "What about your missus?" he asked.

"I'll write and tell her. If she wants any more money you

fix her up, and if she wants to come home before young Dan gets back you can camp in the buggy shed."

"And what about that bloody gin? I'm tellin' you straight, Ben, if I get up there and find her in the house I ain't stoppin' long enough to unroll me swag. Either that or she goes. One of us has gotta get out. See?"

"Like hell I see!" Ben roared. "You listen to me, Dan Clancy. Apart from my family you and Biddy are the two best friends I've got. I wouldn't see either of you stuck for anything not even if it was me last penny, and things are pretty crook if you're gunna start tellin' me you can't get on together. Nobody's turnin' Biddy out of my house, not even you!"

Poor old Dan! The confirmed misogamist who liked to roll out his single swag and sleep where he could look up and see the stars! He was beaten and he knew it. Very miserably he said, "Righto, righto. If that's how yer want it that's how it'll be. When are you movin' off?"

"Now. Run me in the best horse you've got and I'll get started."

"You better have a bit of a camp first, after the ride you put up last night."

"I don't need any sleep. The sooner I get away from here, the better."

As he saddled the horse Dan caught for him Ben said softly, "Say good-bye to the lad for me. And see if you can talk him into staying with you. I'd feel a lot better if I knew you were together."

Three weeks later, as one of a party of raw recruits, he marched into Broadmeadows Camp, on the outskirts of Melbourne. There was nothing military about the bearing of the recruits. Despite the barking efforts of the sergeant in charge, they straggled self-consciously down the long rows of bell tents, greeted everywhere by shouts of "You'll be sorry" as groups of dungaree-clad men lounged forward to look over the new arrivals.

Outside a bell tent marked "Orderly Room" the sergeant halted them. The usual group of onlookers called the usual "You'll be sorry," but one youngster slipped forward with a welcoming grin. There was no mistaking the broad shoulders, the fair hair, and the hooked nose.

"Hello, Boss," he called. "I reckoned it was about time you showed up."

Well, there they were, both "in", and there was nothing either of them could do about it. Each had signed away his liberty "for the duration of the war and three months thereafter". Much as he felt like abusing his headstrong son, Ben merely said, "I might have guessed you'd spring this on me."

Comparing notes that evening they found that each had played safe with his age. Dan giving his as twenty-one and Ben putting his down as thirty-five. The relationship of father and son being ruled out for such obvious reasons, they became the McReady brothers, Boss and Dan, for the nickname took on and stuck to Ben throughout the war.

Together they marched and drilled, hating the discipline, but afraid to draw attention to themselves by kicking against it. If others could put up with it they could, and at least they could laugh at the discomfort their less toughened mates suffered in the primitive camp conditions. Sleeping on the ground was no hardship to them, even when the rain seeped through the tent and turned the hard clay to glutinous mud. Their reluctance to go into town on leave was put down to the fact that they were strangers in a strange town.

"You never know," Ben said to his son once. "Even down here they might be on the look-out for us."

Not until the night before they embarked did he write to Anne, and as he carefully wrote his future address, "1056 Trooper B. McReady. A Squadron, 8th Australian Light Horse Abroad," he felt he had at last put himself beyond Inspector Ryan's reach. Anne would get small comfort from that halting letter, but it was the best he could manage. Acting on Dan's advice, he tried to explain his callous desertion by saying that their son had enlisted first and he had joined up to keep an eye on him. He was sorry as soon as he had done it, he lied, but once in the Army there was no way out. Still, they didn't expect to be away very long. Every one said the war would be over before they got there.

How little those poor fools really knew! There were times

during the next few years when they felt the war would never end. It became so much a part of their lives that they found it difficult to recall or picture a form of existence unconnected with military discipline and desert sand. Gallipoli was only a memory, a senseless interlude that had cost them so many mates. And all for what? they asked each other.

At least the desert had given them back their horses. For the rest it offered nothing but flies, sand, blistering heat, and soul-destroying monotony—the dull monotony of long, seemingly pointless patrols where nothing ever happened and they saw nothing except sandhills and still more sandhills. Even more pointless were the camel escort duties where a section of troopers escorted a small string of mangy camels and their Egyptian drivers to some outlying post. No one knew the reason for the escorts; the camel-drivers could have delivered their loads equally well without them, for there was never anything to molest them. The troopers hated them because their horses hated the camels and never grew used to the smell and the rumbling, belching protests of those aloof, supercilious beasts.

Once Ben said, "One of these days a camel is gunna look down his nose at me with that sneerin' look and be sorry for it."

"What'll you do about it, Boss?" his section mates asked.

"Shoot the bloody thing," Ben declared grimly. "Fair between the eyes. I'll be up before the colonel again and in debt for six months, but it'll be worth it."

Up before the colonel! Since they landed in Egypt he and Dan had been up on various charges so often that the colonel had taken an intense dislike to the two big Queenslanders. They were, he felt, a disturbing element in his unit. They bucked against all forms of discipline, they overstayed their leave passes when the regiment was stationed on the outskirts of Cairo, and rarely came back from an evening in town without having been involved in a brawl, usually with M.P.'s. The colonel was not fond of M.P.'s, but he was not going to have the good name of his regiment spoiled by the McReady brothers. Some allowance could be made for the younger, the wildness of youth and all that sort of thing, but it was high time the elder brother learned sense. Unfortunately it was impossible to punish one without the other, they stuck together in everything. The only solution was to confine them to camp each time they appeared before him, and fine them so heavily that they would always be broke. Even in the desert they were frequently in trouble for insubordination.

The only bright spots in those early desert days were the all too infrequent arrivals of mail from home. Anne wrote regularly, long, gossipy letters telling of her life in Sydney, Anthea's progress in school, and items of news she thought might interest them. If the abrupt news of their enlistment came as a shock to her she never revealed it in her letters. She was proud, she said, that her two men were away fighting for their country and for her. Naturally she worried over their safety and felt scared every time a new casualty list appeared. For certain reasons she could not go back to Coolibah for a while, but old Dan had written to say he was managing quite well.

Ben supposed the "certain reasons" had something to do with her sister's affairs, and when the explanation finally came it shook him so badly he could only pass the letter over to Dan without comment.

> My darling [Anne wrote] I didn't tell you before because I knew you would worry. But it's all over now and we've got another son. Just fancy! At our age it seems rather indecent, doesn't it? At least that's how I used to feel whenever I went shopping during the last few months. I could feel other women staring and saying, "Look at her! She must be at least forty!" (Which I am.) I thought of calling our new son Kenneth, after my father, unless you particularly want him to have another name. Anyway, I won't have him christened until I hear from you.

How typical of Anne! All those months and not a word about her condition in case he worried! Why couldn't he learn some of her unselfishness? He wrote at once, telling her that neither he or Dan could think of a better name and that she mustn't worry about them because they were not in the least danger. In fact the only thing likely to kill them was the monotony of doing nothing and seeing nothing except sand.

Sand, sand, sand! Sand that drifted into their blankets and formed a grit in everything they ate. Sand that burned fiercely by day and chilled them at night. It enveloped them. Eventually it would drift over them, suffocating them, until only their bleached bones remained to remind a passing camel-driver that an army had once camped here.

And then one morning the Turk, the elusive enemy they had long regarded as a myth created by "the Heads" to keep them on the alert, attacked the Suez Canal at Romani. Hard on the heels of the order to saddle up in full marching order came the spate of "furphies." The enemy had smashed through the Tommy infantry positions and was over the Canal! The Second Light Horse Brigade had been cut off! The First had suffered appalling casualties! The enemy was being driven back!

The truth was anyone's guess and only one thing was certain. They were going into action at last! And action meant an end of the dreary monotony. Moreover it would be open warfare, the type of fighting their training and whole upbringing fitted them for. Instead of being hemmed in by trench walls they would be going into action as highly mobile mounted troops. As they rode out of camp that evening there was scarcely a man who did not feel something like affection for the enemy who had given them this opportunity. And strangely enough, despite all the propaganda, that feeling was to persist throughout the long campaign. They fought the Turk fiercely, knowing that they must win each desert battle or perish of thirst in this land where possession of the meagre water-supplies meant everything. But they never hated him.

Throughout the long night ride to Romani they speculated on what the future held for them. Had some one been able to tell them the truth—that from tonight until the campaign ended in far-off Tripoli years later they would sleep in the open or under such crude shelters as they themselves could devise, live on a diet that would seldom include anything but bully beef and iron-hard biscuits, and go for weeks at a stretch without baths—they would not have cared. The very independence of such a nomadic existence, the freedom from official routine, would have appealed to them.

And as the campaigns progressed they accepted as normal all these conditions and worse. They wore their uniforms to threadbare rags because replacements were luxuries that had evidently been overlooked. They sat in the sun and plucked lice from the seams of ragged, dirty clothing that could never be washed in this land where rain never fell. They drank the dark, foul-smelling water from the desert wells, water that filled men and horses with revulsion without ever really quenching their thirsts, and they cursed luridly when the lack of it parched their mouths and brought cruel torture to their wounded.

Their first desert action was by no means a brilliant one. In fact, they came out of it badly mauled and feeling they had achieved nothing. At daylight they came in contact with the enemy. The shell fire was light and scattered and the rifle fire harmless because of the extreme range. Advancing in open squadron line, first at a trot and then at full gallop, they reduced the range until they reached a shallow depression under a line of low sand ridges. There, only partially protected from an intense hail of fire, they dismounted and handed over their mounts, one man in each section taking four horses and galloping for the comparative safety of some deeper hollow. Casualties up to that point had been surprisingly light, doubtless owing to the speed of the advance and the equally swift withdrawal of the horses. The few badly wounded horses left behind were quickly put out of their misery either by their owners or the enemy machine-gun fire.

But once the dismounted troopers lined the sand ridges and started to return the fire the Turkish shooting became embarrassingly accurate. Moreover it soon became evident that the entire squadron was the victim of some one's blunder. The Turk was firing down on them from the desert's nearest approach to a mountain and between the opposing lines there was, as Ben remarked sourly, "Not enough cover to hide a bloody bandicoot." An attempt to advance would be suicidal, a withdrawal over the bare, exposed rise behind them equally dangerous. They were trapped in a hollow from which they could neither extricate themselves nor evacuate their wounded.

"Keep your head well down and save your ammo'," Ben advised his son. "There's no sense in playin' the big hero in this show. The bloke that shoved us into this trap ought to take one more pick and then give the war away."

Like the rest of the squadron he was lying in a hollow he had scooped out at the base of a stunted camel-bush. Dan lay three or four yards to his left and on his right, about the same distance away, was the troop sergeant, a tough old Boer War veteran named Weiss.

The day dragged on. The sun blazed down on their backs and the sand grew searing to the touch. Bullets whined and snarled through the camel-bush a foot or two above their heads or kicked up spurts of sand in front of them. When a man was hit his mate bandaged his wound as best he could with a field-dressing, dragged him back to the hollow, and left him. There was nothing else he could do.

At noon the order to conserve ammunition was passed along the line and a few hours later Weiss called to Ben, "Pass the word along for a volunteer to go back to headquarters with a message."

Ben glanced to his left. If the words reached Dan's ears he certainly would not give anyone else a chance to volunteer, but fortunately his whole attention was focused on some movement in the enemy position.

"It's about time some one woke up and did something," Ben growled. "No need to pass the word along. I'll go."

"Good on you, Boss. Work your way around to my right. The major's here. He'll give you your instructions."

The major's instructions were short and clear. If—and he emphasized the "if"—Ben succeeded in getting up the exposed slope he was to locate Regimental Headquarters and tell the colonel that Major McAllister wished to withdraw his squadron because they were nearly out of ammunition and their casualties were in urgent need of water and medical attention. Given good covering fire from a hill on his right the major felt sure the withdrawal could be achieved without undue loss. They would bring their wounded out with them.

"I'm passing the word for rapid fire when I sound two blasts of the whistle," the major finished. "It should help to keep their heads down while you're getting up that rise. Good luck to you, McReady. I won't forget this."

And I'll bet I won't either, Ben thought as he waited for the whistle. That's if I get up that rise alive.

The whistle blew, an intensified crackle of rifle fire broke out along the line and he set off. The heavy sand, churned up by the galloping horses, came nearly to his ankles, slowing him down to little faster than a walking pace. The whine of bullets increased until they sounded like a swarm of angry bees buzzing around his ears. To the anxiously watching major he seemed to be crawling. To Ben it seemed as if the whole Turkish army was firing at his sweating back. It also seemed a hell of a long way to the crest of the rise.

But he made it. And in the protected hollow beyond it he sat for a few minutes regaining his wind.

"Old Dan was right," he panted aloud. "A man's legs were made to fit over a horse, not for running up sandhills."

When he eventually located Headquarters and saluted the colonel it occurred to him that for once he was facing his commanding officer without wondering how many days' pay the interview would cost him.

The colonel listened to his message with obvious impatience. This, apparently, was one more worry in a day of worries.

"All right, McReady," he said curtly. "Report back to your squadron and tell Major McAllister we'll arrange for his withdrawal, but he'll probably have to hang on until after sundown."

Report back to your squadron! Just like that! He might have been saying, "Report to the cookhouse and peel spuds for the cook!"

The offhand manner in which the order was given made Ben temporarily forget himself and say, "His chances of gettin' that message are about one in fifty."

"Are you refusing to obey an order?" the colonel barked.

"Me, sir?" Ben's face registered exaggerated surprise. "Not me. I've been too long in the Army to come at that. The thought just passed through me mind that a man can't be lucky twice in one mess-up."

★ II ★

YET, incredibly, his luck had held. He topped the final rise of his trudge back to the squadron expecting to be met with a concentrated hail of fire, but only a few stray bullets buzzed past him.

"They must have knocked off for smoko," he remarked when he delivered the colonel's message. "Or else they don't reckon I'm worth wasting any more ammo' on."

"They could be like us," the major said. "Running short of it. Their fire has slackened considerably since you went out. Possibly they're saving what they have until we make a move."

The move came at sundown when the led horses galloped up. With their wounded draped like sacks of corn over the pommels of their saddles, A Squadron rode out, and only a few scattered shots came to speed them on their way. Not until next day did they learn that shortly after Ben's dramatic dash the enemy had started to withdraw because of a threat to his right flank.

"If I'd known what was going on along the rest of the front I wouldn't have let you take that risk," the major told Ben. "We know now that it was unnecessary, but that doesn't detract from your action. I'm recommending you for the Military Medal."

Choosing his words carefully Ben said, "I'd rather you didn't do that, sir. I don't want any medals and I wouldn't like to see you get on the wrong side of the colonel on my account. He'd cross out anything with the McReady name on it, unless it was a defaulter's charge."

This speaking in two tongues was already becoming a habit with him. If he liked or admired a man he spoke as Anne had taught him to speak, but when he disliked a man and wanted to annoy him he deliberately lapsed into the rough speech of his droving days. He liked the major and he had an idea that in spite of his bad record the feeling was mutual.

Both were big men, both were bushmen with the bushmen's broad outlook, and there were no frills about either of them. Had the big difference in rank not kept them so far apart they might have been good friends. Mainly because of his red hair and freckles the major often reminded Ben of old Dan. Admittedly he lacked old Dan's easy-going tolerance, but he would be the same loyal friend in adversity. And in spite of his reputation as a strict disciplinarian he was popular with the men. They called him Red Ned—behind his back.

"I'll decide what recommendations I'll put before the colonel," he said stiffly. "Your name is going in." He turned, but before he walked off he unbent enough to add, "Our communication system let us down badly yesterday, McReady. The lack of it got us into a lot of trouble and nearly cost you your life. They say, 'live and learn.' Well, if we live we'll learn."

They did. They learned to adapt themselves to desert conditions, to live on its meagre and obnoxious water supplies, to take advantage of its scant cover, to boil a mess-tin or quartpot of tea on a handful of dry camel-bush twigs and to find their way with unerring accuracy across its undulating sandy wastes. They learned to shave and wash in a mess-tin of brackish water and go for weeks without the luxury of a bath. Bit by bit they developed an eye for the country, so that never again were they caught in a trap of their own making. Nor could the Turk ever set a trap that could do anything more than delay them despite the fact that the battlegrounds were always of his choosing. Like the jackals that slunk around their outposts on moonlit nights, they moved silently across the desert to attack when the time best suited them.

To Ben McReady, reared in the big open spaces, the desert presented no great problems and few real hardships. His ability to find his way anywhere, his calmness under fire, and his mature appreciation of the possibilities in any situation made him an obvious choice for promotion. His troop leader recommended it, the major was strongly in favour of it, and even the colonel might have been persuaded to overlook his earlier record if Ben had been willing to accept promotion.

But Ben refused to have anything to do with it. He was quite content to stay where he was, he said. Let some one else take on the responsibility.

"I know what's behind your attitude," Red Ned snapped when he sent for Ben one morning. "It's this mistaken sense of loyalty to your young brother. You won't accept promotion because it would mean being separated from him. That's the position, isn't it?"

"Near enough, sir," Ben admitted. There were the other two members of the section to be considered also, but he thought it best to say nothing about them.

"You think a lot of him, don't you?"

"They don't come any better, sir." Ben hesitated a moment before adding, "And he's a damned good soldier."

"I agree, up to a point. He's young and wild. Doubtless he'll grow out of that wildness. You should be helping him by setting him a good example. Instead you encourage him."

"The way I look at it, sir, it's better for him to have his fling while he's young and get it out of his system."

"It's taken you a hell of a long time to get it out of *your* system."

"I've led a pretty rough sort of life, sir." It sounded a weak excuse, Ben realized, but he was unable to think of a better one. He was not enjoying the interview. Red Ned had a reputation for getting what he wanted, and he obviously wanted to turn a reluctant trooper into an efficient N.C.O. Well, this time he had the job ahead of him.

"A damned poor excuse." Red Ned was getting a little terse. "Any other reason for refusing to accept a bit of responsibility?"

"No, sir." There *was* another reason but he could not give himself away by telling the major that his only wish was to remain unnoticed. As Trooper McReady, without stripes or decoration, he was safely tucked away as one of the mob. But if he started the ambitious climb up the ladder of promotion who could say where he would end? The Australian papers were printing anything and everything about the men in the front line. Suppose his name got into the papers? Inspector Ryan would be on to it like a shot. Could Ryan's authority reach him here on the Sinai Desert? Ben was not sure and he had no intention of deliberately putting it to the test. He had got this far without making himself conspicuous, thanks to the colonel running true to form and effectively squashing the Military Medal recommendation.

"I notice you have given your civil occupation as drover," Red Ned went on. "Did you have your own plant?"

"Yes, sir." Not strictly true, but near enough to it.

"Would you say you were a good drover?"

What the hell was Red Ned leading up to? He was as bad as Ryan with his apparently harmless questions. Fired them at you in the same way, too, and didn't give you much time to think out the answers.

"As good as the next, sir."

"And that was good enough for you, eh?"

"Yes, sir."

Reasonable enough answers. He couldn't find any fault with them, surely?

But he did. "Dammit, McReady!" he exploded. "Do you expect me to believe that? Do you mean to tell me you never had any ambitions, never wanted to build up a reputation as the best drover in Queensland, or own your own property?"

"I never gave it a thought, sir."

"That," Red Ned declared emphatically, "is a deliberate bloody lie, McReady. And you know it." He brushed his stiff red hair back in a swift gesture of disgust. "All right, Trooper McReady, we seem to be wasting our time. But before I dismiss you I'll put it to you in a different way. What you did in civil life is no concern of mine; you could have been a bushranger or a cattle-duffer for all I care. But what you do here is very much my concern. I've offered you promotion twice now and each time you've refused it because you wanted to stay in the same section as your brother. You're fond of your brother. That's understandable. It may interest you to know that I'm fond of him too. I have an idea he put his age forward a couple of years when he enlisted, but that's his affair. I admire his spirit. Unfortunately he's got a little too much. He's wild and he's headstrong, but he's a likeable youngster with the makings of a first-class soldier, given the right leadership. And that's my point. What happens to him if that leadership is lacking? We're short of good N.C.O.'s and supposing casualties in some future action leave your troop in charge of a not-so-good junior N.C.O. and that N.C.O. makes a stupid blunder that costs your brother his life? Would you feel that you were responsible? You needn't answer now. Think it over, and don't take too long about it either because it's the last chance you'll get while I'm in charge of the squadron."

Ben saluted smartly and said, "Thank you, sir, I'll do that."

He told Dan about the interview when they were out on outpost duty that night. Officially known as Cossack Posts, those desert outposts were called more unprintable names by the men who manned them. They were small warning posts with orders to fire a few warning shots and gallop back to the main line if an attack developed. Since their lives might depend on the speed of their withdrawal blankets were banned no matter how cold the night. But a single blanket can be concealed under a saddle blanket and the ban was seldom observed.

The duty troop rode out at sundown, and as darkness fell they split into sections of four, each section riding independently to take up a position on some more or less prominent sandhill. The posts could be anything from a few hundred yards to half a mile apart; it all depended on the contour of the country.

Ben's section rode as they aways did, with Ben as number one, Dan number two, and a lean, hard-bitten ex-horsebreaker named Barney White number four. Number three, the horse-holder, was the runt of the section, an undersized but extremely tough little ex-jockey named Charlie Turner. They had been together and had ridden in that order since the regiment was formed, and unless Ben accepted promotion they would stick together until a Turkish bullet removed one of them.

Aided by a rising moon they reached the foot of their allotted sandhill, dismounted, and handed their horses over to Charlie. Officially he was supposed to stay awake all night while the other three took turn-about on duty on the crest of the hill. In actual practice Charlie did what every other horse-holder was doing along the outpost line. He slipped all the reins over his arm, thrust his hand deep into the pocket of his greatcoat, and settled down for a night's sleep. It would be an uneasy sleep, broken at intervals as one restless horse after another tugged at his bridle arm or stepped over him to nibble at a clump of camel-bush. He dozed rather than slept and the first shot from the rise above would bring him to his feet, sorting out the reins in readiness for his mates.

While he made himself comfortable the others climbed to the crest of the rise and drew lots to see who would take the unpopular last shift. In a section where no one owned a watch the last shift was bound to be unpopular, particularly on moonless nights. Each of the other two stayed on duty for what he honestly considered a third of the night and a little extra for good measure. But time drags wearily when a man has nothing to do except lie on his belly and stare out across the empty desert. Minutes seem like hours, and what he is firmly convinced has been a four- or five-hour stretch may turn out to have been little over two hours. When daylight came the unlucky last shift always swore he had been on watch since midnight, or earlier.

But that night the rising moon gave Ben a fairly accurate idea of the time. He was on first watch and he decided to wait until the moon was directly overhead before calling Dan. He was not sleepy. Lying there with his rifle thrust out in front of him, ready for immediate use, he was thinking of a number of things—how Anne and the new baby were getting on, how old Dan was feeling about being left so long on Coolibah with two women, how long it would be before he himself saw them all again, and whether he would eventually return home to be met by a policeman with a warrant. He also gave some thought to Red Ned's final words.

At regular intervals he checked each sector of the undulating, moonlit desert in front and on each side of him, not staring intently minutes at a time because long experience of night watching had taught him that you only had to stare at a bush for long enough and it would do all manner of weird things, like standing erect and crawling around. And before long every bush within sight would be on the move, giving the poor, harassed sentry the impression that the entire enemy force was performing some complicated manœuvre in front of him.

The moon crept slowly towards its zenith and nothing broke the silence of the night except the howling of a pack of jackals and the occasional jingle of a bit from the horses behind him. Once a horse shook himself vigorously with a noisy clatter of stirrup irons and saddle-flaps that brought a growl of, "Shut up, ya noisy b—" from Charlie.

The howling of the jackals came closer and closer until Ben judged the pack to be only yards away, practically ringing the little post. He could see no movement, nothing that could possibly be identified as an animal except the occasional gleam of a pair of eyes. Cowardly little brutes that would sit waiting for a wounded man to die, they would scatter instantly from any sudden movement. The temptation to put a bullet between a pair of those gleaming eyes was strong, but it was a temptation that would have to be resisted. The crash of the rifle shot would put the whole chain of outposts on the alert. It could cause one or two nervous sentries to open fire on some fancied movement and within seconds shots would be cracking out along the entire front. As far as Ben was concerned the jackals were perfectly safe.

Although he had heard them night after night he had never actually seen one—until that moment. He glanced back at his two sleeping section mates and was wondering whether to call Dan or let him sleep a little longer when he saw the jackal. It was sitting on its haunches scarcely two yards from Dan's feet, its ears were pricked and its whole attention was focused on Dan's motionless form. Aware that any movement on his part would send it scurrying, Ben lay still and watched.

The jackal moved a little closer, and now its tongue was lolling expectantly. This still form, wrapped almost to the eyes in a blanket, *must* be dead. A few more patient minutes, another move forward, and it could verify that before lifting its nose and summoning its mates to the feast. The minutes dragged on and the jackal edged warily forward. Its nose was less than a yard from Dan's feet when he came to life, not with the sluggish movements and yawns of a sleeper drowsily regaining consciousness, but with the speed of a striking snake.

In one swift, lithe movement his blanketed figure came partially erect and shot forward, landing with grasping, outspread hands where only a second before his feet had been. The end-for-end movement, so unexpected and so explosive in its speed, reminded Ben of an occasion when the spring had flown out of an alarm clock he had been tinkering with. The spring had shot out with a resounding twang; Dan had shot forward silently and only when he landed did a grunt of "Got ya!" escape.

But the jackal had gone. Ben was prepared to swear that it did not turn and race away. It simply vanished as though it had melted into the sand, and Ben was still trying to figure out where it had gone when Dan crawled to his side and whispered: "I bet that put the wind up him, Boss."

"I'll bet it did," Ben agreed. "How long had you been watching him?"

"A fair while. Ten minutes or more, I reckon. I woke up with a feeling some one was watching me, and there he was, squatting down with his bloody tongue out, waiting for me to die. I played 'possum,' never even winked, just to see how close he'd come. Musta been pretty hungry, eh?"

"Musta been, to come that close, but I'll lay a shade of odds he won't come at that stunt again for a while." Ben grinned at the memory of Dan's startling leap. "It's a wonder that act of yours didn't wake Barney."

"It takes more than that to wake him once he gets his head down."

"You're right there. He'd keep on sleeping if a battery of eighteen pounders opened up on us." Ben yawned and stretched himself. "You can take over now if you like. It's past midnight and there's nothing out in front except camel-bush and jackals."

"Righto, Boss. You get your head down."

"I will in a minute. Red Ned was on to me again this morning about taking stripes."

"I guessed it was that. Why don't you?"

"I hate the idea of breaking the old section up. If I pulled out who would you get to take my place? Some new reinforcement who'd get lost if you turned him around twice! Some city bloke that'd get on your works all day long! No, we've been together so long we might as well see it out together now."

"D'you want my opinion?"

"I can listen to it."

"Well, here she comes. You're a mug if you don't take the stripes. If you don't they might give 'em to some crawler who'll do his block the first time we get into a tight spot. How'd you feel then, Boss? I can't see you taking orders from some windy mug that didn't know what he was yelling about. What if Landser was to finish up troop sergeant? What a bloody mess *he* could get us into if things got tough. You take the stripes, Boss, and we'll know we're getting pushed around by a bloke that knows what it's all about."

"I'll think it over," Ben promised.

He was thinking, as he wrapped his blanket around himself, that young Dan, despite his headstrong youth, had put forward the same mature viewpoint as Red Ned had done that morning. And he was right about Landser, of course. Somehow or other Landser had got himself two stripes. Probably had a bit of pull. But he was bumptious and unpopular, a mean little man who threw his weight around when the regiment was resting safely behind the front line, and always managed to be away when there was a big stunt on. It was often said that the surest way of telling when a stunt was brewing was to watch Landser. If he reported sick and got himself sent off to hospital it was safe to bet that the regiment would be in action within forty-eight hours. As Dan had said, what a mess things could get into with him as troop sergeant! Ben could not imagine anything worse.

Two weeks later he put up his corporal's stripes, and when they crossed into Palestine a few months later he was a troop sergeant, a very efficient N.C.O., twice mentioned in dispatches. For the first time in his life Ben McReady was really facing up to his responsibilities.

His old section had vanished, gone the way of most of the original sections. Barney had been killed in the first Gaza stunt, Charlie was in Cairo hospital recovering from a shrapnel wound in the leg, and Dan had been appointed Brigadier's Galloper, a position that suited him perfectly. The old Brig' had not earned the name of "Galloping Jack" by riding around at a sedate walk or trot. When there was a stunt on he galloped everywhere and saw everything. And as his galloper Dan had to keep right on his heels. Ben felt that although the job did not keep him out of danger it at least kept him out of mischief by providing an outlet for his restless energy.

If he had only stayed in that position how different everything might have been! But Galloping Jack was transferred, the new Brigadier brought his own galloper with him, and Dan came back to his old troop.

★ 12 ★

"MR MCREADY! Mr McReady!"

Old Ben was back in hospital, and the night sister was bending over him, a wraith-like white form illuminated only by the glow of her shaded torch. "It's time for your injection."

Automatically he extended his arm and the suffocating smell of ether filled his nostrils.

"Damn and blast it, Sister!" he grumbled. "Doesn't anybody ever get any rest in this joint?"

He felt the chill of the ether on his arm, the sharp stab of the needle, and the brisk rubbing as the night sister withdrew it.

With a professional smoothing of the pillows she asked, "Are you quite comfortable?"

"What a stupid bloody question to ask a man!" Ignoring her "Ssh! You'll wake the other patients" he went on, "Look, Sister, how would you feel if I sneaked into your bedroom in the middle of the night and shoved a blunt darning-needle into your backside and asked you if you were feeling comfortable? You'd go crook on a bloke, wouldn't you?"

"I gave you your injection in the arm," Sister reminded him tartly. "And the needle was not blunt."

Too experienced to let him get in the last word, she switched her torch off and slipped silently out of the room.

Old Ben was wide awake now, fully aware of his surroundings. He was in a hospital bed in Stonehaven, a damned uncomfortable bed too. Yet only a few moments ago he had been in Palestine, fighting the First World War over again! What the devil had started him on that almost-forgotten chapter of his past? Oh, yes, old Charlie's visit, of course. Charlie and his casual mention of that night at El Burj!

Good, staunch little Charlie! He had rejoined the troop the day before the attack and had immediately filled a vacancy as number four in Dan's section. No more number three for him, he declared. Jacko always shelled the led horses. He ranged his batteries on to them as soon as they galloped out, and he never let up until the action ended. Let some one else be the mug horse-holder from now on.

The truth of the matter was that he only wanted to be back with his old mates, the McReady brothers, and since Ben was no longer one of a section he would settle for the next best thing and team up with Dan in any capacity.

"It's good to be back with the old mob again," he confided to Ben. "But there's not too many of the old hands left. I thought they must have shoved me in the wrong squadron when I lobbed back this mornin'. New faces everywhere."

How true that was! They had advanced a long, long way since that first desert battle at Romani, fighting their way across the Sinai Desert, through Palestine, and almost to the gates of Jerusalem. But their dead lay under every battlefield and the hospitals were filled with their sick and wounded. New faces replaced the old, and they in their turn were replaced by newer ones.

"They've been flat out keeping the reinforcements up to us lately," Ben agreed. "Some of the poor cows only see one stunt and they're on their way back to hospital. Either that or we're buryin' 'em."

"You'd be flat out buryin' 'em around here." Charlie looked across the horse lines to the rugged granite slopes that hemmed them in. "Nothin' but bloody hills and rocks! Blowed if I know, Boss; I can't help thinkin' we was better off back on the old desert."

Strange how so many of them had that feeling. When they were on the desert they cursed it with monotonous regularity and longed for the day when they would cross into Palestine, the Promised Land, with its orange-groves, green fields where the horses could graze, and firm ground where they themselves could walk erect as men should walk instead of dragging themselves wearily through the heavy sand.

But now, with the desert far behind them, they remembered only its good points—the cool shade of an oasis where great bunches of ripe dates hung from the sheltering palms, the brilliant sunsets, the crisp freshness of the early mornings, and the yielding softness of its sands under a blanket at night. They forgot the way the sand gritted between their teeth with every mouthful they ate, forgot the way it drifted in streamers before the *khamsien*, the merciless desert wind that blew for days and nights on end, and forgot how that wind piled the sand inches deep over them as they slept so that it trickled down into mouths and ears.

Yet there was not a man who could not vividly recall their entry into this Promised Land. The horses, long unused to green feed, suffered griping attacks of the scours. The hard ground that at first lent spring to their steps caused their fetlocks to swell so badly that the entire mounted force was immobilized for days, and to acclimatize them to the new conditions limping horses were led out for daily exercise by limping troopers with shins swollen from walking and bones that ached from sleeping on the hard ground. Yet, at least in retrospect, the desert had its good points.

"What are we here for, Boss?" Charlie asked. "What's the latest furphy?"

"We're taking over the front line tonight," Ben told him. "And there's no furphy about it; it's the good oil, straight from the horse's mouth. We're relieving the Jocks at a place called El Burj, about three miles ahead. There's another thing that'll interest you, Charlie; we're leaving the horses here and walking up."

"*Jesus*, Boss!" Charlie made an agonized plea for reassurance. "You wouldn't be kiddin' a man, would you? Walkin' three miles over them bloody hills!"

"Not unless the new major's been kidding me. Did they tell you we've lost Red Ned? Stopped one in the chest on the last stunt. They reckon he's in a pretty bad way, poor cow."

At sundown they relieved the Highlanders on a prominent ridge. It was an excellent defensive position with a good field of fire. From the protective stone sangars the Highlanders had built they could look down a slope devoid of all cover until it fell sharply into a valley several hundred yards away. The Turk held the ridges beyond the valley, announcing his presence with an occasional *rat-tat-tat* of a machine-gun.

"Mon!" a burly Highland sergeant sighed as he handed his sector over to Ben. "If he'd only attack while we're here together! We'd gie him somethin' for his corner, eh, Aussie?"

"My oath we would, Jock," Ben agreed feelingly. "But old Jacko's a bit too shrewd to come at that. He'll sit back in a good strong possie and wait for us to attack him, the way he's always done."

"Aye, mair's the pity. But, mon, it'd be a braw wee scrap if he tried it on!" The Scot took a last hopeful look down the barren slope. "We'd a wee post oot there, but we're nae usin' it now. It's nae a weel-sighted position. Nae field o' fire, ye ken, and nae line o' retreat except up yon bare slope."

A summing-up Ben was soon to find only too accurate, for the Highlanders were scarcely out of sight when his troop lieutenant returned from Headquarters.

"Get the troop ready to move, Sergeant," he said. "We're on outpost duty for the night. Taking over a post the Jocks established."

In bright moonlight they moved silently down the slope—a lieutenant, a sergeant, and twenty men, not counting the two Headquarters signallers who followed up laying a field telephone line. Finding their allotted post was simple, the moon illuminating with all too embarrassing clarity the rough stone sangars. Against the darkness of the valley they stood out like a row of jagged grey teeth. While the men took up their positions and the signallers established contact with Headquarters, Ben and his lieutenant summed up the situation. And neither of them liked one single thing about it.

It was sited a little back from the lip of the valley, and while it commanded an excellent view of the opposite ridge it revealed no part of the valley or the vitally important steep slope in front of the sangars. An enemy patrol could approach to within five yards of it without being detected, it could easily be outflanked if a general attack developed and the only line of retreat lay uphill without a vestige of cover. There was one other disadvantage about it, but that was only a normal hazard of warfare; a machine-gun on the ridge had its range to perfection as it soon proved by traversing the line of sangars with a burst of uncomfortably accurate fire.

"I've never seen a situation I liked less," the lieutenant told Ben when the machine-gun stopped firing. His name was Taylor. He was young and only recently commissioned from another regiment, but he was a capable soldier with an excellent record as an N.C.O. "No field of fire and no observation valuation whatever."

"And no bloody chance of getting out of it alive if Jacko attacks," Ben added.

Taylor said, "He's never attacked before, so let's hope he runs true to form tonight."

"But where's the sense in it?" Ben was finding it hard to suppress an uneasy feeling that tonight Jacko would *not* run true to form. "What are we stuck out here for? What are we supposed to do?"

"Our orders are to report any signs of activity in the enemy line, to fight a short delaying action in the event of an attack and then withdraw to the main line."

"Anyone explain how we were going to get back?"

"No. I don't think the C.O. realized how badly the post was sited."

"Sited!" They had been talking in whispers, but now Ben's voice rose to a grumbling growl. "It's not sited; that's the trouble." He paused for a moment. Taylor had come to them with a good record, but he still had to prove himself as a troop leader. It wouldn't hurt to see how he reacted to a bit of advice. "Look, Mr Taylor, I'm not trying to tell you your job, but if I was in your place I'd call up Headquarters and tell 'em this post is about as useless as eunuch in the Wasser. Tell 'em we can't see a thing and won't see anything until it's too late."

"You're right, Sergeant," Taylor admitted. "I'll do that

straight away." He moved into the next sangar where the signallers had set up their telephone and when he came back a few minutes later he shook his head. "Nothing doing. I was reminded that my job is to obey orders, and told to keep a sharp look-out because they're expecting an attack tonight."

Ben growled, "Me too. I've got a sort of a feeling. Will it be all right with you if I take a bit of walkabout out in front?"

"I think it might be a good idea, so long as you don't take any unnecessary risks. I'll warn the post not to fire until you get back. In fact I'll tell them not to fire until I give the order. There's no sense in letting Jacko know the post is occupied."

When Ben returned fifteen minutes later he had nothing to report beyond the obvious fact that everything seemed quiet on the enemy front.

By midnight it was anything but quiet. Machine-guns were hammering away steadily, rifle fire crackled all along the enemy-held ridge, and salvoes of shells whined over to burst in the hollows behind the Australian lines. The artillery was searching the hollows for the still-silent guns of the Royal Horse Artillery, the machine-gun and rifle fire was directed at the main Australian line, and even the machine-gun that had traversed them when they first manned the post had shifted its fire to another target.

"There's something brewing over there," Lieutenant Taylor said to Ben. "Can you hear that other noise?"

"Yes." For minutes now Ben had been striving to identify it, an indefinite, undefinable undertone to the incessant crackle of small-arms fire. He had tried to shrug it off as imaginary, some hallucination bred out of taut nerves. Yet it was there; every man on the post could hear it.

"What do you make of it, Sergeant?"

"I dunno. It's got me beat. Can't make it out at all. What do you reckon?"

"My guess is that there's a big movement going on over there and all this firing is just a cover-up for it. They could be moving fresh troops in for an attack or they could be withdrawing. Take your pick."

"I'll pick the attack. D'you reckon it'd be a good idea if I went for another walkabout to see if I can find anything out?"

"I'd be damned grateful if you did, Boss. I'd prefer to have something a bit more definite to go on before I report it to Headquarters."

Pleased that Taylor had at last substituted the familiar "Boss" for the more formal "sergeant," Ben moved cautiously down the hillside. He was, he admitted to himself, scared stiff, too scared to stay in that dangerous post waiting for things to happen and even more scared out here probing into the unknown all alone. Nevertheless he crept forward until he could peer down into the floor of the valley. He could hear the noise plainly now, recognize the clatter of accoutrements and even distinguish individual voices, probably commands. Unfortunately clouds were obscuring the moon, making visual confirmation impossible, but he knew beyond all doubt that the sounds were coming from the floor of the valley, directly below him. The Turks were massing down there for an attack and they were making no effort to disguise the fact.

"I can't tell you how many there are," he said when he reported back. "But there's a hell of a big mob of them down there."

"Thanks, Boss." Taylor turned to the signaller crouched over his phone. "Tell Headquarters the enemy is massing for an attack on the floor of the valley below us. Say that I suggest the artillery start shelling the valley and then ask permission to withdraw the post."

Relayed through the signallers the reply came back in the form of a reproof. The enemy, Headquarters stated, was concentrating troops on the ridge and *not* in the valley. Lieutenant Taylor would be informed when he was to withdraw, and in the meantime would he remember that his was a fighting post and would he please use his fire power to silence the machine-gun directly opposite his position?

"So we don't know what we're talking about!" Ben growled.

Taylor shrugged and said, "I s'pose there is a reason for

keeping us here, but I'd certainly like to hear it." The efficient soldier in him took over then and he gave his orders confidently. "Work your way along to the left and take over that end of the post, Boss. I'll take the right flank. Tell every one to fix bayonets, tell the Hotchkiss gunner and every second man to fire at that machine-gun each time it opens up. Tell the others to hold their fire and keep a sharp look-out on their immediate front. When I blow the whistle we withdraw. Keep the men well together on the way back because the big danger will come from the flanks."

Working his way along the post Ben made sure every man understood his orders and fully appreciated the situation. He took up his position in the end sangar then and settled down to wait. Dan was on his immediate right and Charlie next to him. At least he had a good dependable flank.

The next half hour, he admitted afterwards, was the worst he had ever put in his life. The suspense of kneeling there behind the rock barrier and waiting was almost unendurable. Action, any action would have been preferable, an almost welcome relief.

Their own supporting batteries had opened up and their shells were bursting all along the enemy-held ridge. None fell in the valley and Ben wondered whether Taylor had risked another rebuke by asking for the range to be dropped. Not that it would have made any difference. Headquarters had evidently made up their minds that the post was so windy that their information was worthless. Well, they were right about the windy part of it, at least as far as he was concerned.

The moon came out from behind the clouds and lit up the men crouching behind their crude stone shelters. It shone on the pale grey granite boulders, it spread its cold light over the enemy-ridge where the orange and red flashes of the shell bursts emphasized its coldness, but it failed to reveal the mysteries of the valley, the one place that really mattered. Rifle flashes flickered like fireflies along the ridge and occasional prolonged jets of flame revealed the presence of machine-guns.

Sometimes their own Hotchkiss and a few riflemen opened

up, but their fire remained unanswered. It was as if no one, neither their own side nor the enemy, was interested in this insignificant little post. A war was going on around them and over their heads, leaving them isolated between the opposing forces. Small wonder the feeling of tension gripped every man on the post!

Every man except one, Ben would have said. In that small group of anxious men Dan alone remained unaffected, mocking anxiety with his unquenchable exuberance of spirit. He had always been like that in action, either completely unconscious of danger or else treating it as a joke created for his entertainment.

He was having some trouble with his bayonet tonight, a defective catch causing it to fly off, not with every shot he fired, but often enough to be irritating. Twice in twenty minutes he called cheerfully, "Here we go again," and vaulted over the breastwork of his sangar to retrieve it. After the second time Ben asserted his authority and ordered him to cease firing.

"You'll lose the damned thing just when you need it most," he snapped. "And that won't be too long now."

"You reckon he'll really have a crack at us, Boss?" Dan sounded quite hopeful.

"I don't reckon. I'm dead certain."

"Good on him! Let him come. You know, Boss, we've been in every stunt since Romani, we must have fired thousands of rounds and neither of us could ever claim we'd killed one Jacko. Not for sure. If they come over tonight I'm gunna get one if I have to strangle him to death."

"And cut his bloody ears off and take 'em home for souvenirs, I s'pose?" Charlie chipped in dryly.

"Shut up, you two," Ben ordered. "Listen! Listen to that!" A noise, little more than a deep murmur at first, was drifting up from the valley. But as they listened it gradually swelled in volume until it filled the night, forcing even the crashing of gunfire to play the role of supporting music.

"Allah, Allah, Allah," the massed voices shouted in unison. "Allah, Allah, Allah!" The single word became a chant, rising in volume and tempo, an impassioned plea to God to lead them to victory.

It was weird and it was incomprehensible. To the newcomers in the troop it may have been unnerving; perhaps it was intended to be. But to the older hands it was a ridiculous gesture, a display of lack of confidence, and sheer bad tactics on the part of the enemy. Why advertise that he was about to launch an attack and have the whole front standing-to in readiness to meet it?"

"Well, can ya beat that?" Dan laughed. "They're holdin' a bloody corroboree down there!"

"Cease firing on the ridge," Taylor called. "Set your sights back to zero and hold your fire until the enemy appears."

The chant died away, fading out like the last notes of the overture as the curtain rises on the first, and last, act. Well, the curtain was up, but the stage was empty and poorly lit. A good dramatic opening! Crouched behind their stone sangars the audience waited tensely, knowing that within the next few minutes one of two things would happen.

Either the order to withdraw would come or the enemy would appear right under their noses. Only two things, but one meant life and the other almost certain death. No matter how well they fought two dozen men could not hold out for long against two thousand. The post would be overrun, swamped under the torrent of the attack.

Two minutes and the tension broke. A lone figure, possibly an officer leading his platoon, appeared like a grey ghost directly in front of Ben, seeming to rise up out of the rocks not six yards way. A single rifle shot crashed out, beating all the others by seconds. The grey figure crumpled and fell and Dan's voice rang out in a triumphant yell:

"That's one to me, Boss!"

Every man on the post was firing then, blazing furiously into the mass of grey figures swarming up the rise. The accuracy of the fire and possibly the complete unexpectedness of opposition so far in front of the main line temporarily halted the advance and sent the enemy in front of the post to earth. Taylor's whistle shrilled out and Ben roared:

"On your feet, boys. Make a dash for it and stick together."

He knew, even before a quick glance confirmed it, that they had done nothing to check the main advance. On either hand the attackers were streaming up the slope and already they were yards ahead of the retreating post.

Dan too had grasped the situation, because he yelled, "God, Boss! The bastards are all around us!"

With the two flanks converging to cut them off and the second wave of the attack now pressing up behind them it was close enough to the truth.

Running, pausing to fire a few shots at the nearest enemy troops, and running again the outpost fought its way up the slope. Men fell and were left behind because from the start it had been obvious that only the lucky few would win through.

Less than fifty yards to go and all hell broke loose as the Australian machine-guns and rifles opened up, and the nearest Turks began hurling hand-grenades at the retreating outpost.

Twenty yards to go and Ben heard Taylor shouting, "Outpost coming in here," in a desperate attempt to help the defenders distinguish friend from foe. How in hell *could* they distinguish individuals in this wild, flaring shambles lit only by a pale moon and the flashes of bursting grenades? Taylor's voice sounded close. He *was* close, Ben said. No more than eight men between lieutenant and sergeant on opposite ends of the ragged line! Ten left out of twenty-four! Dan was still beside him and beyond Dan he could see little Charlie and hear him cursing luridly. The next moment Dan was cursing as his bayonet flew off and he leaped forward to retrieve it.

Ben roared, "Leave it, son! Leave the bloody thing!"

Too late! One second too late!

The grenade exploded under Dan as he bent down. Ben shot the thrower, fired wildly at the next two figures, and was lifting his son before anyone except Charlie realized what was happening. His rifle was impeding him and he hurled it savagely aside, concentrating every ounce of his strength on the one thing that mattered now. Dimly he was aware that Charlie was beside him, firing rapidly and yelling:

"Come on, Boss! Come on! For God's sake, let's get out of this!"

He was erect with Dan draped over his shoulder when the grenade burst at his feet. The blast of it almost lifted him off his feet and made him stagger about, as Charlie said later, "like a chook with its head chopped off." He felt as though some one had smashed him on the jaw with a rifle butt, no pain, only a numbness that left him dazed and stupid. But he stayed on his feet, still clinging to his precious burden and only Charlie's frantically urging shouts drove him up over those few remaining yards. Good, stout-hearted little Charlie, behind him and blazing away to cover his retreat.

The mists in his brain cleared a little as he staggered between the sangars so that he retained for ever a confused but vivid memory of that moment. Lieutenant Taylor, minus most of one foot and using a rifle as a crutch, limping like a wounded kangaroo to safety, another man half crawling along behind him, and finally Charlie, good little Charlie, reeling past him whimpering:

"I can't do no more for ya, Boss. They got me too."

He had no rifle and both his arms were flapping uselessly as he ran.

In a protected hollow behind the lines Ben lowered his son gently to the ground. "We made it, Danny," he said, the numbness in his jaw slurring the words so that they were almost unintelligible. "We made it, son."

Dan opened his eyes and smiled. "Good old Boss," he said. He spoke calmly and clearly. And a moment later, in the same normal tone, "I'm done, Boss. They got me properly. But she was a good show while she lasted, eh?"

A kilted figure loomed up and knelt beside them, his Red Cross armband clearly visible in the moonlight. "Let's hae a look at him, Aussie," he said. Swiftly and expertly he slashed away the tattered, blood-soaked tunic, exposing gaping wounds far beyond his capacity to dress. He took up a limp wrist, held it for a few moments and said softly, "I'm afeared he's gone, Aussie. There's naethin' we can do for him. Was he a crony o' yours?"

Was he? Was! The dreary, lonely, utter finality of that one word!

"Yes," Ben mumbled. "He was my cobber. My best cobber."

"Mon, but that's bad." The Scot clicked his tongue in sympathy. "Ye're nae wounded yersel', are ye?"

"No." Had the stretcher-bearer been on the other side of him he would have seen the blood spurting from the great hole in his jaw. "No. I'm right thanks, Jock."

"Then I'll be on ma way." A kindly, understanding hand pressed down on Ben's shoulder. "Nae doot he was a braw laddie, but dinna grieve too much o'er him, Aussie. There's fightin' tae be done up yonder."

Fighting? Oh, yes, they were still at it, making the night hideous with their racketing machine-guns, their cracking rifles, and their slam-banging grenades. All right, let them fight if they wanted to, but they wouldn't drag *him* into it again. He'd had this lousy army after tonight's example of how *not* to use an outpost. Four men left out of twenty-four! What a turn-up! What a howling mess! And what had they achieved for it all? Nothing. Not one damned thing. In fact they had only caused confusion to the men in the line by racing up the hill all mixed up with a mob of Jackos. Probably half the outpost had been killed by their own machine-guns. What a lovely bloody thought!

Well, at least Danny hadn't been killed that way. But he was dead, wasn't he? Murdered by some brainless Headquarters mug who kept them stuck out there until it was too late. If they expected Sergeant Ben McReady to go back into the line and fight after that they had another think coming. Let them come back here and put him on a crime sheet for refusing to obey an order. Let them take his bloody stripes away. He didn't want the rotten things. When he got his wind back he'd find Headquarters and tell 'em so. Tell 'em what he thought of the whole show. Take a swing at one or two of 'em for good measure while he was about it. Lay 'em out cold with a decent sort of crack on the jaw. He'd get six months in the cooler for it, but it would be worth it.

He still felt no pain, only a numbness in his jaw and a dizziness that kept sweeping over him. He was not even conscious of the fact that he had been wounded. He only knew, with dreary, unescapable certainty, that Dan was dead.

The regimental stretcher-bearers found them there at sunrise, the McReady brothers, the younger one rigid in death, and his older brother slumped across his body, still breathing but almost dead from loss of blood.

★ 13 ★

"ARE you all right, Mr. McReady?"

It was the anxious voice of the night sister. She was standing beside his bed, one hand holding his wrist and the other shading her torch so that the glare did not shine in his eyes.

"Yes," he muttered drowsily, still unable to drag his mind back from the distant past. "Yes, I'm all right, thanks, Joan. What made you ask?"

"You called out. You shouted and you swore."

"Did I? Sorry about the swearing, dear. It's that damned nightmare again." He was speaking quietly, gently almost, with no trace of the barking rudeness the Stonehaven hospital staff were already regarding as his normal speaking voice. "That blasted grenade! It explodes right underneath me. I can see it coming and I can't do a thing about it. My feet just won't move."

"Try not to think about it. Would you like me to bring you a sleeping-tablet?"

"No, thanks, Joan. I don't want to sleep." He reached for her hand, held it and stroked it gently. "Sit down and talk to me."

"I haven't time now. One of the other patients is wanting me." She tried to pull her hand away, but his grip tightened.

"Let him wait. Switch that torch off, Joan, and sit down."

"I can't, Mr McReady. I must go." With a swift movement she freed her hand. "Why do you keep calling me 'Joan'? That's not my name. You must be confusing me with someone else."

"Eh? You're not Joan?" The abruptness was back in his tone now and he was wide awake, only needing some scrap of assurance or evidence to enable him to shake off the past. "Look, Sister. Would you mind shining that torch on your face, just for a second?"

Obligingly she let the torchlight flicker over her face, a

youngish face and quite an attractive one, but not the one he had been dreaming of.

"No," he growled. "No, of course you're not Joan. Nothing like her at all except for the uniform and the way you wear your veil. She wore hers like that, too, pulled down so that it hid most of her hair. Blast it, I must be getting doddery in the head! Time they used me for dingo bait. Don't take any notice of me, Sister. Go and see the other bloke."

But now that he was speaking rationally and making no attempt to detain her by force she was in no hurry to leave. The excuse about the other patient needing her was merely a stock excuse. All her other charges were sleeping soundly and the book she had brought on duty was the dullest thing she had ever tried to read.

"This Joan you were mistaking me for, is she a relation of yours?" she asked.

"No, Sister. No relation at all. Just a nurse I knew a long time ago, a hell of a long time ago. Away back in the First World War."

Her feminine interest in a possible romance aroused, she asked, "Was she young and beautiful?"

"No. Not very young. And not really beautiful either. Not nearly as pretty as you are."

"Now you're just trying a bit of flattery! I suppose you knew her before the war and the two of you met again over there?"

"No. I never set eyes on her till they dumped me into hospital with a smashed up jaw and a few odd bits of hand-grenade scattered around the rest of me. The big base hospital in Cairo, it was. She was on night duty in the ward they put me in."

"Aha! I see now! She used to sit on your bed and the two of you played handies! Mr McReady, you naughty old man. I'm surprised at you!"

It took a lot to make old Ben feel embarrassed, but this girl was certainly doing it. To hide his confusion he said, "Well, er, I was in a pretty bad way for the first couple of weeks and she, er, she did a lot for me."

"I'll say she did! Carrying on a flirtation with a patient

while she was on duty! It's just as well for the two of you the night super' didn't walk in and catch you at it. Or did she?"

"She didn't." He had recovered his composure now and was able to hold his own with her. "Would you let the night super' catch you smooging?"

"Mr McReady! I don't do that sort of thing. At least, not on duty. You'd better get some sleep now. And no more nightmares. If you're going to dream concentrate on your glamorous night sister."

She slipped quietly out, leaving him with one more memory. Not one to be proud of either, one that he had kept locked away and never shared with a soul until tonight. Yet, after all, it hadn't really done any harm.

Glamorous night sister! There had been nothing glamorous about Sister Joan Sutherland, no striking beauty, no frills, and no pretensions. He had never seen her out of uniform, of course, nor could he ever picture her in an ordinary frock. She was small and trim, not pretty, but certainly not plain. Trying to picture her now the only things old Ben could remember were that her small nose had a defiant upward tilt and her mouth was too big for beauty. He couldn't even remember the colour of her hair except that it was one of those indefinite colours you didn't notice much. She had a personality that made her popular with every one in the ward. They were a great bunch of lads, but for some unknown reason he had been her favourite right from the start.

But hold on now. It was not strictly true to say the reason was unknown. He was the favourite because he was by far the worst case in the ward, and she was, before anything, a woman dedicated to her profession. Secondly, she was older than any of the other patients, a woman in her early thirties.

And he needed her. By heaven he needed her and her gentle understanding during those first hellish nights. The days were not so bad because there was always something to distract him, doctors and sisters coming and going, patients exchanging ceaseless banter, and Charlie to sit beside him, giving him all the latest news; Charlie with both arms immobilized in splints, but still unfailingly cheerful and anxious to keep his mate from brooding.

But the nights, with all the other patients sleeping peacefully! Pain and memories flooded over him then. Memories of Dan going off for a walk with Biddy, Dan riding his first buckjumper, Dan grinning as he waded into a brawl or laughing in the hottest action. Dan, always Dan, right up to that last tragic, futile night.

When sleep came it would be an uneasy, feverish sleep, a sleep of nightmares that varied in minor details and always ended with the blinding flash of a bursting grenade. Sometimes he would be staggering under Dan's limp weight, at others he would be callously abandoning him to the oncoming enemy. But the culmination would always be the same—the one grey figure standing out from all the others, arm swinging up, the grenade curving slowly over in suspended slow-motion and floating gently down to his feet while those useless feet remained glued to the ground. Straining with all his strength he never managed to move one step before the grenade exploded with a deafening crash and a blinding flash of light. The crash never failed to awaken him to the realization that he was lying in a hospital bed with pyjamas and sheets saturated with sweat. Too weak to do anything about it, he could only lie there until the night sister came along and changed his pyjamas and put fresh sheets on his bed. Sometimes it happened twice and even three times in one night.

"Sorry about this, Sister," he apologized once. "I'm making a hell of a nuisance of myself. If I could only stay awake it wouldn't happen."

"Stop worrying about it," she ordered. "The sweats will stop as soon as you get some strength back."

"I wouldn't feel as bad about it if you'd leave the wet things on me."

"And have you catching pneumonia!" she scoffed. "Now stop talking or we'll have the whole ward awake."

Nevertheless she fell into the habit of carrying on a short, whispered conversation to cheer him up before she left him to another troubled sleep. Charlie, of course, had told her all about the outpost and Dan's death, but Charlie had not known that Dan was his son.

Under the circumstances it was not surprising that a certain intimacy developed between them, still only a nurse-and-patient intimacy, but a special nurse and a special patient. If she sometimes held his hand and gently stroked his bandaged head it was done professionally because the soothing effect was good for him.

And then they moved his bed out on to the balcony. The night sister, he was told, had reported that it was difficult to give him the constant attention he needed without disturbing the other patients. That was undoubtedly true and he had often asked Charlie to apologize to his ward mates for him. Out on the balcony he was not disturbing anyone and the knowledge helped him. During the day-time Charlie and the other walking patients saw that he never lacked company and at night there were the frequent visits of the night sister.

"How's my big sergeant tonight?" she would greet him when she came on duty.

And he would manage a lop-sided grin and say painfully, "Good-oh, Sister. Much better now you're here."

After a few nights he fell into the habit of listening for the rustle of her starched uniform when the lights went off and the ward had settled down for the night. Also, he was aware that he was forming a habit of reaching out for her hand when he heard that rustle. And the hand was always there.

Withdrawing it one night she said, "I must go and write up my reports now, Boss."

All the other patients had adopted Charlie's form of address, but she had never used it before.

"It sounds funny, hearing you say that," he told her. "But I like it. I wish you'd keep it up."

"Do you?" She gave his shoulder a light pat. "Then if you're good and don't have too many more of these night sweats I might consider doing it more often."

"That'll do me, Sister. I'll stay awake all night to make sure of it."

"You're to go to sleep at once."

"I will, as soon as you tell me your first name."

"Sergeant McReady!" she reproved. "This is a military hospital. You will address me as Sister or Sister Sutherland."

Although he saw her twice more that night she kept their relationship on a strictly nurse-and-patient-footing.

But the following night she greeted him with her usual, "How's my big sergeant tonight?"

And he said, "Still the same old answer, Sister. Better every time I see you."

"Because you can't think of a better one?"

"Because it's true."

"You'll have me believing it if you keep it up much longer." She rearranged his pillows expertly. "I'll come back and see if you need anything when I get the ward settled down. Comfortable?"

"Never felt better."

A deft tuck of the sheets and she said, "It's Joan." She was gone before he had time to answer.

There was nothing of the nurse-and-patient about the way their hands met when she at last came back, nor was there anything professional about the way she bent and kissed him before she left.

They were very discreet about their affair, for a time, and Ben was certain no one had the least cause to suspect anything until the night sister from the next ward shattered his illusions. She came along the balcony one night and when she was still some distance off she gave a long, low whistle, obviously a warning of her approach.

Joan took her time about getting to her feet. "It's only Smithy," she whispered, not in the least flustered until the other sister said:

"I just heard Matron's on her way round. Don't ask me what she's doing in the wards at this time of night, but I thought I'd better warn you."

"Oh, my gosh!" Joan gasped then. "I wonder what on earth got her out of bed. Thanks, Smithy."

The two hurried off, leaving Ben feeling distinctly uncomfortable. Obviously the other sister knew what was going on and it was on the cards that other members of the staff were in the know. What if it got to Matron's ears? She couldn't do anything to him, but she could make things very awkward for Joan, couldn't she?

Make things awkward for her! Hell, what else had he been doing for the last two weeks? Making up his mind to tell her every day and then postponing it every night through sheer selfishness, because he so badly wanted the comfort she gave him.

The same old Ben McReady! he told himself bitterly. Think of yourself first and to hell with every one else. You never change. Well, this is the one time when you're going to do the right thing.

He told her when she came back later that night. "Look, Joan," he said, coming straight to the point before he weakened again. "I should have told you this before. I meant to, but I kept putting it off and putting it off because, well I didn't have the guts to do it. I'm married."

He had been trying to guess what her reactions would be—whether she would reproach him gently, be bitterly scathing about it, or walk off without even a word of contempt.

She did none of those things. She took his hand in hers, squeezed it tightly, and said, "I know."

"You know!"

"Of course, you poor, dear old fool. If you hadn't been so sick you'd have realized I'd be sure to know. It's in your record, on the ward file. Your next of kin. But I've been hoping you'd tell me. I'm glad you did."

"I can't see that it makes such a hell of a difference."

"Can't you? It makes this much difference. It proves that I was right in my opinion of you, that you were honest and decent."

"I wouldn't say it was exactly decent for a married man to be leading a girl up the garden path."

"You weren't leading me up any garden path. I knew what I was doing. I was helping you over a bad time and I enjoyed doing it because it was helping me as well. You see, Boss, I'm married too."

"Oh!" He was too astonished to say anything else.

"Not that I can actually claim to have a husband. He

walked out on me. Left me for another woman, one with the good looks I didn't have, even if she was nothing but a bitch underneath it all. That's why I went back to nursing and joined the Army."

"A pretty tough break! Did you manage to get a divorce?"

"No. I'm a Catholic. Didn't you know? Our Church doesn't recognize divorce. With us a marriage is for life."

"Anyhow, you're entitled to have a bit of a fling, but I can't claim the same excuse. I'm not a Catholic. I could probably get a divorce if I wanted to, but I don't. I've got a wife any man could be proud of, one that's a lot too good for me."

"See what I mean about you being decent? Another man would have started the old story about his wife not understanding him and all that sort of thing. But you don't." She was silent for a moment, and then, with a defiant toss of her head, she said, "All right, Sergeant Boss McReady, we've cleared the air with our confessions tonight. What are we going to do about it?"

"I dunno." Now that he had faced the issue he was too bewildered to think clearly. "Cut it out, I s'pose."

"I wouldn't exactly call that a helpful contribution, but no doubt it's the right one." She made a swift pretence of arranging his pillows. "You must get some sleep now; it's after midnight."

And she was gone.

Get some sleep! How the hell could he sleep now? Why couldn't he have kept his big mouth shut and let things ride along the way they were? The spell was broken now, the pleasant interlude was over, and surely it had been a harmless enough interlude? But he'd wrecked it because he had suddenly developed a conscience.

He did not see her again until she was going off duty in the morning. She came through a doorway a few yards down the balcony then and called cheerfully:

"Good-bye, Sergeant. I'm going off now."

Cheerfully! Impersonally! The way she said good-bye to every other patient in the ward!

"Sister," he called. "Could you spare a moment before

you go?" To anyone listening it would have sounded a harmless, reasonable request.

She walked down the balcony and stood beside his bed, smiling brightly. "Yes?" she asked. "What is it?"

"Tonight," he said quietly. "Can't you—er—you won't leave me in the lurch, will you?"

"It's my night off. Remember? But Sister Jackson will look after you. She's much more efficient than I am. Be good now." With another bright smile she left him.

That was not a good day. He was uncomfortable and he was grouchy, even snapping at poor little Charlie when he strolled along for his morning chat. The ward doctor had the dressings taken off the wound in his jaw and spent half an hour probing around for a bit of bone. The doctor was brusque and irritable. He appeared to take it as a personal affront that the bit of bone kept eluding him, and the probe felt like a crowbar. The day sister was inclined to sympathize with the doctor rather than the suffering patient, and she, too, seemed to take it as an affront when his temperature went up that afternoon.

"You're to take these," she said, putting two tablets into his hand. "I've filled your water-bottle and you're to drink plenty of water and keep on drinking it until you get your temperature down."

Her tone implied that if it was not down by the time she was due off she would report him for insubordination. She went off that evening without carrying out her implied threat and Sister Jackson took over—plump, cheerful Sister Jackson, telling him she'd heard he'd been a naughty boy and hoping he'd be good and settle down for a good night's rest.

Naughty boy! In one way and another he was a bit fed up with the lot of them. And with himself. The night had to be faced—a long, dreary night, and he had to face it alone. In fact, he grudgingly admitted, he was indulging in a good, old-fashioned bout of self pity simply because he wanted Joan.

He was still doing it when the quick tap-tapping of her footsteps made him turn his head painfully. She was beside him then, standing there in her off-duty uniform, the severe grey tunic and skirt tending to emphasize her plainness rather than enhance her good points. Not that he noticed that. To him she looked beautiful, the most beautiful thing he had seen for years. And as she bent over him his arms went around her, holding her tightly for a full minute without either of them saying a word. After all, what *was* there to say that her presence was not proclaiming for both of them?

It was typical of his awkwardness with women that when he finally released her and broke the silence he said, "Didn't you have anything else to do tonight?"

"Sergeant McReady!" She straightened up and ran the back of her hand quickly across her eyes. "I'll have you know I refused two perfectly good invitations in order to visit you tonight. A captain asked me to dinner at Shepheard's, and a major invited me for a drive out to the Pyramids—to view the Sphinx by moonlight, he said."

"And you knocked 'em both back?"

"Yes."

"Why?"

"Well, for one thing I dislike the captain. Secondly, I happen to know there won't be any moon tonight. And thirdly, I wanted to come and see you because I heard you'd had a bad time today. Any more questions?"

"You won't get into trouble for coming here?" He had both her hands and his voice was anxious.

"Heavens, no. I'm off duty and I got permission to come up and visit an old friend. I didn't have to say what ward he was in and I'm allowed to stay until ten o'clock. Are you pleased?"

"Pleased! If you know how I felt before you came along and the way I'm feeling now you wouldn't need to ask that."

"Still, a girl likes to hear it."

"I'll shout it for the whole ward to hear if you like."

"I don't think that would be a good idea, somehow." She held his hand against her cheek. "Did the doctor give you a very bad time today?"

"My oath, he did! A horse doctor wouldn't have treated a horse the way that cow treated me."

"The callous brute! I'd have had something to say to him if I'd been on duty." She waited until her indignation simmered down before saying, "I had a bad day too. I thought of asking for a transfer to another ward, but I was fairly sure I wouldn't get it. Then I thought of having you moved back inside and I had to admit that wouldn't work either. In the end I decided to come and talk things over with you."

He started to tell her how happy that decision had made him, but she interrupted him.

"Wait a minute, Boss. I haven't finished yet. I'd faced up to the fact that we could either keep on as we are or make a complete break and I was even honest enough with myself to admit that the break would hurt me more than it would hurt you because you've got some one to go back to after the war. It was then I decided to come over here and talk things over sensibly. We've enjoyed being together, we've been a big comfort to each other without pretending we're hopelessly in love, and we haven't done anyone any harm. We're tangled up in this war, cut off from every one and everything at home, and since we can't get out of it we might as well get this scrap of pleasure out of it. And it's a very harmless pleasure, darling, because, after all, it's not as if we were going to do something we'd really be ashamed of afterwards."

He grinned at that last bit and said, "Now hang on a minute, Sister Sutherland. I wouldn't bank on that. You've only known me as a broken-down old crock, too weak to do anyone any harm. But I'm improving pretty fast now and once I'm up out of this bed I'll take a bit of stopping. Wait till *I* take you out to see the Sphinx by moonlight!"

"You're improving a little too rapidly," she reproved. "It's time I had you put back into the ward."

It was another two weeks before he was allowed up, two happy weeks during which he kept his mind on the immediate present, shutting out the past and deliberately avoiding all thought of the future. Red Ned and Taylor, both confined to bed in the officers' ward, had sent him messages of sympathy over Dan's death and congratulations on his conduct at El Burj. He had been recommended for the Military Medal again, they said, and this time it would go through. He had also been recommended for a commission.

Ben wanted neither their medal nor their commission. He was recovering from his wounds, but not from the feeling that had swept over him before he lost consciousness that night—the bitter hatred of a system that allowed senseless waste of lives to go unpunished. By accepting promotion he would, he felt, be making himself an active part of that system. And he wanted no part of it. He did not want to go back to his regiment or take part in any further action. When he was mended to their satisfaction they would undoubtedly want to send him back, but in the meantime he preferred to shut his mind to the possibility and think only of Joan.

"This is what you might call a trial run, Sergeant," the M.O. said as he signed Ben's first leave pass. "If you do anything silly, like getting drunk, don't expect another. You're a long way from fit yet."

Ben smiled at that. His plans for the day were already made and they did not include anything like a round of the pubs with Charlie and a few of the boys. He had timed his leave to coincide with Joan's day off. They would go in to Cairo, have lunch at Groppi's, and then hire a *gharry* to take them out to the pyramids. They would stay to see the Sphinx by moonlight before their leave passes expired that night. And this time neither of them would care whether there was a moon or not.

★ 14 ★

THE letter came next day.

It obliterated all thoughts of war, of military hospitals, and convalescent camps from his mind. It pushed Joan into the background, out of his life for ever. In its way it eased the pain of Dan's death because it brought Ben a new set of worries.

It was from Anne and it contained tragic news. Old Dan was dead, killed while mustering. His horse had fallen with him, crashing down on him and breaking his neck. He was dead when his two blackboys brought him in.

His death had been a tragedy to Anne, who had grown very fond of the old drover. It had also posed two big problems for her. The first, what to do with a body that has been placed on your verandah thirty miles from the nearest township, was solved by the timely arrival of a young parson, the Reverend Mr Coudrey. He had called at Coolibah once before, and Anne had found him shy, nervous, and difficult to entertain. This time, however, he had proved a tower of strength because he knew exactly what to do and was prepared to do it with the minimum of help from Anne. All he wanted was two fresh horses for his buckboard. Biddy ran the horses in for him, helped him harness them, and then she and Anne helped him lift Dan's body into the buckboard. Mr Coudrey afterwards drove off to Baranda to notify the policeman and arrange for Dan's burial. Two days later he returned, did his best to comfort Anne, and stayed with her while the policeman questioned the witnesses and inspected the scene of the accident. No one, Anne said, could have been nicer or more competent.

The second problem—finding a replacement for old Dan—was more difficult because most of the active men were overseas. But Ben was not to worry. Biddy had got a half-caste named Toby Warren to act as head stockman until they found some one better. The ticks had been bad lately and

Toby was dipping now. The bank manager had promised to look out for a suitable man, and Anne's greatest regret was that she knew so little about cattle-work.

"I feel such a useless fool of a wife, dear," she wrote. "After all these years on a cattle property I should know how to run one, but I don't. Biddy is much more knowledgeable and has been such a wonderful help. I don't know what I'd do without her."

Yes, Biddy would know. She'd know all about the mustering, dipping, and branding, know every inch of the country and where to look for the cunning old breeders that tried to dodge a muster. But Toby would never take orders or even advice from her. He just wasn't the type to take directions from anyone except a man strong enough to knock him down.

Old Dan, who had once hired Toby Warren one day and fired him the next, described him as a horse-killing flash buck, all spurs and skite. He would try to lord it over Anne, and his bragging presence would make her life a misery. As if it wasn't miserable enough already! By now she would have received the official notification of Dan's death as well as his own none-too-helpful letter telling her little more than the bare fact that he had been killed in action. Even if he had felt well enough to write more fully, the censor would never have passed a description of that fatal night.

Something must be done to ease Anne's burden and it must be done quickly. But the big problem was what to do and how to go about it. Would they release him from the Army and send him home if he put the facts before the proper authorities? He doubted it. The troops always said that the Army only released you in two ways; they invalided you home when you got too badly shot up to be of any further use to the them or anyone else, or they wrapped you in a blanket and buried you where you fell. Still, he had heard of one or two releases being obtained on compassionate grounds. In the end he decided to take his troubles to Red Ned.

Poor old Red Ned! He was in a bad way, lying there in his hospital bed, looking like the pale ghost of the big robust major who had talked Ben into accepting promotion and responsibility.

"Sit down, McReady. Sit down," he said, obviously pleased to see his visitor. "I'm glad you came along. I've had some excellent reports about you lately. Lieutenant Taylor can't say enough about your conduct on that outpost. A damned poor show, by all accounts."

"It was, sir," Ben agreed. "The greatest muck-up of all times."

"So I understand. A whole troop gone and nothing gained for it. Can't understand it, damned if I can. Still, 'ours not to reason why'. You got our messages?"

"Yes, thank you, sir."

"I know how you must feel about young Dan's death. I felt the same myself when I heard of it. As I told you once before I was very fond of the lad." He coughed painfully in an effort to cover an awkward pause. "How much longer do you think they'll keep you in here?'

"Another week or so at the most, sir. I'm well on the mend now."

"That's good because your commission should be through any day now. You'll go out of here an officer with M.M. after your name and I'd like to be the first to congratulate you."

Ben wanted to tell him that the authorities could shove their commission and their medal, but he could not bring himself to say anything that would hurt this sick man. He tried to thank him, aware that his words lacked conviction.

"You don't seem very pleased about it," Red Ned said.

"No, sir. I'm not feeling very pleased about anything. Dan's death rocked me pretty badly, and today I got more bad news from home." Ben took Anne's letter from his pocket and held it out. "I'd like you to read this and tell me what you think I should do about it."

Red Ned took the letter. During his years of service he had become used to men awkwardly handing him letters and asking for his advice or help. Usually they followed the same old domestic pattern—wives transferring their affections to other men because they were tired of being left alone while their husbands were enjoying themselves overseas! The letters were usually illiterate and the excuses the writers made were old and timeworn.

But this one, he soon realized, was unlike any of the others. The writer was cultured, she had strength of character, and her personality showed in every line. Moreover there was no "other man" involved. This woman was unselfishly in love with her husband and concerned only for his safety and peace of mind.

"I take it this is from your wife?" he said when he finished reading.

"Yes, sir."

"You wouldn't care to explain why you put your occupation down as 'drover' when this letter shows you're a property owner—a grazier, in fact?"

"I had reasons, sir, but I don't think they'd interest you."

"*You* don't think!" Red Ned exploded, almost rising to his old form in his indignation. "You're not asked to think! I'll be the judge of what will or won't interest me. You've come to me for advice and you can either come clean with the whole truth or take your letter elsewhere."

The outburst made him gasp for breath and while he was recovering Ben said, "That's fair enough, Major. You might as well know the full score."

"Right. What size is this property?"

"Near enough to thirty thousand acres."

"Good heavens! That's quite a big station."

"It might be in Victoria, but up in Queensland it's only a selection. There's a fair bit of waste country on it."

"How many head of cattle does it run?"

"Round about fifteen hundred, in the average season."

"Quite a sizable herd. Nearly as big as mine. Now let's get down to the root of the matter. What made you leave a very nice wife and a good property to enlist?"

"The police were after me."

"Cattle-duffing?"

"Yes, sir."

"I might have guessed it. I never could see you as an ordinary drover. Always reckoned there was something you were covering up. Was your young brother in this with you?"

"In a way. But the police never really had anything on him."

"Well, we won't go into that. The point is, what's going to happen to your property now your manager is dead? What sort of a man is this half-caste your wife mentions?"

"I wouldn't give him a job on a pig farm. He used to be a professional pug in his day. I don't think he was ever any great class at it, but it's gone to his head. Now he's a real flash buck, the sort of bloke that'd give a horse a sore back and a girth-gall today and saddle him up and sink the spurs into him again tomorrow. The sort of bloke you'd have to stand over all the time because if you didn't he'd stand over you."

"I see. Not very nice for your wife, having a man like that around the place, especially if he has been given a bit of authority."

"You're dead right there, Major. That's why——" Ben hesitated for a moment and then decided to come straight to the point. "Look, Major, what I want to know is, have I got any chance of being sent home?"

Red Ned gave his answer without hesitation. "With this letter and your Army record to back it up," he said, "I'd say a very good chance. By the way, how old are you? Not your military age."

"Forty-six, sir."

"Good heavens! You certainly carry your age remarkably well. Forty-six, eh? I'd put that in with your request; it'll all help. If you like I'll get some one to draft out your application for you. I'll add my personal recommendation, of course."

"That's very good of you, sir."

"There's one other thing. How will you stand with this cattle-duffing charge when you get back? You say you cleared out because the police were after you. Have they a case against you? Will they be waiting for you?"

"That's more than I can say, sir. I dunno how I'll be. I've done a fair bit of worrying over it, but it hasn't got me anywhere."

Red Ned studied him for a while before saying, "In one

way and another you seem to have done your best to make a thorough mess of your life, McReady. I'm not sure that you deserve it, but I'll do the best I can for you. Ask the ward sister to take you along to Captain Coudrey. He's a Queenslander. He's a lawyer and he also owns a cattle property, so he should be able to tell you where you stand. Tell him everything, everything, mind you. I'm supposed to sleep now, but come back tomorrow and let me know how you got on."

Coudrey was an up-patient, and Ben found him sitting out on the verandah. Small, neat, with a closely clipped moustache and neatly brushed hair, he looked more the lawyer than the cattleman. His manner was abrupt, yet friendly.

"McReady?" he said when Ben introduced himself. "One of McAllister's boys, eh? Heard all about you from him and young Taylor. They took Taylor's foot off, did you know? Rotten luck. Bloody bad business that outpost show. Some one ought to get it in the neck over it. But they won't. That's the bloody trouble with this Army; too much hush-hush when a high-ranker pulls a bad one. Still, you don't need me to tell you that. Pull that chair up and let's hear your trouble."

Ben sat down. Red Ned had advised him to tell this man everything but even without that advice he would have realized that Captain Coudrey was not a man to be satisfied with half-truths. His "let's hear your trouble" proved that he was aware that this was not a social call. His questions were the abrupt, searching questions of a man trained to sift the real truth from the evasive half-truths. When Ben finished talking he felt he had related the story of his life, omitting nothing.

"And now," Coudrey said, running a finger over his clipped moustache, "you want to know where you stand with the law? That's it, eh?"

"That's about the strength of it, Captain."

"Speaking as a cattleman I'd say you'd come out of it a damned sight too well. I know your sort. You prowl around like dingoes, fattening your miserable carcasses on your neighbour's cattle, and then when the law catches up with you, you squeal like a dingo in a trap. I'd like to see all you cattle-duffing scoundrels given ten years without the option. That's the only way to settle you."

Ben started to rise, his indignation showing in his flushed face. He was not going to sit here and let this slick city lawyer liken him to a trapped dingo.

But Coudrey grinned disarmingly and said, "Sit down, man. You haven't heard the legal man yet. You've only been listening to the outraged station owner, and his opinions don't count for anything because he lets his feelings run away with him. You want coldly practical legal advice, don't you?"

"That's right."

"Then speaking as a lawyer I'd say you haven't a thing to worry about, unless you pinched these cattle from a particularly vindictive owner, one who's had it in for you over a period of years, say. Are you old enemies?"

"I've never set eyes on the bloke, and I was never on his property before. But you're missing the point, Captain. The owner of Carina doesn't come into the picture. The bloke I've got to worry about is this Inspector Ryan, and he's the most vindictive character I've ever struck. Told me once he'd get me if it took him ten years."

"I'm not missing any points," Captain Coudrey said coldly. "I'm not in the habit of missing points. And it so happens that the owner of the cattle comes very much into the picture. Unless he'll press the charge the police can't do a thing. And frankly, I'd be very surprised if he went on with it. He got his cattle back and the police will have advised him to try for a conviction on the 'unlawfully using' charge. Only an optimist would ask a Queensland country jury to bring in a verdict of guilty of cattle-stealing.

"But the big point in your favour is the fact that the incident took place over three years ago and you've spent those years fighting for your country. Don't sneer. It doesn't matter why you joined up. That wouldn't enter into it. You've been wounded in action, you've been decorated for bravery, and you've won promotion in the field. You might as well face up to it, McReady; you'll go home a hero whether you like it or not. If the owner of the cattle has an ounce of brains he'll know that by bringing a pre-war charge against you he'd only stir up public opinion against himself without any hope of securing a conviction." Captain Coudrey smiled. "That satisfy you? Anything else you want to know?"

"No, thanks, Captain. That'll do me." Ben felt himself grinning back at the man who had made his outlook so much brighter. "You've got no idea what a big difference this has made to me."

Coudrey studied him for a few moments before answering. "Perhaps I haven't. I don't know you well enough, but I can't help wondering how much *permanent* good this police scare has done you. Possibly you'll go home and start pinching your neighbour's calves again and end up in court after all. I can't understand chaps like you, McReady, hanged if I can. Apparently you're married to an extremely nice woman, and what do you do to make her happy? Get yourself entangled with the law and then clear out and leave her to fend for herself! But she'll forgive you because that's the way things go. The really nice women all fall for scoundrels like you. Don't ask me why. I wish I knew."

He smiled, a twisted, rather rueful smile. "Compare your case with mine. I've always respected the law, always tried to do the right thing, always tried to live up to the belief that a man should do everything possible to make his wife happy. And what did I get for it all? I'll tell you what I got as a reward for my noble efforts, McReady. A bitch. I'm married to an absolute bitch of a woman and I joined the Army to get away from her."

Ben stood up. "That's tough luck, Captain," he said. "Bloody tough."

And after all, he thought as he walked back to his ward, what else *could* he say?

Six weeks later he looked out across the desert for the last time as his homeward-bound transport steamed through the Suez Canal. Thanks mainly to Red Ned's efforts and influence, everything had gone smoothly and less than three weeks after he signed the application he was in a rest camp with Taylor and a dozen other medically unfit officers, awaiting the first available transport. Charlie had gone back to the front after promising to come up to Queensland and visit him if he ever got out of the war alive. Poor little Charlie! Going back to a squadron where he would be almost a stranger among a host of new faces.

The parting with Joan had been uncomfortable because she had clung to him and shed a few tears when he abruptly broke the news to her. She seemed unable to grasp the fact that she no longer meant anything to him, and when he left her he kept thinking of Coudrey's words: "The really nice women all fall for scoundrels like you."

Had she really fallen for him badly? The possible truth of it worried him for a day or so, and then he forgot all about it.

★ 15 ★

It was morning again in Stonehaven hospital. The day staff were bustling about their duties, Dr Stuart was leisurely ambling through his morning rounds and old Ben was preparing to face another day. There would be visitors, he supposed; some brightly babbling with the special inane brand of conversation they seemed to reserve for hospital patients, and others just plain boring. Ben wished it would rain and keep them all away, but the sky visible through his open window was bright blue without one solitary wisp of cloud. Still, he reflected, he had another two peaceful hours before the first visitor could bluff his or her way past Matron. The old girl was very strict about keeping them out until patients and wards were squared up for the day. And good on her, too! He was all for it.

But he had reckoned without Matron's snobbishness. She not only allowed a visitor in an hour ahead of time but she ushered him into Ben's room herself. As the Anglican Bishop of Stonehaven, this early caller rated special privileges, and Matron was a devout woman who rarely missed a Sunday service.

"Some one to see you, Mr McReady," she announced brightly.

Over her shoulder Ben caught sight of a round, jovial face, and called, "Come in, come on in, you cadging old Bible banger. It's good to see you."

And Alfred, Bishop of Stonehaven, smilingly answered as he stepped in, "It's good to see you too you unrepentant old heathen."

He turned to thank Matron, a rather shocked Matron, who plainly did not approve of the undignified greetings. Stonehaven's leading churchman was entitled to more respect, her starched withdrawal seemed to infer, and in his turn the Bishop should preserve a little more decorum in his retaliation.

Her disapproval worried neither man. Poles apart in many ways, they were firm friends who liked and respected each other as individuals.

"I hope you'll forgive this early call," the Bishop said. "I only got back from my Western tour late last night, and Mary didn't tell me you were in here until we were having breakfast an hour ago. I'm supposed to be doing a dozen different things this morning, but I told Mary I was seeing no one until I'd seen you and found how you were." He paused to study his friend intently, and a worried expression crept over his plump face. "And how *are* you, Ben?"

Ben grinned. "Like they'd tell you downstairs if you rang 'em up, Alf. 'As well as can be expected.' "

"Possibly. But I'm not ringing the downstairs office; I'm asking you, my friend."

"The truth, the whole truth, and nothing but the truth, eh?"

"That's what I'd like, Ben."

"Well, I'm as good as hobbled to this damned bed and, strictly between you and me, I don't reckon I'll ever get out of it until they come to crate me up. Doc Stuart's doing a lot of talking about patching me up for a while longer, but he's not fooling either of us."

"But, but——" The Bishop paused. It was not often he was stuck for words these days, but for the moment he was stumped. Only a month ago he had called at Wavering Downs and Ben had seemed his usual robust self. And now he was lying in a hospital bed, calmly announcing that he never expected to recover. "Ben, I'm most distressed to hear you say this, and I only pray you're wrong."

"I'm not wrong. And don't start putting your Bishop's bedside manner on with me just because you think you've got me thrown and tied with no chance of bolting for the scrub. Wipe it off, or I'll ring this bell and have you chucked out." Ben reached for the bell but withdrew his hand when a smile replaced the look of anxiety on his visitor's face. "That's a bit better. After all, I don't see why you should feel distressed to hear that an old bloke like me is kicking the bucket soon. I'm eighty-two. I've had a fair crack of the whip—more than a fair crack, some people reckon. Anyway I'm not whingeing; I've got no kick coming, except one. I always hoped I'd go out the way old Dan went—arse over turkey, galloping flat out after a scrubber. Not like this. Draggin' it out in a hospital bed, day after day, while the dearly beloved relations hang around like a mob of crows on the killing pen rails. They're getting set for it already, Alf. I can tell by the look of 'em."

"I hope you're exaggerating, Ben. Really I do. I mean, if Dr Stuart doesn't hold out any reasonable hope couldn't you get a second opinion? A younger man, perhaps?"

"What for? I know what's wrong with me. The machinery's worn out. And not before its time. It can't last for ever, Alf, even if you look after it, and I've given mine a pretty fair bashing, especially since Anne died. Now would you mind talking about something cheerful? How's Mary?"

"Oh, she's fine, Ben. In splendid health. She sent her love to you, by the way."

"That was nice of her. Anne always said Mary was the right girl for you, didn't she? 'The ideal parson's wife,' she used to say."

"How right she was! Dear Anne; we always remember her in our prayers."

"She'd like that. Had a lot of faith in prayers, even before she knew you." Ben closed his eyes for a moment and saw Anne as she knelt beside her bed. Then abruptly he shook himself back to the present. Mustn't start drifting into the past again, he told himself. Got a few things to square up first. He grinned and asked, "How'd your trip go? Did you bleed every bird in your flock for his last bob?"

"Not quite, not quite. I—er—well I was a *little* disappointed. Although, mind you, the response in many places was quite generous. Possibly I was just a little over-optimistic when I started out."

"You mean you still haven't got enough for the new church?"

"Not quite, I'm afraid. But I think I can persuade the committee to start building. The rest of the money will come,

I feel sure. That's one of the matters I have to go into this morning."

"How much are you shy?"

"Roughly, about a thousand pounds."

"Well, you've got it. You can shove me down for that thousand quid and get on with the job."

"But, Ben! Really, I mean to say, you've been extremely generous already and I couldn't——"

Ben heaved himself on to one elbow and scowled. "Listen," he snapped, "do you want to build this bloody church or don't you?"

"Yes, yes. Of course I do. It's been one of my dearest dreams for years."

"Then shut up and stop humming and hawing when some one offers you the dough. Fish around in that locker and find my cheque-book. Make out the cheque for a thousand and give it to me to sign. No time like the present. I might snuff out before you get around to asking for it, and you'd be a bit uphill tryin' to drag it out of Anthea or Gregory."

He signed the cheque, handed it to his visitor, and said, "There you are, me boy. Do you reckon our debt's squared now?"

"Ben!" the Bishop reproved. "If I didn't know you so well I'd feel offended at that question. You know there has never been a debt. I did what little I was able to do because it was my Christian duty and also a pleasure. I thought we'd agreed not to mention it again?"

"We did, but for the life of me I couldn't help dragging it up when I looked at you, standing there with your little purple Bishop's shirt and that holy, sanctimonious look on your dial, sayin' a black eye was a pleasure!" Ben chuckled. "But I must say, Alf, it was the best 'stinker' I've ever seen. And I've seen a few."

Bishop Coudrey laughed, too, as he said, "An honourable but temporary scar earned in the service of the Lord. I only wish I could have worn it with more pride. But I mustn't tire you, Ben. I was only allowed in as a special privilege and I mustn't abuse that privilege. I'll drop in again in a day or two, but in the meantime, is there anything I can do for you?"

"Nothing at present, Alf. Later on, perhaps next time you come, I might ask you to do me a big favour."

"Ask and it's yours, if it's within my power to do it."

"Oh, it's within your power all right, but it's against your principles, something I've heard you say you always refuse to do these days because it cuts your offsiders out of a fee they need more than you do, or something like that. This may not crop up until after I'm dead. It may never crop up, but if it does I want to know I can count on you."

"You can always count on me, Ben. You know that."

"It's about young Jane, my grand-daughter. I've an idea she'll be getting married before long and if she does I want you to forget your principles and do the ceremony for her."

"Who's the lucky man?"

"Young Reid Calder, my overseer."

"Does her mother approve?"

"No flamin' fear, she doesn't. It's not her idea of a good match at all. But if Jane's determined to marry the lad I've an idea it will soften Anthea up a lot if she hears you're doing the honours."

"Do *you* approve?"

"I think so. He's not good enough for her, of course, but he's a hell of a nice lad and I'm very fond of him. So long as I'm sure he's not after her for the money I might leave her I'd feel happy about it. And I'll find that out. Now will you do your whack?"

"I will, Ben. I most certainly will. In this case I'll make an exception. Anything else I can do? Any—er—help I can give you?"

"No, thanks, Bishop." Ben's tone was lightly bantering. "I know what you're thinking. You'd love to convert me before I croak, wouldn't you? But you're not in the event. I've been a bloody heathen all my life, and it'd be a pretty crook show if I squealed and wanted to reform now, just before the saddling bell rang for the last race, wouldn't it? It'd be like tryin' to square off with the stewards to let an unregistered bush colt enter for one of the big Southern classics. No, Alf,

I've been a brumby this long and I reckon it's up to me to die one."

Bishop Coudrey smiled and grasped Ben's hand. "I can only say, my very dear friend," he said, "I wish I had a few brumbies like you in my congregations."

And, Ben thought, as he watched the rather portly figure withdraw, it's a pity there weren't a few more parsons like you.

He remembered this one as the Reverend Coudrey, the young curate Anne had described as shy, nervous, and difficult to entertain, and had later praised for his efficiency when old Dan was killed. Never would he forget his first meeting with young Coudrey, not only because the minister was his first link with Anne when he returned from the war, but also because of his unusual appearance. Anything less like a shy young minister of religion Ben found it difficult to imagine.

He had written Anne from Egypt, giving her the news of his release, his approximate sailing date, and the approximate date of his return. Unfortunately he had forgotten that the censor would cut those dates out of the letter, and Anne would not know when to expect him. His telegram from Melbourne fared even worse, for it missed the weekly mail coach from Baranda to Coolibah and was still lying in the Baranda post office when he arrived there.

Baranda had grown since the day he and Anne first set out from it in their springless dray. The railway now connected it with Stonehaven, three stores, a new hotel, and more than a score of neat weatherboard homes now faced its broad main street. It even boasted a Shire Hall and a tiny church.

But it held no attractions for Ben. Within an hour of leaving the train he was headed for Coolibah, riding a horse borrowed from the proprietor of the mail run.

He was a little more than half-way home when he met the young man driving the buckboard and pair. Each would have liked to pass on with only a casual nod, Ben because he was anxious to get home before dark, and the young man in the buckboard because he was anxious to hide his face. But since custom demanded certain courtesies when two strangers met on a lonely bush road, both reined in.

"Good day," Ben called, and then, urging his horse closer, "My God, mate! You had a bloody accident?"

His glance travelled swiftly over the buckboard, saw no signs of damage there, and returned to the driver's face, a battered face, distorted by a badly swollen upper lip and further marred by the vivid purple of a completely closed black eye.

"God!" he breathed again, his tone changing to one of admiration. "She musta been some brawl, mate! That's the best bloody stinker I ever laid eyes on!"

Through distorted lips the owner of the stinker mumbled, "I wish you wouldn't joke about it. It was a most regrettable affair."

Only then did Ben notice the clerical collar.

"Sorry if I swore," he apologized. "I didn't notice you were a padre."

The young minister managed a twisted smile. "Please don't apologize," he said. "I know how I must look to a stranger, but actually I've had a terrible time, a most trying time for a man in my position." He wondered whether this stranger would be satisfied with that and let him pass. The fellow looked like a bushman in spite of the new, obviously ready-made suit he was wearing. He certainly sat his horse with the lounging ease of a born horseman. "My name's Coudrey," he finished. "I'm on my way to Baranda to enlist the help of the police."

"Coudrey? Coudrey?" Ben pushed his hat back and scratched his head thoughtfully. "Hold on a minute. You must be the bloke my wife wrote to me about. You helped her out, didn't you? When Dan Clancy was killed. I'm McReady. Ben McReady."

A look of relief showed on the battered face. "Oh, Mr McReady, I'm so glad you're back. I've just come from your place. Your dear wife has had trouble with her head stockman. He was most insolent and actually threatening to her. I—er—intervened on her behalf, but I'm afraid I only made matters worse."

Bit by bit Ben got the mumbled story from him. Toby Warren had been loafing around the house for weeks, making no effort to earn his money, and when Anne had at last plucked up the courage to reprove him he had turned nasty. The Rev. Mr Coudrey had arrived to find an indignant Biddy doing her best to console her weeping mistress, and once again he had taken charge. He had insisted that Toby must be dismissed at once. He had gone further than that. Knowing that the job was too much for Anne, he had located Toby over at the horse-yard and told him to pack his things and leave. Toby had abused him and started off to have the matter out with Anne. And when the young parson had tried to bar his way Toby had used his fists. He had done a fair amount of damage and might have done a lot more if Biddy had not intervened.

Good old Biddy! Loyal, stout-hearted Biddy! Always it was Biddy who came to the rescue of the McReady family when things were tough. Biddy had helped Ben rescue old Dan from the police, Biddy had risked her own life to come to Anne when Anthea was born, and Biddy had stood by Anne through her lonely war years. And in this case Biddy had saved Anne's champion from being battered into a pulp.

Typically she had wasted no time in entreaties or hysterical screams. She had simply grabbed a long-handled shovel, loomed up behind Toby, and laid him out with one well-aimed wallop. Later a sullen but chastened Toby had saddled his horse and ridden away, and only when horse and rider had disappeared down the road did Biddy put the shovel away and say disgustedly:

"Them bloody half-castes alla same dingoes. He left his swag behind, but I bet he don't come back no more."

But the Reverend Coudrey was leaving nothing to chance. He was hurrying to Baranda to demand police protection for Anne.

"Don't worry about the police," Ben told him. "I'll take care of Anne, and I'll take care of Toby later on. I know his sort. He'll lie low for a while, but I'll catch up with him. Maybe I'll never be able to pay you back for all you've done for my wife, Padre, but at least I can square up for what that bloody half-caste did to you."

"Please, Mr McReady," the minister pleaded. "Please

don't get involved with him on my behalf. Perhaps I was wrong to adopt such a belligerent attitude. I had no right to antagonize the man the way I did, and I feel that he has been fully punished for all he did. That blow on the head! I mean, his skull could very easily have been fractured."

"I wouldn't worry too much about his skull," Ben told him. "You'll have enough troubles of your own with that eye for a day or two. I'll push along now, Padre, but before I do I want you to know there'll always be a feed and a bed for you at any time you show up at Coolibah, and if there's anything I can do for you at any time you've only got to let me know."

They parted then, each knowing he had formed a friendship that would endure.

For two happy weeks Ben put Toby out of his mind. He had Anne, a radiant Anne now she had her husband back. Her once raven-black hair was now grey, but she was still beautiful because hers was a beauty that came from deep down inside her, the type of beauty that would never fade. And then there was the difficult job of winning the confidence of the three-year-old son he had never seen before. Young Ken had the McReady sturdy independence, but in looks he took after Anne. He had her dark hair and showed no sign of developing the McReady hooked nose. Of course he adored Biddy, who was doing her best to spoil him.

It was Biddy who dragged the full story of Dan's death out of Ben. At first he was reluctant to talk about any aspect of his Army life, but in the end he found himself talking freely, giving both Anne and Biddy a vivid picture of Dan's laughing, reckless soldiering, right up to the end.

Ben's feelings about his property were mixed. The season was good, the cattle were in prime condition, and although the fences had been neglected since Toby took over, they could be put in order in a couple of weeks. What really alarmed Ben was the spread of the prickly pear. There had been patches of it along the river frontage before he went away, but now it was everywhere. It thrived on the rich river flats and flourished even in the densest brigalow. What, he wondered, could a man do to check such an alarming growth? At this rate it could choke them off the property in another ten years. What did other cattlemen think of it? What were they doing to check it?

It struck Ben that he was badly out of touch with all the vital aspects of the grazing industry. He would have to move around, talk with other cattlemen and have an interview with his bank manager. Why, he wasn't even sure how his bank balance stood! He was aware that he was richer than he had ever been before, though that was nothing to boast of. Anthea was still away at her expensive school and Anne had lacked for nothing while he had been away. Cattle were bringing higher prices than ever before. But would those prices stay up? What would happen to the cattle market when the war ended?

"You should go down to Stonehaven for a few days, darling," Anne said when he discussed the matter with her. "It's the only way to find out what's going on, and we'll be quite all right until you get back." She ran her fingers lovingly through his hair, the thick mane of fair hair that still showed no sign of grey. "And, Ben dear, I want you to promise to buy yourself some good clothes as soon as you get down there. That suit you came home in isn't nearly good enough for my big, handsome husband."

There was one other matter to be finalized, she pointed out. Toby must be paid the few pounds still owing to him and his swag must be delivered to him in Baranda.

★ 16 ★

Next morning Ben hitched two horses to the buggy, tossed his suitcase and Toby's swag into the back, and turned to say good-bye to Anne.

"You'll be careful, darling, won't you?" she asked anxiously. "You won't let Toby start anything, will you? Now that he's gone I'd rather you paid him everything we owe him and let the whole beastly matter drop."

"Don't worry, dear." He took her in his arms and gave her a hug that left her breathless. "I'll pay him everything we owe him and I promise you I won't give him a chance to start anything rough." He kissed her, waved to Ken and Biddy, and drove off.

He found Toby in front of the hotel. The big half-caste was squatting on his heels in a patch of shade, rolling a shapeless cigarette while he carried on a desultory conversation with a lean, sun-dried white man, evidently a stockman or a drover.

"Good day," Ben said, reining in his sweating pair, the heels of the near-side horse only a few feet from Toby's knees. "You're Toby Warren, ain't you?"

He had only met the man once before, but there was no mistaking the broad dusky face with the thick, cruel lips and the dark, bloodshot eyes. He still had the wide, heavily muscled shoulders of the trained pugilist, the hips were still slender, but the belly bulging over the sagging belt told its story of the athlete out of training.

"Yair, that's me." Toby came to his feet in a lithe, effortless movement, his dark eyes flickering and watchful. He had been expecting this meeting for two long weeks and no one was going to catch him off-balance or unprepared. He recognized the man in the buggy, had recognized the two horses as soon as they swung into the street, and he was ready for anything. Big Ben McReady had made a name for himself as a bush fighter years ago, but he was no longer young. If the old bloke was mug enough to start something he'd get what that interfering parson got with a bit more chucked in to make up for the shovel.

Ben reached behind the seat, lifted Toby's swag and flung it carelessly out. "There's your swag," he said.

Toby could have caught it. Instead he stepped back and let it fall to the ground, not even glancing down as it landed with a soft thud and a swirl of red dust.

He's nervous, Ben thought. He said contemptuously, "Better go through it and see there's nothing missing. Your cheque's in there, too."

He flapped the tired horses with the reins and drove around to the hotel stables without bothering to see if Toby was taking his advice.

He had unharnessed the horses and put them in the stables when Toby sauntered up to him and said, "Where's this cheque you bin talkin' about? There ain't no cheque in the swag." His attempt at arrogance was not quite convincing. Behind it was the faintest trace of uncertainty.

This big McReady had him guessing, and so far all his guesses had been wrong. He had expected Ben to challenge him as soon as he reined in, he had expected him to follow the carelessly tossed swag with a flying tackle from the buggy, and when neither move eventuated he had been certain the suggestion that he check the contents of his swag was a ruse calculated to throw him off guard while McReady leaped into his attack. And again this man had proved him wrong by driving off without even looking at him. Surely he would say *something* about the way he had behaved on Coolibah? Surely he wasn't going to let the whole matter drop? But perhaps he'd got wise to the fact that it wouldn't pay him to pick a brawl with Toby Warren, a bloke with a reputation for belting every man in the district. That must be it. Big as he was, why would McReady start a fight with a man fifteen or maybe twenty years younger than himself, an ex-heavyweight pug only a pound or two lighter than he was?

"Well," he said, getting quite a lot of truculence into his tone now, "it ain't in the swag, I said. What you tryin' to do? Chisel a man outa 'is wages?"

"Hell, no!" Ben's tone was almost apologetic. He patted his side pockets and then felt in his hip-pocket. He drew out two folded accounts, examined each one, and dipped his hand in again. This time he pulled out the cheque. Not once had he looked at Toby or even faced him. He had promised Anne he would pay Toby everything they owed him and he had promised her he would not let Toby start anything. Hell, he couldn't afford to let this swaggering flash buck start anything! Toby was years younger than he was, he had the advantage of professional ring-craft, and he had made a name for himself as a dirty fighter.

"Here it is," Ben said passing the cheque over. "The missus wanted me to pay you everything you had coming to you, but I didn't make the cheque out for the full amount."

Toby grabbed the cheque, held it open with both hands, and glanced quickly at the figures.

And in that fleeting second Ben hit him. His uppercut connected cleanly with Toby's chin with a smack that was heard by the cook in the hotel kitchen. It dropped Toby to his knees, but it by no means knocked him out. Nor had Ben expected it to. All along he had known that if he could get the first big hit in it would go a long way towards levelling the difference between their ages and physical conditions. In spite of his big belly Toby had been leading an active life while Ben lay in a hospital bed in Cairo.

Don't give him a chance to start anything or he'll murder you, Ben had reasoned as he drove in from Coolibah. Hit him first and hit him hard. Never mind about the ethics of the game because you'll be dealing with a bloke who'll come at anything and try every dirty trick in the fight game. You've got to start this fight and you've got to win it. Knock this bloke groggy with the first hit and then keep at him, force the pace from start to finish and give him no chance to recover.

Toby's ring training showed in the way he came up, crouched in a perfect smother and lurching straight for his opponent. He needed time, a minute or two close in where he could hang his spinning head over his attacker's shoulder and let his weight sag heavily on him while the numbness cleared from his brain and the stars stopped dancing in front of his eyes. This bush mug would know nothing of in-fighting. He would waste his strength and tire himself out trying to push off the heavy, hampering weight, his short body punches would lack power, and there was no referee to force them apart.

Toby never got that respite. Sensing his intentions Ben eluded each rush or kept his man off with a barrage of punches. He was aware that Toby was taking most of those punches on his arms or rolling with them to take the power out of them, but he *must* keep forcing the pace. Apparently Toby guessed what was in his mind, for he ceased trying to bore in and simply stood his ground, crouched over with arms raised to shield his face and elbows tucked down in the perfect defensive smother. He took the next two punches without moving and then flashed out with a cracking left that opened a gash on Ben's cheekbone.

Time and again he repeated it, absorbing punishment for a while and then suddenly opening up with that deadly left that flashed out with speed of a striking snake and scored more often than it missed.

Men talked about that fight for years after. In the bar of the Baranda Hotel it cropped up whenever fighting was mentioned, told and retold as a battle of giants.

At some stage of it Ben was dimly aware that they were surrounded by spectators. Some one, his voice high and shrill with excitement, was yelling, "Go on, McReady! Give it to the black barstid! You got 'im rattled!"

Another less-excited voice called, "Oh, yeah! I'll have a coupla quid on the boong."

And someone else accepted the offer with, "Yer set, mate. Make it a fiver if ya like."

At that moment Ben would not have backed himself with bad money. He was not giving in. He would never give in, but he was taking some terrific punishment. Toby's flashing lefts were shaking him badly, his face was a mass of cuts and bruises, his wind was giving out, but he was still on his feet and still attacking. Dazed and bleeding, he at least had the satisfaction of knowing that some of his punches were leaving their mark on Toby's face.

He heard the shrill-voiced barracker yell, "'It 'im in the guts, McReady! Ya can't 'urt them bloody boongs' 'eads. 'It 'im in the guts!"

Toby must have heard the advice, too, because he lowered his guard sufficiently for Ben to score with a right to the already damaged jaw. The force of it dropped Toby to his hands and knees again, but he came up with a blind, bull-like rush, charging forward with head lowered in an attempt to butt and bring his opponent to the ground.

Instinctively Ben avoided the rush and was slamming punches into Toby's body as he turned. Mainly because he was finding it increasingly difficult to focus on any single point, he no longer cared where he hit the vague mass in front of him so long as his fists met something solid.

Toby was definitely groggy now, staggering in a vain attempt to weave in the elusive manner instilled into him by his late trainer. One more good crack on the chin would finish him. And knowing it he nursed that chin, keeping it tucked into his chest and guarded with an arm while Ben slammed punch after punch into his ribs.

Keep at him, keep at him, Ben's fuddled brain kept repeating. Don't let up on him or he'll murder you.

But Toby was already beaten and was backing away from Ben's punches, seeking only to protect his injured jaw until he could break off the fight and cry quits. Never in his life had he taken such a belting.

"Tha's enough, tha's enough," he panted. "Lay orf, lay orf. I'm done."

The man who had backed Ben for a fiver yelled, "Don't let 'im dingo on ya, mate. Finish 'im off!" Evidently he had a grudge against Toby.

And again the shrill-voiced barracker screamed his advice, "Now's yer chance! 'It 'im in the guts now yer got 'im rockin'."

This time his words took effect. Ben crashed a right into Toby's solar plexus and had the intense satisfaction of hearing the ex-professional scream with agony as he doubled up and fell forward on his face.

"Get up," Ben panted, standing over him. "Get up and take what's owin' to ya."

A firm hand grasped his arm and a voice said, "Save yer breath, mate. You won't get him on his feet again. He's had it."

Every one was trying to shake his hand at once and even the man who had backed Toby was congratulating him. "I done a fiver on ya, mate," he said. "But it was worth five quid to see that fight."

Ben pushed them aside and looked down at Toby. There was little doubt that he had been paid in full, for he still lay face-downward, moaning, vomiting, and spitting blood into the dust. Some one rolled him on to his side and poured a jug of water over his face. He was not a pretty sight.

Just beyond the reach of one outflung arm the cheque lay, a worthless scrap of paper now, trampled, torn, and as unrecognizable as its legal owner.

"It was his wages," Ben explained, grinding the battered remnants into the dust with his heel. "Tell him to come and see me before he goes home and I'll write him another one."

Half an hour later, washed, changed, but painfully aware of his cut and bruised face, he was about to join the crowd in the bar when a small boy tugged at his arm and said, "Hey, Mr McReady, the copper wants ya down at the p'lice-station."

"Righto, son." Ben grinned stiffly at the upturned freckled face. "You lead the way, eh?"

Hell! he thought ruefully. Home two weeks, in town for an hour, and I'm in trouble with the police. Just can't seem to keep out of it. He wondered what the charge would be. Disturbing the peace, he supposed. Oh, well, this sleepy one-horse town could do with a bit of disturbing. Liven it up a bit.

"Gee, Mr McReady!" The admiring voice of his small guide cut in on his thoughts. "You're pretty good, ain't ya? Nobody ever belted Toby Warren before, but you done 'im over proper didn't ya?"

"Just a bit o' fruit for me, son," Ben said, playing up to the hero-worship. "This the police-station? I'd better go in and see what I'm wanted for. Thanks for showing me the way."

Under other circumstances he would have taken an instant liking to the smiling policeman who answered his knock, but since the man represented a force that had always been a threat to him he reserved his decision. Police Sergeant Forster was a bushman and he looked it. Tall, loose-jointed, deceptively casual in dress and manner, he could have been a cattleman.

"Good of you to come along so soon, Mr McReady," he said, extending a hard capable hand. "Come in and sit down for a few minutes if you can spare the time."

"The kid said you wanted me." Ben was still a little bit wary. This friendly opening mightn't mean a thing.

"Must have got my message a bit mixed-up in his excitement. I told him to tell you to drop in any time you were passing. Didn't think you'd be feeling up to it for a day or so, but I'm glad you are. Sit down and take a weight off your legs." Sergeant Forster waited for his visitor to sit before lounging into his own chair. "Nice job you did on Toby Warren. Congratulations. I saw most of it from the pub back-verandah. Couldn't come any closer because it's my job to stop brawls." He smiled, a lop-sided, likeable smile that showed nothing but friendliness and admiration. "And I'd have stopped this one if it had looked like going the other way. I've been dwelling on that buck for a long time. He's caused more trouble than any man in the district, but he's always been too smart to start anything while I'm around. I stayed until the finish this afternoon, just to make sure he got what was coming to him. If he'd started to get the upper hand I'd have nabbed him and locked him up for starting a brawl."

Thinking it over and choosing his words carefully Ben said, "You'd have been making a blue there, Sergeant. I started it."

"Oh, no, you didn't," Forster contradicted. "As far as I'm concerned Warren took the first swing when he did poor young Coudrey over. I wanted to pick him up for that but the parson wouldn't bring a charge against him. A nice lad, though. His brother was a cobber of mine. He's overseas now with the Light Horse. Did you ever run across him?"

Careful now, Ben was thinking. Better start with a clean sheet and finish with the past altogether. Why admit something that could end up in a confession that the elder Coudrey had helped him with advice about a cattle-duffing charge?

"No," he said slowly, as though trying to place the name. "Can't say I did. But I wouldn't be likely to, except by a fluke. I was with a Victorian unit."

Would this apparently friendly copper be satisfied with that or would he want to know how a man from the Baranda district came to be tangled up with a Victorian mob?

But evidently the sergeant was only making polite conversation for he went out to a cooler on the verandah and came back with a bottle of beer and two glasses. "You wouldn't knock one back, would you?" he asked.

No, Ben definitely would not. He needed a drink to steady himself down, something to dull the ache of his many bruises, and he preferred to drink it sitting here, rather than face the noisy crowd in the hotel bar. The soft gurgling as his host filled the glasses was in itself an assurance that this was nothing more than a friendly social call.

And a very profitable call it proved. Sergeant Forster was an easy talker. Lounging back in his swivel chair, occasionally sipping his beer, he yarned about his district in a casual manner and yet revealed a surprising knowledge of it. He knew every station owner, knew how well or how badly each property was run, and had a very shrewd idea of values. He thought Coolibah easily the best of the small holdings and he expressed admiration for the way Dan Clancy had managed it. Wavering Downs, he declared, was a lovely bit of country, the pick of the big stations.

"And," he added dryly, "it's the worst run. In fact I'd say it wasn't run at all. Old Delacy never seems to do anything except sit in his office and rave about Queensland only being fit for the blacks. He might have been all right in the old days when he could get plenty of cheap labour from the camp on the creek, but now that we've got all the aboriginals in missions he's half the time without a stockman on the place."

"What about his kids? The place used to be lousy with 'em. Don't any of 'em take an interest in it?"

"They've all drifted off. Some of the boys went away to the war, one or two of 'em got city jobs, and even the girls left when their mother died. Can't say I blame 'em either. Half an hour with old Delacy is too much for me."

"How many head of cattle is he carrying?"

"That's more than he or I or anyone else could tell you. His stock returns are nothing but a pain in the neck to me. I'd say he just thinks of a number, adds two hundred, subtracts three hundred, and puts down the answer. The only way to tell how many head he owns would be to put a good team of men on and do a bang-tail muster. And you'd need good men because the cattle are as wild as brumbies."

"What about horses? He used to run some good bloodstock."

"He still does. Man, they'd make your mouth water. He sold some to the Army and some to the police remount depot, but the place is still overrun with unbroken stuff, and any one of 'em could clean up a country race meeting."

"Why doesn't he sell out?"

"Search me. I'll ask him next time I see him if you're interested."

"Me!" Ben laughed at the idea. "Where would *I* get the money to buy a place like Wavering Downs?"

Nevertheless he was already thinking of the possibility. He had envied Delacy from the first day he scaled the Jump-up.

"There are such things as bank loans," Forster reminded him. He refilled Ben's glass. "Think it over. Why not have a yarn about it with your bank manager?"

"I might do that." Ben studied first the froth on his beer and then his host's face. He was thinking it strange that a police sergeant should be offering him, a complete stranger, advice about buying a property—one that, as far as either of them knew, was not even on the market. "You sound more like an agent than a copper," he said, his disarming grin robbing the words of any sting. "You got an interest in Wavering Downs?"

"I have," Sergeant Forster laughed. "Not a financial one, worse luck. I wish I had the money or the backing to buy it. No, I'll tell you why I'd like to see Wavering Downs in the hands of a good, live-wire cattleman. The place is a menace the way it is, what you might call a potential trouble-spot for me, and I'm a great believer in preventing trouble instead of sitting back and waiting for it to develop. The cleanskins on Wavering Downs are a temptation to any cattleman, even if he isn't a cattle-duffer already. The fences are down everywhere and the stock is straying on to the neighbours' properties. See my point? Get those cleanskins branded and the temptation's removed. If you owned the place would *you* leave 'em unbranded?"

"No bloody fear, I wouldn't!"

"That's what I mean. No cleanskins, no duffers. And no trouble for me, trying to catch 'em."

Ben was thinking, do I know what's in the back of this bloke's mind? Does he know about all the Wavering Downs calves I lifted? Does he know about the Carina mob? No harm in trying him out anyway.

"I see," he said, his tone lightly bantering. "But how do you know I wouldn't go in for a bit of duffing myself, Sergeant? You know how it is. With so much temptation bang up against me you couldn't blame a man for slipping, could you?"

"Mr McReady," the sergeant said, matching Ben's tone with his own. "If you owned Wavering Downs there wouldn't *be* any temptation."

Ben stood up, put his empty glass on the desk, and held out his hand. "Thanks for everything, Sergeant," he said. "The beer and the yarn. They both did me good. I'm catching the morning train to Stonehaven, and I'll let you know how I got on when I get back."

★ 17 ★

THE healthy state of Ben's bank balance was revealed in the effusive manner in which Mr McBeath, the manager, ushered him into his office. And McBeath was not normally an effusive man. In fact he was a cold, cautious little Scot, a pessimist of the banking world, who saw good rises in values only as forerunners of their ultimate slump. Ben, however, saw him only as a quietly cordial banker who produced figures to show him how well Coolibah was paying. Compared with other properties of the same size, Mr McBeath said, it had shown outstandingly satisfactory results.

Smiling to himself, Ben wondered what the little man would say if he knew most of those "outstandingly satisfactory results" had come from other people's cattle. But his banker was rambling on about surplus capital and safe investments.

"Put that surplus into something solid," he advised as he saw Ben out. "Think it over and if you decide to do it come back and see me. I'll be only too pleased to advise and help you in the matter."

During the next few months Ben's family saw him only at irregular intervals. He made several trips to Stonehaven and he spent a great deal of time on Wavering Downs, simply riding about and observing. Each time he scaled the Jump-up the irony of the situation struck him. The cleanskins were more plentiful than ever up there and instead of simply taking them he was planning to buy them!

"Delacy'll sell," Sergeant Forster had told him. "In fact he's breaking his neck to get out of the place now that it's been suggested to him, but I don't think you'll get him to put a price on it until he's been down to Stonehaven and talked it over with his bank manager."

"Fair enough," Ben said. "I'm in no hurry anyway."

Prospective buyers came to Coolibah, rode over the property with him, and left behind a mildly curious Anne, who was, or seemed, content with Ben's explanations that he was getting the stock valued.

And then one evening he returned from a trip to Stonehaven and calmly announced that he had sold Coolibah.

"Oh, Ben!" Anne looked horrified. "You haven't! You're joking, aren't you, darling?"

No, he was not joking, but until then he had not realized how his wife had grown to love her home. She had watched it grow from a two-roomed hut without even a proper floor, to a house with five rooms and a verandah. No, she had done more than watch its growth, she had been responsible for it, planning each addition, building always to a plan she carried in her mind. She and Biddy had planted every shrub and seedling in the garden so that the house was now surrounded by shady trees, shut in from all except the view across the lagoon and the river flats beyond it, the view she had admired that first morning. She had left some of her personality in every room in the house and now her husband was telling her it was no longer theirs!

"But, Ben!" she pleaded, fighting hard to keep the tears back. "This is our home. We've been so happy here. I—I just couldn't bear to leave it. Where would we go if we left it?"

"Don't look so miserable about it," he comforted her awkwardly. "I'm buying a better place, much better."

"It couldn't be better than this."

"You wait. I'm not going to spoil everything by telling you now, in case there's some last-minute hitch, but I'm going down to Stonehaven to finalize things next week."

"Stonehaven!" She looked at him anxiously, aghast at her sudden thought. "Darling, you're not planning to move to town, are you?"

"Town!" He threw his arms around her and hugged her until she gasped. "Can you see an old bushwhacker like me settling down to live in a town? That's one thing I'll never do, or at least not until you say you're fed up with the bush."

"You'll wait an awful long time for that, my sweet. Don't forget I'm a bushwhacker too." He thought she was crying, but she was only gasping a little. "Ben, darling, would you mind if I breathed? And just sort of felt myself to see how many broken ribs I've got? You forget how big and strong you are."

It needed more than physical strength to close the deal for Wavering Downs, he discovered, when he returned to Stonehaven. His negotiations so far had been conducted through an agent because he feared that if Delacy recognized him he would probably refuse to sell to the man who had once threatened to throw him in the creek. But with his own price finally agreed to and a firm offer in his pocket Ben anticipated little trouble in obtaining the extra finance he needed.

He found a lot. He found that it needed moral courage, assurance, and a grim tenacity of purpose to get what he wanted, and at one stage it looked as though he faced certain defeat.

He found a very different Mr McBeath this time, a coldly aloof banker, who listened to his strongest arguments and remained unmoved. Under no circumstances, he said, would the bank consider Ben's request for such a substantial overdraft, particularly to put into cattle at such a time. Cattle prices were at their peak. The war would soon be over, prices would drop drastically and there would be a general tightening-up in the financial world. *Some one* would have to pay for this reckless war expenditure. He had never seen Wavering Downs, but he knew all he needed to know about it. It had always been badly managed, and the fencing, yards, and even the homestead itself had been allowed to deteriorate badly. And then, he added as his final argument, there was the prickly pear. At the rate it was spreading it would choke the cattlemen off their runs in a few years. Either that or the Lands Department would enforce such heavy clearing conditions that the owners would go bankrupt trying to comply with them.

Ben put forward his own arguments. He knew exactly what the fences and yards were like. Moreover he had the Crown Lands ranger's report on them and had used it to force Delacy's price down. He also had the ranger's report on the pear situation. Wavering Downs, being mainly open downs with patches of scrub, was still only lightly infested. A determined man could keep the pest under control, whereas on Coolibah it had already got beyond that point. Annual floods kept spreading it over the river flats, and it was firmly established in the brigalow.

But the cattle were the crux of this deal. He had agreed to buy on a book muster—that is, he would accept the numbers Delacy showed in his books and stock returns. Delacy's estimate was six thousand grown head. He had originally asked market price for them, but had subsequently agreed to accept two pounds a head less when it was pointed out that the cattle were so wild that many of them might never be yarded, and that the standard of the herd had been allowed to deteriorate.

"At the price I've got him down to it's not a bargain," Ben declared. "It's a gift. I've spent the best part of three weeks riding over that country, just poking quietly about, and I'll guarantee to muster and yard over seven thousand head. That's a thousand head of grown cattle free, and there'll be more on the neighbouring properties. There are fat bullocks on Wavering that Delacy hasn't seen since they were branded. They'll bring eight or nine quid a head more than I'll be paying for them."

"Why hasn't Delacy sold them to the meatworks?"

"Because they're living in the scrubs and they were too wild for his musterers to bother about."

"If he couldn't get them out how do you expect to?"

"*Jesus!*" Ben exploded. "I'm a bloody cattleman! The scrubber I couldn't throw and tie hasn't been born yet."

Ignoring the outburst McBeath said, "Going back to these numbers you have quoted, Mr McReady. If Delacy based his figures on the numbers he had yarded and branded I doubt whether you could make a more reliable estimate simply by riding over the country. Don't you agree that it's highly probable that you counted the same cows twice or perhaps three times over in some cases?"

Ben was about to explode again, but realizing that only tact could help him, he said, with all the self-control he could muster, "Look, Mr McBeath. Don't try to tell me I wouldn't recognize a cow when I saw her. You recognize blokes that come in to your bank; it's part of your job, isn't it? The same goes for me with cattle. I see a cow today and I'll recognize her next time I see her, even if it's a month later and she's ten miles away from where I first spotted her." Having made his point clear he got back to business. "I'm asking you for fifty thousand pounds, a lousy fifty thousand!" In his enthusiasm he made it sound like pocket-money. "And by selling off the extra thousand head I'll yard, and a couple of thousand of the ones I'm paying for, I'll wipe off most of that debt in the first year."

"And still need money for fences and other improvements," McBeath pointed out acidly.

"I've allowed for that."

"I'm sorry, Mr McReady. The bank would not be interested in that kind of speculation. You appear to have been carried away by supreme optimism in this case. But if you decide to buy a smaller property, one more within your means, I would strongly recommend that you insist on a proper muster and count before taking over. Your proposed method—er—well it amounts to wild-catting."

Ben stood up and said, "So you won't play?"

"No, Mr McReady. I'm extremely sorry, but——"

"Like bloody hell you're sorry! You know what you are, McBeath? You're a piker. A lousy little piker! When I had a few quid to spare you told me to invest it in something solid. Righto. Show me something as solid as land, good land, first-class cattle country. Prices are gunna drop. Righto, let 'em drop; I'll be finished selling by then. But they'll come good again because people have gotta eat. Even you, though a bloke wouldn't think it to look at you and listen to you. A big feed of juicy steak would do you a lotta good. Put a bit of blood and guts into ya."

Mr McBeath started to rise. He was indignant and he could put his abusive client in his place more authoritatively once he was on his feet. But the client had other ideas. He leaned over the desk and held up a restraining hand, a big, hard hand that looked only too capable of pushing him back into his chair.

"Save it," Ben said. "Save it for some bloke that wants to buy a dairy farm. And you know what you can do with your advice and your bank, don't ya?" He was outside before Mr McBeath had grasped the enormity of the suggestion.

Where next? Ben wondered as he stood for a moment on the sun-drenched pavement. Disappointed and angry, he was still far from defeated. If necessary he was prepared to put his case before every banker in town. Sooner or later he would find a man who would share his enthusiasm and belief in the country's future, some one who would see the force of his reasoning and agree that Wavering Downs, at the price agreed on, was a gift.

His next interview looked promising from the start. Mr Hamilton was genial and he shared some of Ben's enthusiasm, but it took three days of interviews and searching questions before he agreed to take over the new account and make the necessary finance available. Like the pessimistic Mr McBeath, he pointed out that prices were bound to fall soon.

"Start selling as soon as you can," he said when everything had been finalized. "Especially those fat bullocks you've been talking about. And I only hope you're right about those extra numbers. If things turn out to be the other way around you and I will be in for a lot of trouble."

"I *am* right," Ben assured him. "I've been too long in the cattle game to make a blue like that."

Two evenings later he leaped from the buggy at Coolibah, lifted Anne high above his head, and said, "How does it feel to be a big station-owner's wife? I've bought Wavering Downs and you can move in any time you like."

In later years he sometimes wondered whether Anne would have been just as happy if they had stayed on Coolibah. With her it was difficult to tell, because she invariably made the best of everything, even accepting the neglected ruin that was Wavering Downs homestead without complaint. She and Biddy would make it comfortable in no time, she declared. For of course Biddy moved with them. A home without her would always lack something for both of them. She was, and always would be, one of the family. During the next two years they all worked harder than they had ever worked in their lives. Anne and Biddy had a team of hungry stockmen to feed, and Anne had to plan and oversee the building of the new house. Beyond providing her with an elderly bush carpenter who turned out to be a perfect craftsman, Ben took no interest in the building. He had no time to spare for anything except the cattle and the fences.

"Let old Andy pick out the best timber in the old buildings and then order anything else you like," he told Anne. "We're so far in debt that what you spend on the house won't be noticed."

From dawn until dark he and his stockmen mustered, drafted, bang-tailed the grown cattle and branded the cleanskins. With the help of the neighbours they scoured the adjoining properties and roughly patched the boundary fences. There were delays while they replaced rotten timbers in the yards, delays while they tailed the cattle to steady them down, and delays while they made the holding paddocks safe for the fat bullocks. Most of these bullocks were touchy old scrubbers that would fret and lose condition quickly in the holding paddocks, but Ben gave them no chance to pine away. Time and again he took small mobs in to Baranda and trucked them down to Stonehaven saleyards, where their prime condition ensured keen bidding and good prices from butchers and meatworks buyers.

Yarding those wild old rogues was hard, fast work, calling for good horses and good horsemen. Often Ben fell asleep before the evening meal was cleared away. But in the end it was worth it all, for the money for the bullocks was in the bank, and the final tally of the muster showed that there were still seven thousand five hundred head of cattle on Wavering Downs—fifteen hundred head more than Ben had paid for.

He started selling in earnest then, culling the herd down and down and keeping only the best breeders, so that when the war ended and the inevitable slump came he had only three thousand breeders, the pick of the old Wavering Downs herd and the foundation of the new one. Most important of all, he had proved the soundness of his judgment, and he had made a lifelong friend of his new bank manager.

A few years later he saw the price of cattle drop until good breeders with calves at foot were being offered for thirty shillings a head. But he was not a seller then; he was a buyer, backing his conviction that the cattle market would come good again. Because he was lightly stocked, the drought that was later known as the Big Drought scarcely worried him. Even the post-war depression favoured him, for with labour cheap and plentiful he was able to renew his yards and fences and fight the ever-pressing battle with the pear. Certainly he never conquered the pear, but he held it in check until the release of the cacto-blastis grub ended pear worries for the whole of Queensland.

The depression did him another good turn. It brought his old section mate, Charlie Turner, up from Melbourne in search of a job—Charlie, the ex-jockey who could do anything with a horse, Charlie the ex-Light Horseman who had so gallantly given him covering fire that night at El Burj. Now he was Charlie Turner, a depressed little member of the vast company of unemployed.

"Things are crook down south, Boss," he said. "Every one reckoned they'd be better up here, but I dunno, they still look pretty tough to me. Jobs are scarcer than hen's teeth where I've been."

"There's a job for you here any time you want it," Ben told him. But Charlie made it clear that he was not looking for charity. He said indignantly, "Now hang on a minute, Boss. I didn't come here to bludge on an old Army mate. I came to Queensland for a look around and I dug you up because I promised to when we was in hospital together, see?"

Yes, Ben saw. And he was not offering charity. He was offering work, hard work, to a man who understood horses. He had been on the look-out for the right man ever since he bought Wavering Downs, and if Charlie wanted the job he could give it a go.

"I'll give anything a go, Boss," Charlie declared. "What's the score?"

Ben explained the score. The Delacy horses were a problem to him, a problem he had no time to tackle seriously. Most of them were thoroughbred stock, but he had bought them at his own figure, telling Delacy that if he didn't like the price he could muster them and shift them off the place. To him they were only working horses and there were far too many of them. There was a limit to the number he could break in and use for stockwork, so the rest would have to go. He wanted Charlie to take charge of them, to draft them, classify them, and break in anything that had not passed the breakable age.

"Some of the old unbroken ones'll have to be shot. A lot of the others'll have to be sold. I'll give you a lad for an offsider, and when you get a mob handled and ready for sale you can let me know and I'll get in touch with a bloke that buys for the Indian Army. I'll hand Delacy's horse-books over to you. Get your nose into 'em and you'll probably find they're right up to date, about the only well-kept things he left behind. I've never had time to look through 'em."

Charlie started work next day, after winning the only serious argument he and Ben were to have in all their years together. He flatly refused to live in the house, and in the end Ben gave in and took him down to the stockmen's quarters.

The big house was finished now, and stood among the trees, a lasting monument to Anne's good taste and the craftsmanship of old Andy. One by one the untidy jumble of old buildings had been pulled down and the best of their timbers put aside for the new house. It was long, low, and immensely solid, with wide verandahs shading its walls, walls of hand-dressed old slabs that gave the building the mellow dignity of age. It had grown slowly but happily, and the only differences of opinion between Anne and her builder were caused through the trees, Andy's idea of homemaking in the bush being to cut down every tree within four hundred yards of the site and then build the house.

"That tree'll 'ave to come down," he would state emphatically. "It'll be right in me way."

"It won't really be in your way, Andy," was Anne's invariable retort. "Just forget all about it."

But Andy could not forget the trees. They were a constant challenge to him. "Them bloody trees," became his theme song whenever anything put him out.

Finally Anne turned on him and said, "Andy, if I hear you

mention 'them bloody trees' again I'll get some one else to finish the house."

That settled the old fellow. The house was his masterpiece and no one else was going to have a hand in the building of it.

Things always worked out that way with Anne. She never demanded, never nagged, and never resorted to tears, yet she invariably got what she wanted. Like the lawn. Long before the house was completed she was planning a garden with a wide sweep of lawn. Ben scoffed at the idea. No one tried to grow lawns in the bush, he said. They needed constant water and constant work. And what use were they? Women seemed to need flowers and he supposed they got some sort of satisfaction out of growing them. But a lawn! It was like pretending you were living in the city.

Yet within a week he was writing away for materials and men to erect an overhead tank, a system of pipes and a windmill to pump water up from the creek. By the time the new house was furnished and they were ready to move in, the lawn was firmly established.

Anthea was home for the housewarming party, and although she was impressed with the house and particularly with the room Anne had furnished for her, she never really cared for Wavering Downs or bush life. When she finished school she spent as much time as possible visiting her city friends.

Mary Rutland, Anne's niece, was also at the housewarming. She had come up from Sydney to help Anne with the furnishing, *and* to look for a husband.

The Reverend Alfred Coudrey was there because no party at the McReady home would have been considered complete without him, and because on this occasion he was to bless the new house. There was a third reason for his visit, although he was not yet fully aware of it. Anne had made up her mind that Mary would never make a good bushman's wife. She was not the type to cope with stockmen's meals and rough conditions. But she would make an ideal wife for a clergyman.

The neighbouring station owners and their wives were there. Mr Hamilton, the genial bank manager, had come all the way from Stonehaven to be present at the housewarming he felt he had made possible. Police Sergeant and Mrs Forster were there, and although the Sergeant was not pretending, even to himself, that he had made this party possible, he was quietly pleased with the way things had worked out.

The idea of inviting a policeman to his house because he genuinely liked and admired him appealed to Ben's sense of humour. Unfortunately he could not share the joke with anyone.

It was, every one said, a wonderful party. Anne was thrilled, firstly because she was happiest when she was giving other people pleasure, and secondly because it was so rewarding to hear the generous praises of her new home. Anthea was thrilled because Mr Hamilton invited her to stay with his wife and daughter during the Stonehaven Show Week festivities. Biddy was thrilled simply to be helping in the kitchen where every one came to have a few words with her.

And as for Mary—she returned from a stroll in the garden with young Coudrey and confided to Anne that she had never before realized how lovely the bush looked by starlight.

"You'll have to give the bride away, darling," Anne said as she undressed that night.

And Ben said, "Stone the flamin' crows, Anne! Give him a go. The poor bloke doesn't even know it's on yet!"

"He soon will," Anne prophesied.

And as usual she was right.

★ 18 ★

WAVERING DOWNS later became famous for three things—its homestead, its horses, and its cattle.

All credit for the beauty of the homestead was, of course, Anne's, and she had the satisfaction of seeing it become the showplace of the district. Distinguished visitors came to look over the house and garden, wasting a lot of her time and occasionally provoking Ben to growl that "anyone'd think the place was a flamin' pub."

The fame of the horses was due to Charlie, who had realized the potentialities of the breed after an all-night sitting with Delacy's horse-books. When he saw some of the horses next day he was even more enthusiastic. He was also amazed that such valuable material should be wasted.

"You blokes have got me beat," he told Ben. "You've got some of the best blood in Australia here. Good stayers. Takin' 'em on breedin', you could stand a chance of winnin' the Melbourne Cup with one of 'em. And what do you do with them? Use 'em for chasin' cows!"

Mildly amused at his scorn Ben asked, "What do you expect us to do with them? Use 'em for ornaments and run the cattle down on foot?"

"You could put some of 'em into trainin' and clean up a few country race meetin's for a start."

"And where would that get us?" Ben put his hand on the little man's shoulder. "Look, Charlie, I'm a cattleman and that's all I ever will be. I dunno anything about racing because I've never had the time or the money to waste on it. As far as I'm concerned there's only two sorts of horses—stock-horses and pack-horses; buggy horses are just about things of the past now. I bought this lot as working horses, at working-horse prices, and they've either got to earn their keep or go."

"What about this bloke you bought 'em orf? Didn't he ever do anything about 'em?"

"Delacy? He was just a mug. A complete no-hoper. He

bred good horses because he liked them—about the only things he *did* like. But he never got around to doing anything with them because he never got around to doing anything—except running the country down. Those horses kept him broke. I dunno what he spent on them, but I'll tell you right now that I'm not the sucker Delacy was."

Charlie pulled a stalk of grass, put one end in his mouth, and chewed thoughtfully on it for a few moments. "Boss," he said at last, "Gimme an open go at 'em for a year or two and I'll guarantee to put you in the money. You'll have to lay out a bit of dough, but you'll get it all back and a lot more besides. I'm talkin' about somethin' I know now."

"You want to start racing some of them?"

"That's right."

"Nothing doing, Charlie. I told you before I'm not going to be like Delacy. I'm out to make money, not spend it, and I'm too busy to be muckin' around with racehorses and race meetings."

"No one's askin' you to. All I'm askin' for is a fair go. I'll do all the work and you cop the profits. I'll clean your horses up for you, and you can sell the culls for whatever they'll bring. I'll get stuck into the young stuff then. While I'm breakin' in I'll pick one or two of the most likely ones and try 'em out. If they're as good as I reckon they are we'll enter 'em for some of the local races. You don't have to back 'em, you don't even have to take time off to watch 'em run. All you gotta do is let me enter 'em in your name, for the advertisement, see? If they win, up goes the price of the whole breed, and all you'll have to fork out is the nomination fees. Get it?"

Yes, Ben got it. And once he saw the logic of Charlie's reasoning he did everything possible to help him. Within two weeks they had a training track measured and marked out on the flat below the house, and the following year they won their first race in Baranda.

As Charlie had prophesied, the prices of the Wavering Downs horses rose as their number of wins increased. Neither he nor Ben made spectacular sums from those wins because neither of them bet heavily. Charlie often attended a race meeting without placing a single bet. Ben never backed a horse unless he was on the course to see it run. He was not greatly interested in racing and saw it only as a means to an end, an opportunity to exhibit his horses to possible buyers.

And Charlie was providing him with every opportunity. He had an uncanny knowledge of horses and a very thorough knowledge of the intricacies of racing. He worked even longer hours than Ben did, sparing neither himself nor his offsider. Ben was always an early riser, but quite often when he arose in the first chilly streaks of dawn he would hear the two of them riding past on their way down to the training track.

Charlie loved horses, he lived and breathed horses, he could and would talk fluently about horses in general, but on the subject of any one particular horse that he was training he was a cautious little clam. No one ever heard what his stop-watch told him on those early morning trials.

Questioned by Ben about a certain filly's chance at the next race meeting he might admit that on her present form she *should* run a pretty fair race, or he might say that she wasn't set to go yet, but the run in company would do her good. Never had he been heard to declare that a horse *would* win.

"There ain't no such thing as a racecourse certainty," he once told Ben. "Too many things to go wrong. The 'orse might be in top form and the hoop's on the level, willin' to ride accordin' to instructions, but the 'orse stumbles before the boy gets 'im properly settled down, and bang goes your certainty. Or some one might slip the boy a few quid to pull him. Or a couple of other boys gang up to knock him off his stride. You got no idea what goes on between them hoops around the back of the course. *I* know. I been in it meself too often."

Occasionally he backed a horse for a pound or two, but he was by no means a regular punter.

Anne, on the other hand, backed every horse he started, even if he told her it could not win.

"You never know," she said once. "I've heard you say there's no such thing as a racecourse certainty. And anyway, I'd hate to think of the poor darling starting without any of us backing it. It couldn't possibly do well if it knew we had no faith in it."

Like Ben she attended few race meetings, but she always gave money to Charlie before he left for one. Her usual wager was ten shillings, and on the rare occasions when she managed to drag a cautious admission from Charlie that a certain horse *could* win she increased the amount to a pound.

Ben bet much more heavily than either of them, simply because he did everything in a big way. He sent Charlie south to buy a new sire, and he paid more for it than he had paid Delacy for his entire mob of horses. The suggestion had come from Charlie, but Ben was quick to realize the soundness of it. He was making money out of the horses and the only way to continue making it was to maintain or improve the standard.

But horses were only a sideline to him. His big interest was, and always would be, in the cattle. He had bought a run-down herd from Delacy, and by ruthless culling and shrewd buying he gradually built up a herd of pure-bred Herefords. He improved the property by building dams and clearing the worst of the scrubs, and when it finally became a recognized thing for Wavering Downs bullocks to top the market, people said he had made his money easily.

The poor, ignorant fools! He made his money by sheer hard work, by spending long weary hours in the saddle, mustering for dipping and branding, tailing weaners, and keeping the cattle always well handled and docile. He supervised all the work that went into improving the property. He drove hard bargains with fencing contractors, dam sinkers, and ring-barkers, stating his own terms and adopting a take-it-or-leave-it attitude that earned him the name of Take-it-or-leave-it McReady.

"That's my price," was his ultimatum. "Take it or leave it."

He fought the tough, thankless battle with the pear, a heartbreaking battle, because no matter how much time and money he spent on its eradication he never seemed to be winning. While men were poisoning it in one place it was springing up in another. The Crown Lands' ranger was never *quite* satisfied with the progress made. He liked Ben and he respected his dogged capacity for work. He knew all about the difficulties of securing and keeping reliable labour, he knew that Ben was making an honest effort to fight the pest, but what he wanted was results—more country free from pear. Without resorting to threats he always left behind him the impression that the leaseholder must either make a greater effort to comply with the clearing conditions or appear before the Land Court.

One more "Show Cause" case! One more cattleman summoned to appear before the Court and show the cause of his failure to comply with the conditions of his lease! And unless he could give a satisfactory explanation he might forfeit that lease to the Crown.

Men were looking for work, any work—except pear-poisoning. The more desperate ones took it on because they were willing to risk anything for a few pounds. They might start off well, but after a few weeks the hopeless monotony of the work would get them down and they would either become fed up with the job or careless. If they became fed up they drew their wages and left. If they became careless and ignored the safety precautions in handling the poison it burned through their clothes and into their skins or ate into nail-beds so that their finger-nails dropped off. In any case, the final result was the same. They left and they never came back.

Until the cacto-blastis grub relieved him of all pear worries, Ben never fully enjoyed a day's side on Wavering Downs. Even in a bumper season, with the cattle in prime condition and young calves everywhere, there was always the pear to remind him of the pessimistic Mr McBeath and his prophecy that the pear would ultimately force all the cattlemen off their properties.

He sometimes wondered how badly it had spread on Coolibah, and though he never visited his old selection he often rode to the edge of the Jump-up. Sitting there on his horse he could look out over the entire selection, across the shimmering, silver-grey sea of brigalow to the coolibah flats beyond. He could trace the winding course of the river by the deeper green of the trees along its banks, and on clear days it was sometimes possible to see the smoke rising from the kitchen of his old home. It was a view that would have delighted Anne. It pleased Ben because it aroused memories and gave him a sense of achievement. He had come a long way since those first Coolibah days—from a thirty-thousand-acre selection without fences, yards, or even a hut, to a well-improved station of one hundred and eight thousand acres! From ninety head of mixed cattle to a fine herd of six thousand head!

But Ben was not there to admire the view or gloat over his success. He was looking for tracks. Coolibah had changed hands twice since he sold it, and the new owner was reputed to be a bit of a cattle-duffer. Did he know about the old pad up the Jump-up? Or had the growth of pear in the scrub made it impossible for a horseman to force his way through? In any case, he could not scale the cliffs without leaving evidence of his visit. Secretly Ben always hoped he would find that evidence, and when he eventually did find it he felt a thrill of excitement equal to any he had felt when he and Biddy had made one of their successful raids. Once again he was about to pit his wits against a neighbour's, only this time the positions were reversed. Now he was the respectable station-owner and the other man was the duffer.

The tracks were several days old, but they were still readable. Some one had ridden his horse up the Jump-up and down again. The some one could only be Downey, the new owner of Coolibah, and his visit had merely been a prospecting ride, for there were no cattle tracks going down.

Would he be satisfied now that he had seen that there were no cleanskins on Wavering Downs these days? Or would he come back with an offsider, muster up some cows with calves too young to be branded, and drive them home? It was an old dodge and a safe one—one that Ben had seldom used. You held mother and calf until the calf was old enough to wean, then you returned the cow to its rightful run and put your own brand on the calf. There was no risk attached to that method of duffing because even if the owner found his cows and calves on your property you could claim that they were strays you had picked up in your last muster and were holding until you found an opportunity to tell the owner to come and get them. The unbranded calves would, in themselves, be proof of your honesty.

Deciding that if there was any truth in the local gossip about Downey this would be the method most in keeping with his character. Ben visited the Jump-up once and sometimes twice a week. On the third week he found more tracks, and the story they told was as plain as a written confession.

Two horsemen had come up, mustered about half a dozen cows with baby calves, and driven them down. The men were poor cattlemen, either inexperienced or impatient, for they had had a great deal of trouble in getting the cattle to take to the steep, downward track. Instead of letting them take their time, the duffers had tried to force them. Scuffed-up tracks showed where they had milled and repeatedly broken back, only to be blocked by the hard-riding horsemen whose mounts had left the deep imprints of their hooves each time they propped and wheeled. The cattle had become overheated before finally giving in. The proof of that lay in the almost liquid dung that had been spattered everywhere.

"The bloody useless mugs!" Ben growled aloud. "A man oughta belt hell outa the pair of them."

He was indignant and very annoyed, not at the actual theft of the cattle, but at the manner in which they had been handled. Why, in the old days he and Biddy would have put that little mob down the pad without lifting their horses out of a walk! He hadn't the slightest doubt that he would recover the cattle, but it would take them weeks to get over the rough handling.

He did not bother to follow the tracks, nor did he call on Downey for another two weeks.

Soon after sunrise one morning, feeling a pleasurable thrill of anticipation, he rode down the steep pad. He'd show Downey he couldn't put anything over Ben McReady, he'd bawl hell out of him for knocking the cattle about, and he'd scare the daylights out of him. But first he would locate the missing cows. He knew exactly where to look for them because there was only one paddock where they would be reasonably safe from observation by men using the road along the river flats. Lord, he'd fenced that paddock himself for that very reason! What a laugh that was!

But as he left the Jump-up behind him and picked his way through the brigalow his mood gradually changed. He was appalled at the way the pear had spread. Here, in the scrub, it had taken complete possession. Tall tree-pear towered up among the branches of the brigalow, and the low variety sprawled everywhere, choking out the bushes and flourishing in great, impenetrable clumps often fifty or more yards through. Cattle had been feeding on it, fostering its spread by knocking the big juicy leaves to the ground and leaving them to take root. Birds were eating the ripe purple fruit and spreading the seeds wherever they flew, so that small seedlings were springing up wherever there was soil to nourish them. No longer was this a scrub of brigalow and wilga-bushes; it was a monstrous forest of pear scantily interspread with the original native scrub growth. A gang of fifty poisoners could work in it for a year without making an appreciable impression on the strangling growth. Even on the open flats it had spread beyond control.

Apparently it had stifled the ambitions of the successive owners for there were signs of indifference and neglect everywhere. The fences had either been left unrepaired or patched in a manner that would have disgraced the laziest black-fellow. The old holding paddock fence had recently been made reasonably secure, and inside the paddock Ben found his cattle—four cows with baby calves and one dry cow that may have been brought along because she refused to leave her mates, or may have been deliberately included to replenish Downey's beef cask.

Satisfied that there were no more Wavering Downs cattle in the paddock, he rode on up to the homestead and dismounted at the horse-yard. Here, too, he noted countless signs of neglect. A great clump of pear grew half in and half out of the horse-yard, its sagging weight bending the rails almost to breaking point. One corner post had rotted off at the ground and was propped up by two inadequate forked sticks. The buggy shed had developed a tired lean, sheets of bark were missing from its roof, and several slabs had fallen out of the walls. The garden that had once been Anne's pride was now a neglected wilderness of weeds. There was even a big tree-pear flourishing against the kitchen tank!

Downey was lounging in a sagging old squatter's chair on the verandah. He was reading a newspaper and sipping a mug of black tea. Evidently he was a bachelor, for the windows were bare of curtains and the verandah was littered with rubbish. A riding saddle was propped against one doorpost and a pack-saddle against another. A bridle lay where it had been flung, the manner in which one rein had been knotted to the bit itself an indication of the shiftless indifference of the owner. Two pack-bags filled the only other chair, and green-hide ropes lay all over the floor like tangled, hairy snakes, waiting to trip the unwary. If Downey owned a broom he certainly ran no risk of wearing it out, for old newspapers and dead leaves cluttered every corner, and dust and cobwebs covered everything.

Downey himself looked as neglected as the house. He had not shaved for a week, his grey flannel shirt and moleskin trousers were wrinkled and greasy, and his elastic-side boots were burst open at the ankles and greenish from dried cow-dung.

After studying him for a moment Ben called, "Good day."

Downey tossed his newspaper to the floor and stood up, revealing himself as a rather pathetic little man with sparse black hair hanging down over a wrinkled forehead, and eyes that seldom looked at anything above the level of his dilapidated boots.

"G'day," he answered. "Seen ya ridin' up but I never took no more notice. Thought ya was Scrubber comin' back. You know Scrubber Jackson? The most useless bloody boong in the Mission. Took the night 'orse and went out to look for the workin' 'orses. Musta been a break in the fence somewhere and they all got out last night." He picked up his mug and was about to finish his tea when he remembered his duties as host. "Wot about a cuppa tea? There's still plenty in the pot."

"I could do with one," Ben admitted.

On his way through to the kitchen Downey called, "Chuck them pack-bags orf that chair and make yerself comfortable."

Ben lifted the pack-bags from the chair and tossed them on to the floor. He also removed a bent stirrup iron, a surcingle, two branding irons, and a rusty bag-needle from the stained canvas before he sat down.

Already he was aware that this interview was not going to be anything like the one he had planned. He had intended to browbeat Downey, throw such a scare into him that he would never come near Wavering Downs again. He had hoped that Downey would turn out to be a tough customer, one who would put up a fight and try to bluff and bluster his way out of the charge. He could deal with a man like that and enjoy doing it.

But the little man shuffling about in the kitchen was not worth wasting time on. You couldn't bawl him out for the way he had mishandled the cattle because he so obviously was not and never would be a good cattleman. Nor was he in any way a fighter. He was beaten before the start, beaten by his own laziness and incompetence, by the run-down state of his selection, by the strangling growth of the pear, and by the smallness of his entire outlook. He might fancy himself as a cattle-duffer, but he would never get away with more than half a dozen calves a year. He had made two trips to Wavering Downs, and what had he got for the trouble? Four baby calves that would never feel the burning imprint of his brand!

Downey came back and put a mug of tea on the arm-rest of Ben's chair. The mug was stained and slightly greasy, the tea was black and bitter from standing too long on the stove, but Downey had been liberal with the sugar.

"Dunno if you like it sweet," he said. "I shoved a fair bit of sugar in it."

"All tea tastes good to me," Ben told him. He took a long swig of the bitter-sweet brew. "My name's McReady, from Wavering Downs."

"Pleased ter meetcha." Downey's face and tone were

devoid of expression as he mumbled the conventional words, apparently to his own feet.

"I came over to see about those cows of mine."

Downey studied his boots carefully and asked, "Wot cows?"

"The ones you've got in your holding paddock. Five head, four of 'em with young calves. Three bull calves and one heifer."

"Oh, them. Me and Scrubber picked 'em up when we mustered the river flats last week. We was gunna turn 'em back on to your property, but the pear's that thick in the scrub ya couldn't drive a wallaby through it. So I says to Scrubber, I says, 'We'll hang on to 'em for a bit and I'll send 'im word they're 'ere next time I'm in Baranda.' "

Without a trace of heat or anger Ben said, "Come off it, Downey. You're not fooling anyone, and I'm just the last man you ought to try *that* story on. Now you just sit tight for a minute and I'll tell you the true story. You and Scrubber Jackson rode up the Jump-up two weeks ago. On Tuesday the fifteenth, it was. You headed for Back Gully because you'd been over there for a look-see three weeks before. You picked up these cows and calves, drove'm back, and shut 'em in the holding paddock. I wouldn't have minded that so much because I knew I could get 'em back any time, but you knocked hell out of 'em, got 'em so overheated it's a wonder they didn't all die before you got 'em down here."

Downey's eyes flickered upward as far as Ben's knees and returned quickly to the contemplation of his own boots as he asked, "Wot if I was to tell ya I've never been on your country in me life, eh?"

"You wouldn't be so bloody silly."

"You thinkin' of puttin' the copper on to me?"

"Not me. I wouldn't waste his time or mine. You've got no chance of putting anything over me, Downey. You're not in the hunt."

"Bloody smart, ain't ya?"

"Too right I'm smart. I've been a long time in the cattle game, Downey. I started from scratch and I didn't make my money by sitting on the verandah while other blokes pinched my calves. I want those cattle back on Wavering Downs before the end of the week." Ben drained the last of his tea and stood up. "Thanks for the tea. It was a good brew. I'll see you in a day or two when you bring the cows back. I want 'em delivered at the homestead yards, too. Nothin' like being sure, is there?" He grinned broadly as he added, "If you turned 'em loose at the foot of the Jump-up they'd find their own way back, but I'd have to take your word for it that you'd let 'em go. I wouldn't have any proof, would I? Because I mightn't recognize 'em again."

"You mightn't!" In the bitterness of his defeat Downey actually looked at Ben's chin. "You'd reckernize one o' them cows if she was cut up and salted away in a beef cask!"

And that, Ben thought as he mounted and rode off, was as nice a compliment as any cattleman could wish for.

★ 19 ★

Ben was dipping the last of a mob of bullocks two mornings later when Downey and Scrubber drove the little mob of cows and calves up to the homestead yards. The morning was hot, and an acrid pall of dust hung over the yards, powdering the leaves of the shade trees, the yard rails, the drying bullocks, and the sweat-soaked clothing of the stockmen.

"You couldn't have timed it better," Ben told Downey. "The last lot's just coming out of the draining yard and the smoko bell's due to go any minute. I dunno about you, but I'm breaking my neck for a cup of tea."

"I don't want no tea—thanks." The "thanks" was a reluctant addition. Downey would have preferred to show defiant rudeness to the man who had so easily outwitted and humiliated him. Having been forced to bring the cows back, he wanted to show Ben that no one could force him to accept patronage in the form of a cup of tea. But the best he could manage was a mumbled, "Me and Scrubber'll boil up down on the creek."

"Why the hell should you when it's already made? I had a cup of tea at your place and I'm damned if I'm going to let you call on me and go away without one." The discordant clatter as Biddy vigorously rang the big kitchen cow-bell lent point to his words, and Ben turned to Scrubber. "I'll bet you could do with one, eh, Scrubber?"

Scrubber's black face split into a wide grin that revealed a pink tongue behind an array of stained, broken teeth. He was a fat, pot-bellied old blackfellow with white hair, white eyebrows, and a white stubble of beard emphasizing the blackness of his face. Downey had referred to him as "the most useless bloody boong in the Mission," a description that was unfair and incorrect.

Despite his age and pot-belly, Scrubber was a good horseman and a good stockman, but like so many of the older aboriginals, he was something of a chameleon in that he assumed the characteristics of the man he was working for. Under a good boss he was a good stockman, under an indifferent boss he was an indifferent one. When working for an honest cattleman Scrubber was a model of honesty. Possessing a photographic memory for cattle, he would push his way through a pen of a hundred calves at branding time, grab one of the milling, bawling youngsters, trundle it to the gate, and say, "This one b'longa that old Walamul cow, boss. Let 'im go, eh?"

"There's no chance of branding a neighbour's calf by mistake when you've got Scrubber in the mustering team," an honest boss had once said of him.

Yet if his boss made a practice of putting his brand on everything he mustered Scrubber would cheerfully play the game his way. When he worked for a lazy boss he invariably outshone that boss in laziness. He even adopted little mannerisms of speech, and it was sometimes said of him that you could tell who he was working for by the way he spoke.

Evidently he had not been long with Downey, for he showed none of Downey's mannerisms as he looked straight at Ben and said, "My crikey, yes, Boss. I wouldn't knock one back."

"Never been known to knock anything back, have you, Scrubber?" Ben joked. He had employed Scrubber on several occasions and was quite fond of the old blackfellow. "Leave the horses in the shade and go up to the kitchen with the boys. And don't try getting fresh with Biddy, you rampin' old scrub bull."

Chuckling like a lazy old kookaburra, Scrubber went off with the Wavering Downs stockmen, and Ben led Downey up to the house.

"I'd sooner go to the kitchen," Downey protested feebly. "I ain't togged up for visitin'."

"Don't let that worry you," Ben told him. He glanced down at his own dusty, sweat-soaked shirt and pants. "You're a dam' sight cleaner than I am."

They washed in the basin under the big tank stand and walked through the garden to the front verandah where Anne, looking fresh and cool in a cotton sun-frock, greeted them. Like the morning-tea table she presided over, she made the visitor think ruefully of his own crude living conditions.

There was no untidy litter about this verandah, yet it was homely and welcoming. Downey had the choice of several uncluttered squatter's chairs. He could relax there and look out through the hanging baskets of ferns to the colourful garden beds and the wide sweep of green lawn. He could drink his fill of tea, fresh tea served in china cups with saucers. He could start off with hot buttered scones and finish up with cake. Yet he would have preferred to boil his quartpot down on the creek bank where he could squat on his heels and yabber with old Scrubber. He felt out of place and uncomfortable here, and even Anne's natural charm and tact failed to make him feel at ease.

"Anne," Ben said, "this is Mr Downey, the new owner of Coolibah. He brought back a few strays he picked up in his last muster."

She came forward, shook Downey's limp hand, and said, "That was very good of you, Mr Downey, to go to all that trouble. You must be dying for a cup of tea. Do you take milk and sugar?"

Downey studied his boots and mumbled something about liking his tea black. Invited to sit down, he achieved the almost impossible feat of perching himself on the edge of a squatter's chair without tipping it up.

"Where's the kids?" Ben asked.

"They had their tea," Anne told him. "Ken's doing his lessons and Anthea's gone off somewhere."

Ben thought, yes, Anthea would. She'd spot Downey walking up from the yards, gulp her tea, and clear out, because one look would have satisfied her that the visitor was an "uncouth type". And Anthea never bothered to make herself agreeable to people she classified as uncouth types.

Anne, of course, treated Downey as a friendly neighbour. She wanted to know all about Coolibah. How was the garden looking? Were the various shrubs flowering well this year? And had the frosts damaged her favourite bougainvillaea?

Downey reckoned the garden was all right, but he didn't know much about plants of any sort—except pear. There was enough of that to keep a man working day and night if he was fool enough to waste his time on it.

"If you don't waste a bit of your time on it you'll loose your selection," Ben pointed out.

"No bloomin' fear I won't!" In his animation Downey forgot his nervousness. "Ya don't hafta worry about the pear no more. That's why I bought the place. They got a grub breedin' up on the Government Experimental Station that's gunna clean up all the pear in Queensland in a coupla years."

Anne smiled at the little man's optimism, and Ben said, "I've heard a few bush yarns in me day, but that's the tallest one I've ever heard."

"But I'm tellin' ya," Downey persisted. "It's fair dinkum. A bloke I know put me wise to it. He was lookin' over this 'ere Experimental Station a while back, and the bloke in charge told 'im they was just about set to let this grub go. They'll put it out next month and there won't be no more clearin' conditions. Ya can chuck away all yer stabbers and poison. In two years ya won't find a bit of pear in the country."

Out of the corner of his eye Ben caught sight of his young son standing in the doorway, staring at Downey in wide-eyed amazement. Ken had just turned ten and had a normal small boy's curiosity about anything new or strange. Evidently Downey's outburst made quite an impression on him, because when the visitor left he asked:

"Dad, is that man mad?"

"I dunno if he's exactly mad, son," Ben answered. "I'd say he's a bit weak in the head. Either that or he's kidding himself into believing anything that'll save him from work."

"The poor little man has probably been living alone too long," Anne said. "I'm sure he's a bachelor. Did you notice how his trousers were mended? No woman would sew like that."

"Do *you* believe what he said about the grub, Dad?" Ken persisted.

"Not me, son. I wish I did. I'd go out and sack every useless pear-poisoner on the place before lunch."

"Anyway," Anne defended. "I think he's mad in a nice way. It was very good of him to come all this way to return our strays. None of the other neighbours bother to do it."

Later they admitted that Downey was by no means mad. He had bought a pear-ridden selection on inside information. Admittedly it was something of a gamble, but the gamble had come off, and Downey was only wrong on one point. It took the cacto-blastis five years, not two, to rid the country of the pest that had threatened to destroy it.

Although he did his best to conceal it, Ben was disappointed in his young son. As father and son they got on well together, but they never achieved the easy, brotherly companionship that had been so outstanding between Ben and Dan. Perhaps it was too much to expect with such a big difference between their ages. Ken was moderately fond of riding. He had his own pony and could even stick its playful, winter-morning pigroot, but he showed none of Dan's reckless horsemanship. If anything he was a sedate, almost cautious rider. In his disappointment Ben was apt to overlook the fact he himself was not the wild, hell-for-leather rider he had been when Dan was young. Certainly it still took a good horse to throw him, but he no longer encouraged a horse to buck. Instead he tended to soothe it and discourage it from showing its spirits. Chasing and throwing a scrubber still appealed to him as a sport, but by the time Ken was old enough to help with a day's muster there were no longer any opportunities to practise it on Wavering Downs. Good fences and good handling had subdued the cattle to a point where reckless horsemanship was seldom called for.

To young Ken horses and cattle were only mildly interesting. His big interest lay in anything mechanical. The rackety little engine that pumped water up from the creek on windless days could keep him absorbed for hours, the car that had replaced the horses and buggy was a constant delight to him, and when he went off to a Brisbane boarding-school he had made up his mind to become a mechanic. Later his ambitions extended to engineering and flying, all of which Ben refused to regard as more than passing phases.

During Ken's fourth year at school Anthea married

Gregory Arnedale. Stonehaven society considered that Anthea had done very well for herself indeed. She was twenty-four, and Gregory was the catch of the season, a young man with looks, personality, money, and excellent prospects. Anne wanted her daughter to be married on Wavering Downs, but Anthea refused to consider what she termed "such an outlandish idea." She wanted a wedding in Stonehaven, a big wedding with all the best people present. One couldn't, she pointed out, expect Gregory's numerous friends and relations to come all the way out to Wavering Downs for the wedding!

Ben agreed, mainly because he did not want Gregory's friends and relations on Wavering Downs. Gregory had spent a week there when the engagement was first announced and that was more than enough for Ben. His future son-in-law disliked the bush, regarded all bushmen as clods, and refused to put a foot inside the stockyard. Moreover he was faintly patronizing.

"One week with him's enough for me," Ben told Anne afterwards. "Gawd! Fancy living with him all the time!"

"I know how you feel, darling," Anne soothed. "But *you* don't have to live with him, and I think he'll turn out to be a very suitable husband for Anthea."

"I'll bet he will!" Ben grinned at his own thoughts on the matter. "Anthea'll see to that."

She did. Starting off with the most lavish wedding Stonehaven had seen for years and ending up as the town's unchallenged leader of society, she achieved the happiness she valued most.

Loyally backed up by Anne, Ben did everything possible to interest Ken in station affairs. He had made Wavering Downs a property to be proud of and he wanted it to stay in the family. Ken could take his time. He could stay on at school as long as he liked; when he left school he could take a job as jackeroo on one of the big Northern Territory stations, put in two or three years up there, learning the tough part of cattle work, and then come back to Wavering Downs.

"But why the Territory, dear?" Anne asked. "It's so far

away and conditions on those big stations are so crude. You've often said so."

"That's just the point," Ben told her. "I want to test him out, see if he's got what it takes. If he can stick out a couple of years up there he'll do me. It'll prove he's a cattleman, and if he is he can step into my shoes and take over here as soon as he's ready. That's fair enough, isn't it?"

Yes, Anne agreed, it was fair enough. And with all her heart she hoped Ken would make good in his father's eyes. If he could only do that he would finally make up for the loss of Dan, a loss she knew Ben would never outgrow.

And Ken did his best. He wanted to make good as a cattleman, not because he knew that by doing so he would inherit Wavering Downs and a very comfortable future, but because he wanted to please his father. He got himself a job on one of the big Territory stations and he stayed there for a full year, although he hated almost every day of it. The hard work and the rough living conditions did not worry him unduly; it was simply that he was bored with cattle-work and the never-ending conversation about horses and cattle. He could work all day on a broken-down old wreck of a car or an obstinate pumping-engine and regard it as a holiday; he could talk of piston rings, carburettors, and magnetoes until long after midnight and still look forward to a daylight start on the mechanical problem. But cattle-work was sheer drudgery.

After his year in the Territory he returned to Wavering Downs and said, "I'm sorry, Dad, but it's no good. I've given it a fair go, but I reckon I'm not cut out for a cattleman. I just can't work up any interest in them."

Irritably Ben asked, "Then what the devil *do* you take an interest in? What do you want to do? Live in a city?" He put a lot of scorn into that last question because he could not understand anyone wanting to live in a city. Nor could he understand the viewpoint of a man who was not interested in cattle.

"The city hasn't got anything to do with it," Ken explained patiently. "I'd as soon live in the bush as anywhere if I could do the sort of work I like and make a living out of it."

"What work?"

"Anything mechanical. Anything to do with engines."

"That's a hell of an ambition, I must say! Muckin' around with the insides of a car all day and comin' home at night stinkin' of oil and grease!"

Ken's smile took the sting out of his words as he said, "I don't suppose it would be any worse than coming home smelling of stockyard dust and cow-dug, Dad. It's just a matter of which you prefer. I like the smell of engines."

The cheerful admission staggered Ben, who regarded cars and all mechanical contrivances as necessary evils. He got into a car reluctantly, he drove it defiantly, and if it broke down he kicked it, cursed it, and declared that it served a man bloody well right for having anything to do with the infernal machine. To have his own son declare that he not only preferred engines to stock, but actually liked the smell of them, was something he found almost impossible to believe.

"Are you sure you're old enough to know what you like?" he asked.

"I ought to be. I'm nineteen and I've been mad about the same thing ever since I was a kid." Ken hesitated a moment before addding, "There's more to it than that, Dad. I want to take up flying. There's a wonderful future in it. But don't get the idea that I want to sponge on you. I've got a bit saved up —enough to start paying for flying lessons and keep me until I get a job."

"What sort of job?"

"Probably general rouseabout or grease-boy in a garage." Ken's smile was completely disarming. "You've got to start at the bottom in these things."

"Too right you have!" At least Ben could appreciate the courage behind the quiet acceptance of such a humble start. "Where were you thinking of kicking off?"

"Stonehaven. It's closest to home and they've got a good flying club there. No need to go farther south."

"Stonehaven!" The humour of the situation struck Ben and he laughed in spite of himself. "Stone the flamin' crows, son, Anthea'll have a bit to say about that! She'll take a pretty crook view of things if some of her fancy friends see her brother knockin' around town in a suit of greasy overalls."

"To hell with Anthea and her fancy friends." Again the disarming smile robbed Ken's words of any sting. "I won't be likely to run into any of them."

Ben knew when he was beaten. Any further objections would only create an irreparable rift between himself and his son. Much better let the lad try this dam' fool scheme and get it out of his system. He was still too young to know his own mind, and sooner or later he would tire of city life and come back to the bush.

"All right," he growled ungraciously. "If you want to give it a go you might as well start now. I'll pay for the flying lessons. You'll be flat out keeping yourself."

Not only was he disappointed, but secretly he was a little ashamed of his son. He felt that Ken was taking the easy way because he lacked the guts to shoulder the responsibility of managing the station and giving the stockmen a lead. Looking back he remembered the youngster's preference for quiet horses and his reluctance to join in a wild gallop through a patch of scrub. Not like Dan. No one could have wrested the lead away from Dan. Even in the densest scrub he used to spur his horse recklessly and laugh for the sheer devilment of it. To Ken a falling horse was a catastrophe, to Dan it had been one more entertaining incident in a day of thrills. Remembering how Dan had laughed his way through the hottest war-time engagement, Ben could not help wondering how Ken would have reacted had the three of them been together.

And reluctantly he decided that Ken would have been the cautious type of soldier, the one who hugged every scrap of cover and took no unnecessary risks.

★ 20 ★

"WE'RE back to where we started, old girl," he said to Anne the day after Ken left to try his luck in Stonehaven. "Just you and me."

"And Biddy," she reminded him. "We've still got Biddy. And don't forget we have a grandson on the way."

Glumly Ben said, "It'll probably be a girl."

Anne scoffed at the very idea. Anthea's first baby would be a boy. She was quite positive about that. When he was old enough he would come out to Wavering Downs for his holidays, he would take naturally to bush life, and he would grow up to be a cattleman like his grandfather.

Undoubtedly it was wishful thinking on her part. Unlike Ben, she had already accepted the fact that Ken would make his own life in the city and never take over the management of the station. Her big hope for her husband's future happiness lay in their yet unborn grandson. But right to the end Ben refused to give up his dream. Some day, he felt sure, Ken would tire of city life and come back and announce that Wavering Downs would do him.

And why wouldn't it satisfy any lad? Things had altered a lot since the old Delacy days. Apart from the improved working conditions and the very comfortable homestead, they now had practically all the luxuries of town dwellers. They had refrigeration and a telephone. They had a late-model car, a utility and good roads. They could reach Baranda in half an hour and Stonehaven in less than five. Baranda had expanded into a thriving township with two hotels, three stores, a garage, a dance-hall, and a picture show. The population had grown to a point where it was supporting a young doctor, and already plans for a new hospital were being considered.

"You should stand for the Shire Council and make them start on the hospital," Anne said one day. "It would be a wonderful thing for the district."

She was preparing for her visit to Stonehaven because she

had planned to be with Anthea when the baby was born and possibly for a week or two afterwards. Ben would be well looked after while she was away for, besides Biddy, they had a half-caste girl named Hilda Dempsey in the kitchen. Hilda was clean and competent; Biddy saw to that.

"Don't worry about me," Ben said. "I could get on all right without either of 'em."

"I know you could, darling." Anne slipped an arm round him and pressed her white head against his shoulder. "You're always so very competent, aren't you, my big, handsome husband?"

"Who are you trying to kid?"

"I'm not trying to kid anyone. I'm simply telling the truth. You *are* competent and you *are* big and handsome. And I hate going away and leaving you because I'm going to miss you like anything."

He bent and picked her up, holding her, despite her struggles, like a child in his arms. "Now I'm gunna tell you something."

"Ben!" she gasped. "Put me down. Let me go. Hilda might come in and goodness knows what she'd think."

"Let her think. She wouldn't be far wrong." Instead of putting her down he tightened his grip. "Now you stop kicking, Anne McReady, and listen to me. I'll get on all right while you're away, but I'll be miserable because I'm gunna miss you like hell."

"Truly?"

"Fair dinkum. And I'll tell you something else. I think you're still as beautiful as ever."

"Oh, Ben, you know that's not true. I'm a white-haired old hag."

"I'm a bit partial to white-haired old hags."

"You're very sweet." She rumpled his hair and gave him a swift kiss on the cheek. "Now will you put me down?"

"When I'm ready. When I get a proper kiss." He kissed her in a way that made her forget all about Hilda, and stood her gently on her feet.

Only rarely did he show his true feelings towards her, but

when he did he showed them with boyish enthusiasm. He was to remember this particular scene with gratitude all his life, remember how Anne had returned his kiss, remember how youthful and pleased she had looked as he set her down.

"You'd better finish your packing," he said. "I'm going out to look at those young bulls I bought last week. I'll be back in about an hour in plenty of time for us to have lunch before I drive you in to the train."

He must have inspected the bulls although afterwards he could never recall seeing them. He remembered stopping at the training track on the way back and speaking to Charlie, who was exercising a chestnut colt.

"You're wanted up at the house, Boss," Charlie said. He nodded towards a frantically waving Hilda. "Something urgent by the look of things."

Ben growled, "Bloody telephone! Every one thinks a phone call's urgent even if the bloke on the other end of the line is only some useless galah tryin' to sell a new brand of dip."

He touched his horse lightly with the spurs and cantered up the rise.

Hilda met him half-way, Hilda wild-eyed, sobbing, and gasping for breath, Hilda on the verge of hysterics.

"Quick!" she panted. "The Missus! She's sick. Bad. Hurry. We dunno what——"

Her voice trailed off in the background as Ben galloped headlong for the house. There had been hysterical fear in Hilda's voice, and there was an answering fear deep down inside Ben as he spurred his horse straight for the breast-high white railing surrounding the lawn.

Years ago, when he was young and supple, he had been an expert at vaulting from a galloping horse to pin down a thrown scrubber. Now, without conscious thought, the years of sedate horsemanship fell away as though they had never been. The horse cleared the fence, galloped across lawn and flower-beds, and as it shied nervously away from the overhang of the verandah roof Ben left it, landing on his feet in a run that carried him across the verandah and through the open door. The horse was loose in the garden, Anne's precious garden, trotting around and trampling over flower-beds, but Ben had forgotten its existence.

Anne was lying on the floor, her head resting in Biddy's lap. She was unconscious. Tears were streaming down Biddy's face, but unlike Hilda she had herself under control. Her thin black hands were caressing Anne's face and gently smoothing the white hair, and as she looked up at Ben she moaned pitifully, "Oh, Boss, what name this one?"

"The doctor!" Ben snapped. "You ring him?"

"Hilda bin ring him. He's comin'."

But Ben was already at the phone, shouting for the number, and when the doctor's wife answered he barked, "McReady here. Has Dr Pike left yet?"

"Yes, Mr McReady," the calm voice answered. "He left nearly fifteen minutes ago."

"Well, for God's sake tell him to hurry."

He slammed the receiver back and as he knelt by Anne the stupidity of his last words struck him. No one could tell Dr Pike anything. He was cut off from any form of communication, driving out along the Wavering Downs road. Possibly he *was* hurrying. He *must* have detected the urgency behind Hilda's hysteria. But supposing he wasn't hurrying? Supposing he was taking his time, treating this as a routine call instead of pressing his foot hard down on the accelerator and roaring along with a cloud of dust trailing behind him? Without him they were helpless since neither he nor Biddy knew what to do. Should they lift her on to a bed? Should they try some form of massage to restore the circulation? She felt cold. Should they try to warm her with blankets and hot-water bottles, or would the heat be bad for her? Ben didn't know. Whatever he did might prove wrong, so in the end he did nothing except kneel beside Anne, hold her limp hand in his, and stroke it as gently as Biddy was stroking her face and hair.

Hilda came in, and above her blubbering and wailing he could hear the nervous whinnying of the horse as it trotted around the strange confines of the garden.

"Stop that bloody noise, Hilda," he ordered. "Go out and open the gate and chase that horse out of the garden. Stay out there, too. When the doctor comes get him in here fast."

"What happened, Biddy?" he asked then.

She raised her dark, wrinkled face and blinked at him through her tears. "Boss," she whispered, as though fearful of disturbing Anne, "I dunno. It just came. We was standin' here talkin' about the new baby. I say might be this first one'll be a girl and she bin laugh and say, 'Nonsense, Biddy. I just know it'll be a boy, and we'll ask Anthea to call him Ben after the Boss.' Then she bin sing out 'Oh, Biddy!' and fall down in a heap." She shook her head to and fro in a bewildered manner. "Boss," she pleaded. "What do you think?"

"I dunno, Biddy. I dunno what to think. It must be her heart. What else could it be?" He was as helpless as she was. "Has she ever said anything to you about a pain in her chest?"

"No, Boss."

No, of course she hadn't. Even if she had felt warning twinges she would have kept them to herself because that was her way. She would listen to the troubles of others, sympathize with them and help them, but never mention her own.

"Blast that bloody doctor! Why the hell doesn't he get a move on?"

"He'll come soon, Boss." That was Biddy, calmly reassuring him despite her own anguish. Good, loyal, dependable old Biddy.

As if to justify her confidence the faint hum of a fast-driven car drifted in to them. It was still a long way off and another ten agonizing minutes dragged by before it pulled up with a shriek of protesting brakes. The car door banged and Dr Pike rushed in. He knelt beside Anne, felt her pulse, and slipped a hand inside her dress. He examined her eyes and after a moment or two he looked across at Ben and said:

"I'm afraid she's gone, old man."

Neither Ben nor Biddy spoke. They looked at each other in dumb, uncomprehending disbelief, and they looked imploringly at Dr Pike, each silently willing him to contradict himself and bring Anne back. They had waited beside her, impotent in their ignorance, counting the long minutes until the doctor arrived, pinning their faith in his ability to perform some professional miracle, to say something reassuring.

And all he said was, "I'm afraid she's gone."

Why couldn't he do something to revive her? That was what doctors were for, wasn't it?

"But that's impossible." The words were jerked out of Ben in spite of himself. How could she be dead? An hour ago he'd held her in his arms and made love to her. Half an hour ago she had been talking and laughing with Biddy. All her things were packed ready for her trip to Stonehaven. She was going down to see her new grandchild.

"Could you get me a blanket?" Dr Pike asked.

He took the blanket Biddy brought to him and gently spread it over Anne, covering her face and her lovely white hair.

Well, at least that was final proof. It reduced Biddy to the loud, wailing sobs of the mourning aboriginal woman, and it reduced Ben to soundless tears.

"You'd better come out to the verandah and tell me about it," Dr Pike said.

Ben followed him and did his best to answer the questions. Only there were no answers. At least no helpful ones.

No, Anne had never complained of any pains. No, she had not been sick. No, she had not been depressed in any way. Rather the opposite. She had been laughing and happy when he left her an hour ago, laughing with Biddy when she collapsed.

In the end Dr Pike shook his head, muttered something about a possible cerebral haemorrhage, and said apologetically that he was afraid a post-mortem would be necessary. Ben nodded his assent. He was still too dazed to grasp anything clearly, even the fact that Biddy's wails were making conversation difficult away out there on the verandah.

Dr Pike said, "I'd better give that old aboriginal woman a sedative. Calm her down a bit." He was new to Baranda and knew very little about aboriginals and their habits.

"Leave her," Ben said. "They're all like that. Got to get it out of their systems."

God, if he could only ease his feelings like that instead of sitting here choking everything back. Biddy could air her grief and not give a damn who heard her. But he couldn't. He had to keep up this pretence, even to himself.

"You need something yourself, old man," Dr Pike shook two white tablets from a bottle and held them out. "Swallow these. I'll get you a glass of water."

Ben shook his head and waved the tablets aside. What bloody fools these doctors were. Little white pills for everything! You took two of these, and you forgot your wife was lying dead in the next room! Bloody rot! Quackery, that's all it was. When it came to a showdown, something big, like saving a life, a doctor was useless. Useless, useless, useless.

Ben was only vaguely aware of the happenings of that afternoon. He knew that Charlie and one of the stockmen had driven off to Baranda in the station utility, taking Anne away, that Dr Pike had followed them, that young Coudrey and his wife, Mary, were here at Wavering Downs, that Mary had prepared the evening meal, and that they had all made a pretence of eating before the Coudreys drove back to Baranda. He had insisted that they leave, he remembered, because he wanted to be alone, and he felt intensely grateful to them because they had helped in practical ways and spared him the sympathetic platitudes he had been dreading.

And when the noise of their car faded away in the distance he followed on foot because he could not bear the silence.

He walked a long way that night—more than half-way to Baranda before weariness and the awareness of the futility of trying to walk away from sorrow forced him to turn back. A mile or two along the homeward trudge he met Biddy. Neither of them spoke. She simply loomed up out of the darkness, turned, and walked beside him.

After another mile or so he said, "Sorry, I can't talk, Biddy. But there's nothing to say, is there?"

"Bimeby we talk, Boss," she answered. "When it don't hurt so bad."

Hell, why hadn't he realized that it was hurting her as much as it was hurting him? Why hadn't he stayed and tried to comfort her instead of walking out and leaving her to face it alone? She had worshipped Anne and she had been more loyal, more unselfish, and more faithful to her than he had been.

"Gimme your arm," he said gruffly. "Lean on me. You shouldn't have walked all this way."

Day was breaking when they reached the homestead. The first long, dreary night was over, but the new day had to be faced.

Charlie returned shortly after sunrise. He slumped into a verandah chair opposite Ben and made his report, going over everything in detail, so that Ben had only to nod his under standing. He had spent the night with the Coudreys because the parson had taken charge of everything, including him. Anne had died of cerebral haemorrhage. She would be buried in Baranda and the funeral service would start at three that afternoon. Mr Coudrey had rung Anthea's husband and Gregory had got in touch with Ken who was driving straight up. He would probably arrive in time for breakfast. Gregory had sent messages of sympathy and had apologized for not coming up with Ken. Ben would understand that it was impossible for Anthea to leave Stonehaven with the baby so nearly due, he said, and he felt it was his duty to stay with her.

"He's all right, that parson," Charlie concluded. "He'll do me."

And coming from that reticent little horse-trainer, that was high praise indeed.

★ 21 ★

KEN stayed for four days after the funeral. He overhauled the engine of the pumping plant and he made minor adjustments to both car engines. None of the jobs really needed doing, but they at least kept him occupied during daylight hours.

"You get back to your job, son," Ben said with a flash of rare understanding. "You're only trying to fill in time here, and things won't seem so bad if you've got something interesting to keep you busy."

Striving to conceal his relief Ken said, "I hate leaving you all alone at a time like this."

"Don't worry about me. I've got enough to keep me busy for a while. I've got to start mustering for dipping tomorrow and after we finish that I'll probably take a run down to Stonehaven to see how Anthea makes out."

Anthea made out very well. As Anne had predicted, she presented him with a grandson, and because Anne had wished it, the baby was named after him. But Anne's other wish never came true. From the very start old Ben and young Ben failed to get on. Perhaps, Ben thought, he was too old to make friends with a baby. Perhaps Anne's death had left him too cold and forbidding. Or perhaps the child in some way sensed the lack of any real love between his parents and his grandfather, and subconsciously resented it.

Whatever the cause, young Ben never outgrew it. Even as a schoolboy he hated Wavering Downs, visited it under protest, and was obviously glad to leave it after each brief visit. He disliked horses, was afraid of cattle, and refused to have anything to do with Biddy.

That was something old Ben could neither understand nor forgive. Children had always loved Biddy. Dan had always sent messages to her in his letters from the front, Ken had always been her ardent admirer, and even Anthea had adored her during her childhood.

Although he gradually recovered from the shock of Anne's

death Ben found it impossible to outgrow the feeling of loneliness. Wavering Downs still absorbed most of his interest, but he had brought it to such a stage of perfection that it no longer demanded all his time. And since he needed another outlet for his boundless energy he began taking an interest in public life. Within two years he was Chairman of the Baranda Shire Council, the most dominant chairman in the history of the Shire. He became a member of the Stonehaven Club, establishing a reputation in that usually sedate gathering of business and professional men that was to grow into a legend. For when Ben drank he did so on a grand scale that swept a few decorous groups of drinkers into one vast, rip-roaring party, with himself as host and pacemaker.

"McReady of Wavering Downs is in town," became the stock excuse of husbands who arrived home late for dinner.

He joined the Stonehaven Jockey Club and moved Charlie and his stable down to town where they could meet competition more worthy of them than anything they could find in the country race clubs.

And reluctantly he installed a housekeeper on Wavering Downs. He did so, not so much because he felt his position demanded it, but because the job was too big for Biddy. Since Anne's death poor Biddy had aged a lot and she tired quickly. Dr Pike diagnosed a heart condition and advised her to give up work altogether, but Biddy refused to take his advice seriously. Some one, she declared, had to look after the Boss. Even when Mrs Phillips took over she continued to do many of the jobs she had always regarded as her own.

At first Mrs Phillips had resented Biddy's attitude. She was a tall, rather gaunt widow who prided herself on her efficiency, and she made the mistake of airing her feelings to Ben.

"I don't know why you keep that old gin," she said. "I could get on quite well without her."

"You could, eh?" Ben lowered the paper he had been reading. "We'd better get this straight, Mrs Phillips. I don't like anyone calling Biddy an old gin. Maybe she is an old gin, but she's been one of this family nearly all her life and she's staying that way for the rest of it. If you can't get on with her just say so, and I'll find another housekeeper that can. There are plenty of good housekeepers, but there's only one Biddy."

And since Mrs Phillips valued her job she accepted Biddy, gradually grew to like her, and scarcely raised her eyebrows when Ken, home for a brief week-end, greeted Biddy with a hug and laughingly asked, "How's my favourite girl?"

With new-found tolerance, Ben eased the domestic situation by relieving Biddy of all household duties and putting her in charge of the garden.

"We'll have to keep it looking the way the Missus always had it," he told her. "I don't know anything about gardening, so you'd better take charge of it. But don't let me catch you doing any heavy work. I'll find some one to do all that for you and you can just see it's done properly."

He got Scrubber Jackson. Scrubber had finally decided that he was getting too old for stockwork, and the gardening job appealed to him as a good, easy way of making a living. He was wrong about the easy part of it. Biddy was a tough, demanding boss, but by the time Scrubber realized it he had settled in to the job and was even taking a certain pride in it.

When young Ben was two years old Jane was born, and old Ben's loneliness vanished. For Jane took to him at once. As far as her parents were concerned Jane was an unwanted baby. Her unscheduled arrival upset Anthea's plans by forcing her into temporary retirement at a time when she was rapidly achieving social success. Gregory was simply not interested in the baby he looked on as an unfortunate mishap. He already had a son and that was enough for him. Only recently he had discovered that racing was an absorbing and lucrative sport for a man with capital and brains—in other words, a shrewd punter like himself. So long as he wasn't asked to give up any of his valuable time he didn't care who looked after his new daughter.

Jane Arnedale. She should have been Jane McReady, for she and Ben were like father and daughter, a very doting old father and a very special daughter. As soon as she was old enough he took her out to Wavering Downs for a short visit.

Two or three days, he told Anthea. The three days stretched to three weeks and Jane loved every minute of them. She loved horses and cattle and she loved Biddy from the moment she leaped excitedly from the car and ran to greet old Blue.

Blue was Ben's cattle-dog. He was old and he was surly, he disliked all strangers, and, like most old cattle-dogs, he preferred to bite rather than bark or growl a warning.

Ben yelled, "Janie! Janie! Come back. Don't touch him."

But he was too late. Jane already had her arms around Blue's neck. Over his scarred old head she could see an understanding black face that smiled and said:

"Leave 'em alone, Boss. These two bin gunna get on together like old cobbers."

Blue's hackles went up at the indignity of the embrace, but he made amends immediately. His pink tongue came out and he licked the child's face enthusiastically and thoroughly.

"Cut it out!" Ben roared. And then, because Biddy was much closer to the child and dog than he was, "Gawdstruth, Biddy, don't let him do that to her. Kick him in the slats."

But Biddy only smiled calmly and said, "He ain't doin' no harm, Boss. You bin feedin' the little girl chocolates and Blue only wants to clean her face up a bit."

The novelty of that viewpoint delighted Jane. Anyone, black or white, who approved of such a method of face-washing was her idea of a real friend. She even raised no objections when Biddy led her off to the bathroom for a proper wash because Biddy clucked in disgust and said:

"That old Blue he don't do such a good washin' job after all. Leaves bits of chocolate everywhere. Must be gettin' old and lazy. Come along and we'll finish it off for him."

"We got the right one this time, eh, Boss?" Biddy chuckled delightedly when Ben brought an enthralled Jane back from the stockyard next day. "She big gunna be proper little bush-whacker, that one."

And Ben grinned and said, "She'll do me."

Blue showed his approval by deserting Ben for Jane, and Jane followed Biddy or Ben impartially. Ageing, with failing heart and dimming eyesight, Biddy could still take a small girl for walks along the creek and show her the most enthralling and exciting things. Maybe they weren't so exciting, but she always managed to make them sound so.

She knew where an old goanna lived and she knew which tree he would scramble up if you sooled Blue on to him. She knew that if you threw a stick at a certain dead limb on a tree it would turn into a bird and fly away. Only mostly you didn't throw sticks at it. You crept past quietly so as not to disturb the poor old mopoke because he had been up all night keeping the mice out of Charlie's horsefeed. She knew where to part the grass and disclose the cunningly built nest of a kangaroo rat. She knew where to find a native bees' nest, and how to extract sips of honey with a twig while the little black bees crawled over your face and hands but never stung. She knew that if you sat very still and watched a certain tiny hole in the creek bank a beautiful rainbow bird would pop out and fly away.

She knew, wily old Biddy, the most amazing blackfellow magic. Like making the emu forget his shyness and walk right up to you. It was a secret known only to certain favoured members of the tribe and you had to promise never to tell it to a soul.

You bent over like a feeding kangaroo, wiggled your arms about like long twitching ears and kept on saying the secret word, "Gunjulla, Gunjulla," very softly, over and over, and he would forget his shyness and come right up to you, so close that you could see the fierce glitter in his brown eyes as he turned his head from side to side, so terrifyingly close that he could almost stretch out his long neck and peck you. Admittedly it was a frightening experience, but, as Biddy promptly demonstrated, if you got scared of that cruel-looking beak you only had to stop saying the magic word, stand up and shout "Birramin!" and he would race off in a panic.

It was years before Jane learned that she had been the victim of one of Biddy's numerous fascinating confidence tricks and that the emu was an exceedingly curious bird, incapable of resisting the attraction of anything new or strange to him. But even when she grew up she still laughed and said, "Gunjulla, Gunjulla," every time she saw an emu.

As soon as she was old enough to ride Ben presented Jane with a pony. He paid for her education at Anthea's old school and he and Biddy did their best to spoil her each time she came to Wavering Downs. But Jane was unspoilable. She remained charmingly natural, called Wavering Downs "home" and Ben "Bossy". She went for long rides with Ben, helped with the mustering, and openly adored Biddy. To Ben's intense delight she quickly developed that rare and valuable cattleman's ability to recognize and remember individual beasts.

Since she was only seven when it broke out the Second World War made very little impression on her. Ben was of the opinion that it would have no effect on him, beyond boosting the price of cattle. He was too old to take any active part in another war and he felt sure Ken would never enlist; he was completely wrapped up in his job of instructor to the Stonehaven Flying Club.

"There's a big future in the air, Dad," he said on one of his week-end visits to Wavering Downs. "The time's coming when every big station will have its own landing strip and probably its own plane. Look at the way the airlines are expanding. In a big country like this flying is the logical way to travel. Look at the time it saves."

"That's the bloody trouble these days," Ben answered irritably. "Everybody's in a hell of a hurry to get to some place or other. And blowed if I can see where they're any better off for it. In the old days every one had time to spare. Every one pulled up for a cup of tea and a yarn. Now they go tearin' past in a bloody great cloud of dust. Not even time to say good day."

"That's true enough, Dad. But being air-minded isn't so much a matter of being in a hurry. It's a matter of keeping up with the times."

Well, Ken had more than kept up with the times; he had led the way. To Ben's intense surprise he was one of the first to enlist. He joined the Air Force, and his enthusiasm when he was accepted as fighter pilot material caused Ben to reverse all his former opinions about his son. Ken was going off to war as if it were a glorious big adventure, created for his special entertainment. Dan had looked on war in that light. Had he been alive then the pair of them would have gone off like two kids on a holiday. Dan had wanted the Turks to attack on that last night. His only fear had been that they would *not* come.

And now his young brother was saying, "We've got the planes and we've got the chaps to fly 'em. I only hope Hitler and his mob don't chuck it in before we get a go at 'em."

Absent-mindedly Ben said, "I don't think they're likely to do that, son."

His thoughts were all tangled up, and to get them sorted out so that he could put them into words he got up and poured two rums. They had been sitting on the verandah, looking out over the moonlit garden, listening to the croaking of the frogs along the creek, and talking quietly.

Ben came back with the drinks and settled himself in his canvas squatter's chair.

"You know, son," he said. "I've been chewing things over lately and I reckon this is as good a time as any to get 'em off my chest. I've been wrong about you, wrong ever since I found you'd never be a cattleman. All the time I had it in the back of my thick skull that you shied off cattle-work because you didn't have enough guts for it. If I'd had any brains at all I'd have seen I was up the wrong gully when you took up flying. It takes guts to fly one of those blasted planes—more guts than I've got. Or it could be just a different sort of guts. That's what I'm getting at. We're all made different, and perhaps it's just as well we are. Wouldn't do if we were all cattlemen, would it? Who'd buy the flamin' beef? It took me a long time to wake up to that, but I can see things your way now. You're just like your brother Dan, only in a quieter sort of way, if you get what I mean. He went to the first war for the hell of it. He reckoned he went to be with me, but he'd have gone anyway because that was the way he was made. I never told you the full score on that, did I?"

Without waiting for Ken to answer he went on, "I didn't join up for the hell of it. I didn't join up because I was a bloody hero wanting to fight for his country. I joined up because the police were after me for cattle-duffing. And I can't claim I liked it once we got overseas. Too many things about the Army got on my goat. Maybe I was a bit too old for a war. But Dan was different. He enjoyed himself no matter how tough the going was. You'll be like Dan; I can see that now. You'll be fighting a different sort of war in a different way, but you'll be Dan all over again."

He sipped his rum slowly and after a minute or two Ken said, "Mother always said you and Dan were like brothers. I wish I'd known him. He must have been quite a bloke."

"He was. He was right out on his own. Funny I never saw it that way before, but you two would have got on well together. You're going off to this war for the hell of it and you'll probably enjoy yourself as much as he did." Ben downed the last of his rum and sighed. "I'm only going to give you one bit of advice before you go, son. If I told you to take care of yourself I'd only be showing you how bloody silly a father can get, because a war is one place where a man can't take care of himself. His superior officers are supposed to do that for him, but the trouble is they sometimes fall down on the job. What I'm getting at, son, is this. Don't knock back any promotion that comes your way. It's not a matter of higher pay. It's a matter of getting to where you're giving the orders instead of taking them. The higher up you get the fewer numbskulls you've got pushing you around and the more chances you have of getting home alive. Dan was killed through the mistake of a dud officer. I wouldn't want the same thing to happen to you."

It was quite a speech for Ben. It called for another drink, so he collected the glasses and went inside to pour it. He poured several more drinks that night, and when they went off to bed at midnight both he and Ken were a little unsteady on their feet.

"We're both full, Boss," Ken announced, adopting Dan's form of address for the first time. "But what the hell! It's our last night together for a long time."

He went off next morning, and although Ben heard from him regularly during the next two years he never saw his son again.

Until the day he was shot down over the English Channel Ken never lost his enthusiasm for flying and aerial combat. He was twice mentioned in dispatches, and only a week before he died he was awarded the D.F.C. Unlike his father and elder brother, whose short, stilted letters must have been poor consolation to Anne, Ken wrote fluently and well. Perhaps the only thing the three writers had in common was their remembrance of Biddy, for every letter from both wars contained some little message for her.

Poor old Biddy. She lacked Ben's iron constitution and ability to withstand shocks. Ken's death hit Ben hard because he felt he had found his son only to lose him, but it aged Biddy noticeably and it worsened her heart condition. Ken had been her baby, the youngest of her trio. Dan had gone, Anthea had drifted away from her, Anne had gone, and now Ken had been taken from her.

Dr Pike took matters in hand and packed her off to hospital. He may not have learned a great deal about aboriginals but he at least knew something about failing hearts. It was on his advice that Ben bought the cottage in Stonehaven where Biddy could be close to good medical attention for the rest of her life.

Biddy protested at the move. She didn't want to leave Wavering Downs, she said. It was her home and she preferred to die there rather than live among strangers in a strange town.

"You'll do as you're told," Ben roared at her. It did him good to have a problem to tackle, and he went about it in his own forthright, bull-headed way. "I haven't got the time to play nursemaid to you. You'll be near the doctor down there and some of your relations are living in the same street. Not that I'd trust them to do anything except sponge on you. I'll keep an eye on you, me gal, so don't think you can put anything over me."

Very meekly she said, "Youi, Boss." And then as an afterthought. "You know I wouldn't ever do anything like that."

"Like hell you wouldn't!" Ben laughed at her worried sincerity. "I know you and your old blackfella ways, and I'm fixing things so you'll always be all right."

How well he knew Biddy and all her old aboriginal instincts and upbringing! She would share everything with the descendants of any member of her tribe because that was the way of her people. He could never stop her from doing that, but at least he could make sure she never wanted for anything.

★ 22 ★

LORD, that was years ago. Ancient history, as the youngsters of today would say. Miraculously Biddy still lived, Jane had grown up and was actually contemplating marriage, her brother was wasting his time at the university, and he, old Ben McReady, was lying in Stonehaven hospital, waiting for the end.

The end of the road, a road that had started off as a rough, uncleared, winding bush-track, gradually developing stage by stage into a broad, straight highway that ended. . . . Where did it end? In a swamp, or at the foot of a mountain? Old Alf Coudrey might know, but if he didn't he'd never admit it. Most likely he'd have some wonderful yarn about the road not stopping at the foot of the mountain, but winding steadily up and up it in beautiful scenic curves. Oh, well, every man to his trade. That was Alf's trade, and there was no denying he was pretty good at it.

But when a man looked back and considered all the facts he could only come to one conclusion. The road ended as it had started—a winding bush-track that finally petered out up a blind gully. Where was the point in starting from scratch and ending up as the owner of the finest cattle property in the district if you had no one to carry on after you'd gone? That was a blind gully, wasn't it?

If he left Wavering Downs to Anthea she and Gregory would sell it to the highest bidder as soon as they got back from his funeral. His grandson would do the same and have a high old time on the proceeds. None of them cared two hoots for the station, apart from the money they could get out of it.

Certainly there was Jane. She loved Wavering Downs, loved it for itself, just as he always had done.

But you couldn't leave a big cattle station to a twenty-year-old girl. The responsibility would be too much for her and she'd be a sitting shot for every go-getter in the country.

She'd be swamped with proposals of marriage because they'd all be after her for her money. She'd get so browned-off with them all that even if she did marry a good, fair dinkum bloke who didn't give a damn about her money she'd always feel a bit suspicious of him.

No, no. That wouldn't work. He wanted her to be happy, and happiness was one of the things you couldn't buy. Somehow, before he died, he'd have to find a way out of it. Perhaps old Bill Amity would know. Bill was not only a good lawyer, he was a big-hearted bloke who understood human weaknesses and problems. Yes, that would be the shot. Talk things over with old Bill. Get one of the nurses to ring him and ask him to drop around for an hour or two as soon as he could spare the time. Better get on to it soon before this gnawing pain made clear thinking too difficult.

Who was on duty this morning? Oh, yes, the plump little first-year nurse with the big dark eyes and the chest like a squatter pigeon's. What the devil was her name? Must find out. It was silly to have a girl washing you and doing all sort of things for you and not even know her name.

He rang his bell and when she came in he said, "Nurse, I want you to do something for me."

"Yes, Mr McReady." She smiled, no longer in awe of this big, domineering old man now that she had been permitted to study his chart. Young and inexperienced though she was, she could at least see through his bluff and appreciate the battle he was putting up. "Sister says you can have two more tablets if the pain is too bad."

"Never mind the pain. I can put up with it. What's your name, nurse?"

"It's Yardley. Nurse Yardley."

"No first name?"

"Yes, Yvette. But you're not supposed to know it. It's silly, isn't it?"

"What, the name or me not being supposed to know it?"

"Both. I hate my Christian name. Simply loathe it. Don't you think it's a silly name?"

"I dunno; I think it suits you. Anyway you don't want to let it get you down. Pretty well every one hates their first name. Look at mine. It's Ben. Benjamin. Sounds like a bloody Jew, doesn't it?"

"Now, Mr McReady, you mustn't start swearing again. You've been very good lately." She was trying to be professionally correct now. "What did you ring for?"

"Oh, yes, I nearly forgot. I want you to make a phone-call for me. Ring Mr W. Amity, the solicitor, at his office and tell him I'd like him to drop around and see me as soon as he can spare the time."

"Will he be at his office this morning? It's Saturday, you know."

"Good heaven! So it is. I'd forgotten that. Never mind. I'll get a message to him on Monday. Sorry I dragged you in for nothing."

"That's all right, Mr McReady. We're not very busy this morning." She glanced up and down the passage and then reassured that none of her superiors was in the offing, abandoned all attempts at professionalism. "Mr McReady, I suppose I shouldn't ask you, but I'm simply dying to know. The suspense is killing me. Do you think your horse, Starry Gold, will win this afternoon?"

Looking at her in astonishment Ben asked, "Why? I mean, what the devil do you want to know for?"

"Well——" She hesitated, bit her lip, and finally blurted out the truth. "I've backed it."

"You've backed Starry Gold! What on earth made you do a thing like that, child? Don't tell me you're a gambler, that you throw your money away on horses at your age!"

"Oh, no, Mr McReady. I've never backed one before. But I heard some of the staff talking about your racehorses and I looked up the racing news in the paper and saw the name Starry Gold. It was such a lovely name."

"And you reckoned that was a good enough reason for you to chuck your money away?"

"Well, it wasn't only the name. I felt I simply had to back it because you owned it and you were my patient." The lashes fluttered over her dark eyes and she flushed. "There's another reason. I've been invited to the Digger's Ball next week and I wanted the money for a new frock."

"How much did you put on?"

"A whole pound. I couldn't really afford it this week, but then I couldn't afford the new frock either, unless I won the money. Ten pounds to one, the bookmaker gave me. Was that good?"

"Oh, real generous! Bookies are like that. He might as well have made it fifty while he was at it. At least you'd have got a bit more kick out of telling your mates about all the dough you *didn't* make." To cover his embarrassment he scowled fiercely at her and snapped, "How much a week do they pay you?"

"Four pounds, four, and sixpence."

"And you chuck away nearly a quarter of it on a horse you know nothing about!"

"I know you own it and you're my patient."

"Dammit, child, don't keep saying that. As if it's a good excuse for chuckin' your money down the drain."

Her eyelashes fluttered, blinking away the tears of dismay. "But, Mr McReady, don't you think it'll win?"

"No, I *don't* think she'll win. She hasn't got a bloody dog's chance. The—er—well, I s'pose you could say some of the other horses are too good for her."

"But why are you letting her start if you know she hasn't got a chance?"

Ben thought that one over. He couldn't disillusion this child by telling her he was one of many owners who instructed jockeys to pull horses up for a number of reasons. Certainly he couldn't tell her that Starry Gold was being deliberately blocked on his orders because he disliked his son-in-law and wanted to teach him a lesson.

"You never know in racing," he said lamely. "As my old trainer always says, 'There's no such thing as a racecourse certainty!'"

"There you are!" Grasping at the straw, Nurse Yardley smiled her triumph. "You're just being modest because it's your own horse. And you're afraid I'll blame you if she doesn't win, aren't you? But I wouldn't do that, Mr

McReady, really I wouldn't. Whatever happens I'll know you wanted your horse to win just as much as I do."

"Aw, skip it." Ben squirmed uncomfortably in the bed. So this was what happened when you pulled a horse! Funny he'd never thought of that side of it before. He'd often chuckled at the idea of a few hardened punters doing their money but they were fair game. Like Gregory. Always thinking they could outsmart owners and bookies. It was a different thing when a youngster risked a big slice of her wages because you were her patient and she thought you were a good, square-shooting old bloke.

"Look, Nurse," he said gruffly. "How about letting me give you your quid back and then forgetting all about it?"

"Oh, Mr McReady!" She looked positively shocked at the suggestion. "I couldn't dream of it. Besides, something tells me Starry Gold is going to win. I've got a feeling about it."

A feeling about it! She had a feeling about it! Could you beat that? A pity her feelings didn't warn her about trusting crook owners. Ben was thinking hard. If he could contact Charlie on the course, get a message to him to give the filly a fair run, she might win. Charlie reckoned she could and he was never an optimist. But what about Gregory? He'd make a big clean-up and go around for weeks afterwards bragging about his shrewdness. Oh, to hell with Gregory. Let him have his win. In the long run it wouldn't make a great deal of difference. He might win a packet today but he'd do it all in the next few race meetings. As Charlie had said, nothing would cure him. There was only a faint chance of getting a message to Charlie in time, but at least he could try. Only a soft, sentimental old fool would do a thing like this. But hell's bells! When a man had nothing to look forward to he was entitled to get a bit sentimental, wasn't he?

"Look, Nurse," he said. "I want you to do something for me. Ring the racecourse and ask them to get hold of a bloke named Turner, Charlie Turner. They probably won't be able to get him to the phone straight away, so leave a message for him to ring you here as soon as he can. You might get him and you mightn't, but if he does ring back tell him you're my nurse, my favourite nurse, and then say, 'Boss McReady says to call Lee off.' Understand?"

"I'm afraid I don't, Mr McReady. Will Mr Turner know what I'm talking about?"

"He'll know." Ben paused, searching for a plausible explanation. "I've got two horses entered for that race. If Turner gets the message in time he'll scratch the colt and give your filly a better chance, see?"

"Is the colt faster than Starry Gold?"

"Eh? No. I mean he's—— Never mind what he is. Don't ask so many questions, there's a good girl. If you want to have a sporting chance of getting that new frock just run along and do what you're told."

"Yes, Mr McReady." Beaming her pleasure she added, "It's terribly good of you to go to all this trouble for me. You must think I'm an awful nuisance. I—er—I'd better go now."

When she came in with his pre-lunch drink she had the air of a conspiratress rather than a nurse.

"I've got a portable wireless in my room," she whispered. "It's only a tiny little one. Will it be all right if I bring it in here so we can listen to the race? The paper says it starts at three o'clock and I'll be on duty then. We could keep it tuned very low, but if Matron did happen to hear it we could say you wanted to listen to the race, couldn't we?"

Ben swallowed his rum, felt its burning warmth spread through him, and asked, "Did you get on to Charlie Turner?"

"No, he hasn't rung back yet."

"Then put in another call for him. Tell 'em it's urgent. Say McReady wants him."

"Yes, Mr McReady. And you won't mind about the wireless, will you?"

"I don't care what you do so long as you get that call through. Now hop it."

Taking his empty glass she hurried off and left him to his worries. What if Charlie couldn't be contacted? He'd be out there for sure, but he'd be a hard man to locate in a big race crowd. Had a habit of making himself invisible by melting into the background like a blasted old curlew. And now that the first race had started every one would be too busy to take much trouble over a phone message. Hell! What was the good of worrying about it? If Charlie didn't get the message Starry Gold would be one of the also-rans and Nurse Yardley would do her quid cold. Serve her right, too, the silly little fool. Teach her not to think she could buy herself a frock by putting a quid on a horse with a fancy name. If she got away with it this time she'd probably end up making a habit of it.

He ate his lunch and then dozed off for a while without once slipping back into the past. The past was over and done with, and only the future remained. The immediate future with a shy, little first-year nurse pinning her faith in him because he was her patient. Damn it all, what difference did that make? It didn't make a saint of him, did it? But she'd come in here with her blasted wireless, all starry-eyed with excitement and full of faith that her patient's horse would romp home a winner and hand her out a new frock for the ball. And what could the patient say to comfort her when their horse finished away back in the tail of the field? "Never mind, dear, I'll buy the frock for you?" That might satisfy some little tart, but it wouldn't go down with this kid. She wasn't that type.

Ten minutes to three, and she was there beside him, putting her little portable radio on his table, plugging it in to his bedside plug and saying, "Oh, Mr McReady, I'm so excited I can hardly wait."

"Have you got on to Charlie Turner yet?"

"No." She was turning the dial expectantly. "He hasn't rung and it's too late to get him now. But it doesn't really matter, does it? I mean it's not that important, is it?"

Oh, no! Not that important! Only the difference between making you happy and destroying your faith in human nature. Why don't you take your blasted wireless to hell out of here and leave a man to feel a low bloody heel by himself without having to face the silent reproach in those big dark eyes? What's a lousy quid anyway. I'll tell you what it is, you big mug. A quid is a new frock for the ball and a new frock could be the difference between your boy friend wiping you off as one of the also-rans or falling for you in a big way.

"The horses are coming up to the barrier for the start of the Maiden Plate."

The voice of the commentator blared across his thoughts and was instantly hushed as Nurse Yardley hastily turned the radio's volume down.

He had to strain to hear the words now. He didn't want to hear them. What could the commentator tell him that he didn't already know? Yet in spite of himself he listened, catching only a word here and there.

"Can you hear?" Nurse Yardley asked. "Is it loud enough for you? I'm scared to have it too loud in case Matron comes in and catches me."

He nodded, hearing faintly the words, ". . . the odds-on favourite Starry Gold, coming into position now."

Odds-on favourite! From tens to odds-on overnight! Gregory must have opened his big mouth to some of his pals or else he'd backed the horse so heavily he'd scared hell out of the bookies. Probably he'd done both. That would be his form. Back the horse clean off the market and then make a good fellow of himself by putting all his pals on to "the good thing." What a cropper he'd come! He'd never live this down. Never. Take a good look at the bright colours above the dancing horses, Gregory, because after this race is over you'll never have the nerve to show yourself on a racecourse again.

The commentator's voice called, "They're off! Off to a good start . . . ." His words trailed off in an unintelligible jumble of names.

Ben closed his eyes. The matter was out of his hands now. He caught the name, Starry Gold, and he opened them again to see Nurse Yardley with her ear only an inch or two away from the radio. Her lips were parted and her eyes were shining with excitement. Scared to miss one single word she put her finger on the volume control and raised her eyebrows. Plainly she was asking, "It is loud enough for you? Can you hear?"

He nodded. He couldn't hear and he didn't want to hear. He closed his eyes, intending to keep them closed until the announcement of the final placings forced him to open them and meet the silent reproach in those big tell-tale eyes.

The voice of the commentator droned on, rising and falling as he reeled off the changing positions, and again Ben caught the name, Starry Gold. Where the devil was the filly anyway? Right back in the tail of the field if he knew anything of her form when she'd been jammed in and stopped from making her early run. She hadn't the guts to fight back and come again.

There it was again, "Starry Gold," excitedly called as though the filly was right up with the leaders. They must be nearly into the straight now.

Ben opened his eyes. Little Nurse Yardley was on her knees beside the table, still with her ear glued to the radio. He couldn't see her eyes, but her hands fascinated him. In her excitement she had clutched the corner of the white table-cover and was twisting it round and round her plump little fingers, threatening at any moment to pull it clean off the table.

". . . into the straight now and Starry Gold has taken the lead." Every word rang out clearly now as the commentator worked himself to the thrill of the finish. "This boy, Spargo, has certainly ridden a wonderful race. The filly's moving away from the field now and looks as if she'll win by a couple of lengths. . . . Yes, they're past the post and it's Starry Gold first by two and a half lengths. Next comes . . ."

Crash! !

Radio, water-bottle, and glass hit the floor, ending the broadcast and leaving Nurse Yardley kneeling in a pool of water she was still too excited to notice. Her big eyes were brimming over and she was looking at Ben with an adoration that made him cough with embarrassment and say:

"I knew you was gunna do that."

"Nurse Yardley! What on earth are you doing?"

Stiff, grim-lipped, like a regimental sergeant major about to bawl out a clumsy recruit, Matron stood in the doorway.

Gallantly Ben came to the rescue. He'd had a grudge against sergeant majors ever since 1914 anyhow.

"It was my fault, Matron," he explained. "I was listening to a race broadcast and I reached over to turn the wireless up and knocked the whole box and dice down."

Matron's lips softened into a smile. "That's quite all right, Mr McReady," she purred. "Accidents happen to us all. Whose wireless is that?"

Nurse Yardley said, "Mine, Matron," and to forestall any further confessions, Ben cut in, "I asked her for a loan of it. And I'm sorry if I bust it, Nurse. Better have it checked, just in case. Take it round to the radio-shop on Monday. Tell them to fix up anything that needs fixing and send the account to me."

Nurse Yardley smiled her thanks. "Mr McReady's horse won, Matron," she said.

"I'm aware of that, Nurse," Matron snapped. And then softening, "I backed it."

"*You* backed it!" Ben stared at her. He simply could not visualize Matron playing the horses.

"Yes, I——Nurse, answer those bells and then come back here and clean this mess up." Matron waited until Nurse Yardley left before explaining. "I came to ask you Mr McReady, if I put ten shillings on Starry Gold yesterday when it was ten to one will I only be paid starting price?"

"Depends on what the bookie quoted you."

"He distinctly said ten to one, but he didn't give me any form of receipt."

"Don't worry about the receipt, Matron. You'll get your money. Five pounds, and your ten bob back as well."

Nurse Yardley came back and said, "It was Mr Harris ringing, Matron. And old Mrs Parker, too. They wanted me to congratulate Mr McReady on his horse's win. They'd both backed it."

Ben turned his head away and sighed. Before the day was over he would probably hear that the whole damned hospital, nurses and patients, had backed his horse. They'd be thinking what a great fellow he was, and no one except little Charlie would know that he had slipped up in the greatest racing double-cross of all time.

He felt the pressure of soft, warm lips on his cheek. Obviously Matron had gone because Nurse Yardley was doing the kissing and saying:

"Mr McReady, I think you're the dearest, sweetest old man I've ever met in my whole life."

★ 23 ★

An hour later he was being kissed again, this time by Jane.

"Oh, Bossy," she was saying. "Isn't it wonderful? I do wish you could have been there to see her win. It was the thrillingest race. You know how timid the poor darling can be in company? Well, Spargo didn't give any of them a chance to crowd her. He kept her on the outside, fairly well up, and then when they came around the turn into the straight he sent her ahead and simply walked away from the rest of the field. I was so excited I nearly chewed my betting slip into a pulp."

"So you backed her too, eh?"

"Of course I backed, Bossy! She's always been my favourite! Don't you remember? I s'pose because she's so gentle and timid. And Charlie used to let me ride her when he was breaking her in." She took a small compact from her handbag and applied a few dabs of lipstick. "I saw Spargo just before the race—isn't he a wicked-looking little man when he turns the peak of his cap up and lets his black skull-cap show underneath?—and I said, 'Don't you dare let her get jammed in Spargo, or I'll never speak to you again.'"

"You did, eh?"

"Yes, and he grinned with that awful leer of his and said, 'She'll be jake, miss. You leave it to me. It's in the bag!'"

Ben muttered, "It just bloody well goes to show."

Bubbling over with happiness Jane bent and rubbed her smooth cheek against his. "What does it bloody well go to show, you naughty old man?"

"Nothing, Janie, nothing. I was just thinking about the way you can twist any of the boys around. If I'd told Spargo to pull that filly up and you'd come along afterwards and told him to win, he'd have ridden the race your way. S'pose I tell you I *did* tell him to pull her?"

Actually he was thinking that it was amazing the way luck

or some slip had stepped in to save him wrecking the day for these two girls. In his anxiety to take a rise out of Gregory he had completely forgotten that the filly had been Jane's favourite from the day Charlie started to handle her.

"What an awful fib, Bossy! You weren't thinking anything of the sort. And I bet you told Spargo to try and win that race, didn't you now?"

"I didn't see Spargo, but as a matter of fact I told Charlie to tell him that if he didn't win he'd never get another ride from me." Even the truth, or at least a half-truth, was working to save him!

"There! I knew it. You do love making yourself out a bad old man, don't you? But you can't fool me."

That was the wonderful thing about Jane. She had such absolute faith in him that she'd never believe anything bad about him. And he valued that faith. Come to think of it, it was the thing he valued most now. Above all else he wanted her love and understanding and her happiness.

Undoubtedly she was happy now. She was glowing with happiness, sitting there with red lips parted and eyes shining as she removed her ridiculous little hat and shook her dark wavy hair out with the toss of the head he had come to know so well. Somehow it reminded him of a horse shaking the tangles out of its mane. She was keeping something back, he knew. There was very little about Jane he didn't know. Certainly she was overjoyed about the filly's win this afternoon, but there was something else, something bigger than that. He could ask her, of course, but why spoil her little surprise by forestalling her? When she was ready she'd tell him, just as she'd always done. Ever since her childhood she had confided her innermost feelings and secrets to him—things she never told her mother or father because, she used to say, they wouldn't understand. But he had always understood. Hadn't he, in his loneliness, put other things aside and trained himself to understand her every mood?

"Hey, Bossy," she said at last. "Guess what?"

There was no need for him to guess now; he already knew. But he mustn't spoil things for her by admitting it. He must play the game her way, talk to her in the language of her generation, the language Anthea detested because she was so blasted snobbish and considered all the modern expressions vulgar.

"Wouldn't have a clue," he answered.

"Reid's coming down tonight. He's driving down in the tilly and he'll be here between eight and nine."

"Reid's coming down? Something gone wrong on Wavering?" He knew perfectly well that nothing had gone wrong on the station, but he could not resist the opportunity of teasing her.

"No, of course nothing's gone wrong. Reid's coming down to see you about an offer for the bullocks, but he's—at least he'd better be mainly coming down to see me."

Striving to impart a convincing intolerance into the words, Ben said, "That's lovely! That's bloody lovely, I must say! Here am I, yarded up in this flamin' hospital, and the useless galah I've left in charge of the place takes the station tilly, fills it up with station petrol, and drives a hundred odd miles to see his blasted little popsy!"

Evidently he was not quite convincing because Jane looked him straight in the eye, kept on looking for fully twenty seconds, and then said:

"Wooff!"

And then they both laughed.

"Bossy," she pleaded after a while. "If he asks you about, well, about me, you'll be nice to him, won't you?"

"Now hold on, young lady." Ben tried to hoist himself up, the better to dominate the situation, but finding the effort too great he contented himself with saying mildly, "If Reid wants to talk to anyone about marrying you it's up to him to see your mother and father. It's nothing to do with me."

"Oh, but it is. It's everything to do with you. You're the one that understands, the one that matters most. Mother doesn't like Reid; she won't let herself like him because he's only an overseer on a cattle station. I don't know what Father's feelings on the subject are, but he's in such a jovial mood after his big win today that he'd probably agree to anything—and then back down in a couple of days when Mother had had time to work him over. But if you say you approve it'll make all the difference. They'll both give in."

"Because I've got the chips?"

"Definitely, Bossy darling. Chips are the things that count with my family."

A nurse came in, put his evening rum on the table beside him, said "Your medicine, Mr McReady," smiled at his visitor, and left.

Jane picked up the glass and sniffed it. "Medicine, huh!" she laughed. "Some medicine, eh, Bossy?" She held it out to him. "Here you are, you old boozer. Down the hatch."

"Not just now, Janie. Leave it on the table. I'll probably drink it later, after you've gone."

"Darling!" She looked at him anxiously, noting for the first time the signs of weariness and strain in his lined face. "You're not feeling worse, are you?"

"Just a bit tired, honey." He fought hard to keep up the pretence to conceal the fact that he was feeling so hellish that even his rum had no appeal for him. "Had a bit of a tiring day."

She bent over, smoothed his white hair, and kissed him gently. "You poor pet. And here have I been pestering you about my affairs and not even noticing how sick you were. I'll run along and let you get some rest now. Is there anything you want?"

"Only a phone call. As soon as you get home ring Bill Amity at his house and ask him to come and see me at nine o'clock on Monday morning."

When Charlie Turner came in half an hour later he was shocked at his friend's appearance. He had expected to be met with a blast of abuse. Instead he got only a listless flicker of recognition. Ben's rum stood alongside his untouched evening meal. He looked drawn and haggard, drained of all his immense vitality.

"Not feelin' the best, Boss?" Charlie asked foolishly. He suffered from a variety of minor ailments himself, but somehow he could never picture Ben as a sick man. "I never got your message until after the last race. Didn't reckon it was any good ringin' the nurse then, so I grabbed a taxi and come straight in."

"What happened out there?" Ben had no energy for conversation. He had lost all interest in the afternoon's events, but Charlie would want to explain.

"In the Maiden? I'm sorry about that, Boss. Fair dinkum; you could've knocked me down with a saddle-cloth when I seen it happen. I did me best, but it looks as if Spargo outsmarted us. Or we outsmarted ourselves. That's racin' for ya. Ya never know until the numbers go up. Spargo got the filly away on the outside and Lee never had a chance to block her."

"It doesn't matter." Ben was panting a little, having trouble with his speech. "Changed me mind anyway."

"Changed your mind, Boss? Ya mean ya wanted her to win?"

Ben nodded. "That's why . . . tried to get hold of you. Never mind. Worked out all right. Tell you about . . . about it next time. Bit crook tonight. Come and see me . . . in day or two. Not tomorrow. Day after, eh?"

"Righto, Boss." Twisting his hat nervously in his hands the little trainer backed away. "Sorry you're not so good. Hope you'll be feelin' better in the mornin'. See ya Monday, eh?"

Ben watched him go and raised a limp hand in farewell. Even that hurt, hurt like hell, as if some one had thrust a bayonet into his chest and twisted it. Twisted it to let the air out and free it, as he had once been taught to do. A long time ago. A hell of a long time ago. Drive it in, twist it, and drag it out ready for the next bloke, the instructor used to say.

Christ, they didn't have to practise on *him,* did they? He wasn't a straw-stuffed dummy. Who the hell was doing it? Doc Stuart and one of the sisters. "Go easy, Doc! Break it down! Once is enough, ain't it? D'you want . . . want to stab a . . . stab a man to death?"

"You'll feel better now, Ben. We're keeping you propped up to relieve the strain. Just relax and take it easy. Too much excitement today. I warned you about that, you old villain. You'll sleep now, and tomorrow I want you to take things very quietly. No arguments with visitors or I'll put a stop to them altogether. Understand?"

"Righto, Doc. You're the boss. But I've gotta . . . gotta see one bloke tomorrow. Gotta straighten out a . . . gotta fix up . . . Blast you and your dope. Tongue . . . won't work. Doped."

Sleep. Hours of peaceful sleep, dreamless sleep, free from pain. And now it was morning, Sunday morning. Breakfast-time, and Sister saying:

"Dr Stuart wants you to take things very quietly today. You're to stay propped up and you can have one or two visitors so long as they don't upset you or tire you by staying too long."

"Yes, Sister." Meekly. Funny how meek and mild they could make you by throwing a scare into you. Not that he was scared of dying. Hell, no! It was just that he had to straighten a few things out first. He *must* find out about young Reid. Make sure he was the right man for Janie and wanted her for herself and not the money she might inherit.

Ten o'clock on Sunday morning and Reid Calder was standing beside him; Reid, tall and slim, with his well-fitting gaberdine pants emphasizing the narrowness of his hips. Without being able to see his feet Ben knew he would be wearing well-polished, tan elastic-side boots. Except when the formality of the occasion demanded a suit Reid always wore those boots. He wore them because he was proud of his trade. proud of being a cattleman, and slightly contemptuous of the less fortunate city dwellers.

Now, above the gaberdine trousers, he wore a white shirt left open at the neck to show a red and black patterned cravat.

Jane thought he was handsome, but that was only the blindness of love. He wasn't handsome. His fair hair was always a little long and untidy, one strand of it usually flopping down over his left eye. His high-bridged nose sat slightly askew, the result of a fall from a horse when he was a boy, before he had learned to land on his feet instead of his face. When he was amused even his grin was askew, a lop-sided sort of grin that twisted his mouth up one side more than the other. His eyes were too blue for the tan of his face and the jaw-line was hard and determined.

Come to think of it, he, Ben McReady, must have looked very like that in his youth. Strange he'd never noticed that before, but then he'd always been more interested in Reid's capabilities than his looks.

And he *was* capable. There was no doubt about that. As well as being a good cattleman he was a natural horseman who rode buckjumpers for the fun of it. He attended every rodeo in the district and put his name down for every event on the programmes—buckjumping, bullock riding, camp-drafting, and any other mounted event that was going. He came from a cattle family. His father owned a property on the Dawson, and young Reid had learned to ride and work cattle before he could read or write. But he wasn't just a raw, ignorant bushwhacker. He had been to one of the best schools in Brisbane, and if it came to the point he could hold his own in any company.

As an overseer Ben had not one single fault to find with him. He got on well with his stockmen and he could not have worked the cattle better or taken more interest in the station if he had owned it.

As a possible husband for Jane he had one big drawback. He had no money and no prospects apart from his wages as station overseer. The best he could hope for was a manager's job, and manager's jobs, except away out in the Never-never, were as scarce as kangaroos in the main street of Stonehaven. He was the youngest of a family of five, and all he could expect when his old man died was a share in the overdraft. No wonder he wanted to marry Jane!

"G'day, Mr Mac." Reid's lop-sided grin flashed on, rather shyly. He was a trifle nervous, not of his boss, but of the unfamiliar hospital surroundings. "Sorry to see they've still got you tied down."

"Drag yourself up a chair, Reid," Ben invited quietly. He was conserving his energy, wasting none of it in gestures or unnecessary words. He watched his visitor pull the chair forward, sit down, and then move the water-bottle to one side of the table to make room for his wide-brimmed felt hat. "What brings you down?"

"The meatworks buyer was on his way through to Shannon's on Friday. He pulled up at the yards just after we'd yarded the bullocks for dipping, and he asked if I'd mind him having a look at them. I told him to go ahead. After he'd had a good look through 'em he asked me what you had on 'em. I told him, and he laughed and asked if we'd been feeding 'em on gold dust. We had a bit of a yabber about it for a while and in the end he said he'd take delivery of 'em next week if you come down five bob a head. I've got to ring the works and give 'em your answer to-morrow."

"What do you reckon?"

"I'd take it, Mr Mac."

"Why?"

"It's a good price and the bullocks aren't going ahead like they should. I don't reckon they've put on anything since we last dipped 'em. I'd say the bullock paddock was going off, especially up the top end. We could do with a drop of rain, and even if we did get rain I'd like to see the bullock paddock spelled for a few months."

Good, sound reasoning, Ben thought. It showed the youngster knew his job and took a real interest in the place.

"Fair enough," he said. "Tell him they're his, and then go ahead and arrange delivery."

For ten minutes or more Reid talked on, giving his employer all the scraps of station news until finally, inevitably, he ran out of scraps and sat staring uncomfortably at his hands.

Ben let him stare for a few moments before saying, "Righto, Reid. What's on your mind?"

"It's about Jane, Mr Mac." Reid took a last look at his hands and faced his boss. "We want to get married."

"So what?"

"Well—er—we'd like your approval."

"Why?"

"Because, well, because you're my boss, and I'd want your permission to bring a wife to Wavering Downs."

"Yes, you'd need that." Having conceded him the point Ben took over the attack. "How much money have you got?"

The question hit home. It brought a flush to the tanned cheeks and a stammering admission from Reid that, with the bit he had in the bank and the wages due to him, he could muster a bit over ninety pounds.

"And you reckon that's enough to get married on?" Ben fairly snapped the question at him.

"I've got my job."

"Yes, you've got your job. How long have you been with me?"

"A bit over four years."

"Four years! And all you've got to show for it is ninety-odd quid, not even enough for a decent honeymoon. If it takes all your wages to support you how the hell do you think you'd support a wife as well?"

"We've talked it over and we're both sure we can manage. I waste a lot of money now, but I'd cut out all that nonsense."

"And what if you lost your job? What if I died and the station went to Janie's parents? D'you think they'd hang on to it just to keep you in a safe job? Not on your bloody life they wouldn't. They'd sell it and you'd find yourself out on your ear."

"There's more than one cattle station in Queensland, Mr McReady. I'd get myself another job."

"What as? A married overseer? Don't kid yourself. There ain't any such jobs unless the wife's prepared to do the station cooking. You're still too young for a manager's job. So what do you do? Park Jane with her parents while you go off to a job as overseer or head stockman to a mob of wild boongs on some station away up in the Territory."

Somewhat heatedly Reid said, "It's not likely to come to that, Mr McReady."

"No. And I'll tell you why you're so cocksure. Because you know I'm soft about Jane. You're counting on that. You've got it all worked out that you can't go wrong by marrying her because I'll look after the pair of you while I'm alive, and when I die I'll leave her enough for both of you to live on."

Reid Calder stood up and picked up his hat.

"So that's the way of it," he said slowly. "You know, I used to have a lot of time for you, used to think you were one of the best. I've even got into a couple of brawls with blokes that called you a hard old bastard. But I can see what they meant now. It sticks out a mile. And you know what you can do with your money and your bloody job too? You can shove 'em. I'll stay on at Wavering Downs until you get another overseer, not on your account, but because I like the place and I'd hate to see it go to the pack. You think I'll be flat out getting another job! That's a laugh. I'll have one lined up before you get your new man, and as soon as I land it I'm gunna marry Jane whether you bloody well like it or not."

He slammed his hat on his head, pulled the broad brim down at an aggressive angle over one defiant eye, and strode out.

★ 24 ★

AND that, Ben thought, was the end of that, the end of his friendship with Reid. Even if he had wanted to call the lad back the effort would have been too great. He was gasping for breath now, gasping painfully. Shouldn't have got excited about it. Should have taken things easier. A man couldn't think clearly with this pain stabbing and stabbing. Reid had gone off hating his guts. A pity. Right stuff in him. No doubt about that. He'd do all right for himself. He and Janie would be happy together wherever they were. They'd have their ups and downs, like all married couples, but in the main they'd be happy because they had the same tastes, the same independent spirits, and they were in love with each other.

Anthea was going to buck like hell. Well, let her buck. Next year Jane would be twenty-one and she could marry without anyone's consent. Wouldn't hurt the youngsters to wait another year. Give Reid time to get on his feet.

Where would Reid be now? On his way to see Janie and tell her the news? Of course, and then *she'd* hate his guts. She'd come in here looking hurt and reproachful and she'd. . . . But she mightn't come at all! Stop thinking about Jane and Reid or any of 'em. Stop worrying. Relax and take it easy. Remember what Doc Stuart said last night.

"It's up to you, Ben. You've had a coronary occlusion and that's a thing you can't fool around with. If you take it easy and don't let yourself get tired or excited you could last for quite a while yet, but keep on acting like the old bull-headed Ben McReady and you're liable to go out like that!" And to illustrate his point Doc had snapped his fingers. "Even a nip of rum could do it. Rum is a stimulant. It could start your heart racing and finish you off as quickly as you could drink the rum."

Yes, he must remember that. No more excitement and no more rum until he'd done what had to be done. After that it didn't matter. Not such a bad way to go out at that. Say

"Here's hoping," swallow the rum, and die with the glass in your hand and the good strong flavour of the rum still in your mouth. There were plenty worse ways to die—when you'd finished all you had to do.

The duty sister came in, felt his pulse and said reprovingly, "You've been getting excited again."

He nodded meekly and when she went off and returned with some vile-tasting medicine he swallowed it without a word of protest.

"There's a youth here wanting to see you," she told him. "He says it's important, but I don't think you're fit to see any more visitors at present."

Still meekly he said, "If it's important we'd better let him in for a minute, eh, Sister? You stay here and chase him off when we've heard what he wants."

The youth she ushered in was a half-caste. His straight black hair was plastered down with brilliantine and the scent of it hung heavily about him. One of the arrogant type in his own element, here, in the presence of Ben and the white-uniformed sister, he was humble enough. Obviously he owned a motor-bike because his black jeans were lavishly ornamented with studs and fancy stitching, and over a red and white check shirt he wore a leather jacket.

"It's me Aunty," he mumbled apologetically. "She's pretty crook. Keeled over outside our place on 'er way down to the bus-stop. Comin' in to see you she was."

"Where is she now?"

"At our place. Mum didn't know what to do on account of it bein' Sundee. She said it's pretty 'ard to get a doctor Sundees, so she arst me to see if you could get 'im to come."

With difficulty Ben suppressed an angry blast. These fools, dithering around and wondering what to do! Me Aunty! Biddy wasn't this lout's Aunt; she may have been some very distant relation, but the whole mob called her "Aunty."

Very quietly he asked, "Have you got a spare room here, Sister?"

"Yes, Mr McReady."

To the youth he said, "Scoot around to the ambulance.

Tell them to bring her straight in here. And get a move on."

"She's Doc Stuart's patient," he explained to the sister. "Do you think you could get him straight away?"

"Yes. He left word that if we wanted him for you we could get him at his home or the bowling club. He'd hardly have gone to bowls yet, so I'll ring the house."

"Thanks, Sister. All her expenses go on my account. And when she comes in do everything you can for her, will you? She's an old abo, but she's one in a million. They don't make 'em like her any more."

Disciplining himself then he dozed off and only awoke when Dr Stuart and the sister looked in.

"How is she, Doc?" he asked.

The doctor held his wrist for a moment or two, studied him thoughtfully, and said, "Pretty low I'm afraid, Ben. It's more or less what we've been expecting."

"Nothing you can do?"

"Nothing except keep her comfortable. I think her relatives should be informed."

"They know, but there's none of 'em close enough to matter. Apart from me there's only one person she'd really want to see before she goes and that's young Jane, my granddaughter. Would you give her a ring, Sister? Ask her to come and see me straight away."

Half an hour passed before Jane arrived. She came in without any of her usual impetuous warmth. Instead she walked sedately to his bedside and said, coldly and impersonally:

"You wanted to see me, grandfather?"

Grandfather! God, she *did* hate his guts. He couldn't remember hearing her call him grandfather in her whole life. Poor little Janie! Poor old Ben, too! It hurt like the very devil to see her standing there looking like a stranger. But there was no time for explanations now.

"Janie," he said gently. "It's Biddy. She's in here and she's very low. I reckoned she'd want to see you before she went."

"Oh, no! Poor darling Biddy." Tears welled into the eyes that a moment ago had been so cold. "Where is she?"

"I don't know, honey. You'll have to ask the sister. And when you've had a look at her I want you to do something for me. You've got the car?"

"Yes."

"Hop in it and get all the flowers you can get hold of. I know it's Sunday, but you'll be able to get some, won't you? Put 'em in her room. She'll know we're thinking of her then even if she can't understand anything else. She and your grandmother always loved flowers."

Dabbing her eyes Jane nodded and went out.

And again Ben dozed. He dozed fitfully until Jane returned and said:

"I got the flowers, masses of them, and put them in her room. It looks like a garden. She can't speak, but she's conscious. She recognized me and she understood what I was saying when I told her the flowers were from you because she sort of smiled with her eyes."

Ben nodded.

"I'm going back to sit with her," Jane said. "Is there any message I can give her?"

"Message? No, I don't—— Wait a minute; just say 'The Boss says he'll follow you up the Jump-up.' She'll understand."

Yes, Biddy would understand. She'd always understood.

Biddy died at three that afternoon. She slipped off quietly and unobtrusively. In that manner she had slipped into his life, into Anne's, and into all their lives. Quietly, unobtrusively, and loyally helping each one when help was most needed, influencing their lives with her gentle goodness. And now she was gone.

"Oh, Bossy, she's gone." Jane's head was down on the sheet beside Ben and she was sobbing with the big, unrestrained sobs of a child. Tears trickled down the wrinkles in Ben's cheeks. He wept, not only because of Biddy's death, but because her influence still remained. Even in her final act, the act of dying, she had reached out and helped him by bringing Jane back to him in spite of what he had done to hurt the child.

"It doesn't seem possible, Bossy," Jane sobbed. "I went

round to see her yesterday morning and she was the same as she always was, ever since I can remember, ever since she taught me to say 'Gunjulla' to the emu."

"Don't take it too hard, honey." Ben's fingers, shaky fingers now, were running through her hair, caressing the dark curls, mussing them up into an untidy tangle that she would presently shake out with that characteristic toss of her head. "It had to come. We've been expecting it for a long time, and she must have gone off peacefully, without any pain."

Words. Empty, comfortless words. You always said them when somone died, even though you knew they did nothing to soften the initial shock. Only time could do that.

Yet he kept on murmuring them and caressing the dark head until Jane stopped sobbing and sat up and shook some of the disorder out of her hair.

The duty sister came in and said, "I think you should go now, Miss Arnedale. Dr Stuart doesn't want your grandfather to get too tired or worked-up." She said it very nicely and added, "I'll be giving him a sedative presently because we want him to have as much sleep as possible."

"Of course, Sister," Jane jumped to her feet and ran a comb through her hair. "I should have thought of that myself." She bent and kissed Ben. "Good-bye, Bossy. I'll come and see you tomorrow."

Alone with her patient the sister smoothed the rumpled bed-clothes and adjusted the pillows.

"Would it upset you too much if I asked you for some particulars of the old lady who just died?" she asked.

"It wouldn't upset me at all, Sister. I wouldn't let it." He grinned at her. "I've reformed."

"I should hope so!" She softened the reproof with an answering smile, and took a small notebook and pencil from her pocket. "Her full name?"

"Biddy—er, I'm blowed if I know, Sister. You'll think I'm not right in the head. She's been with us ever since she was knee-high to a sand goanna, and I'm hanged if I can ever remember hearing her surname. 'Biddy' wasn't even her proper name; we just called her that. But it doesn't matter.

Put down 'Biddy McReady.' She's always been one of the family."

"Next of kin?"

"The only blood relations she's got left are such distant ones that they wouldn't know what the connexion was. Shove me for that. She'd like it."

"Religion?"

"Better make it Church of England, same as my wife."

"Age?"

"Shove down seventy-six. It'll be near enough."

"Funeral arrangements?"

"I pay for everything. I want her buried out at Baranda. When my wife died we had a young parson friend—he's a bishop now—and he bought a family plot. She's to go there, alongside my wife."

"You'll need some one to attend to all the details for you. Who do you suggest?"

"Alf Coudrey, Bishop Coudrey. He'll know what to do. Or my solicitor, Bill Amity. Better let 'em both know, if it's not too much trouble, Sister. Bill Amity's due here at nine tomorrow morning anyway."

"I'll see to all that, Mr McReady." Sister put the notebook and pencil back in her pocket. "I'll give you a sedative now and you must try to sleep. And no more visitors today if you want to be fresh enough to see your solicitor in the morning."

"Righto, Sister. You're the boss. But I'll warn you, you'll have a hell of a job keeping the old Bish' out. Still, I reckon you'll handle him, eh?"

Five minutes to nine on Monday morning and he was *not* feeling fresh. Not after a night of pain, whispering nurses dimly seen in subdued torchlight, drugged sleep, and more pain. And the damnable shortage of breath. The pain came in spasms and when he tried to talk his speech came in spasms because he had to pause and gasp for breath after every few words.

More whispering. "Round the other side, Nurse. Your hand, under here. Now up."

"Struth! Go easy."

"Sshh."

"Sshh, be hanged . . . man can't sleep . . . this way."

"We *must* keep you propped up."

"Righto. Stand on . . . me head . . . if it'll help."

"Sshh! Don't try to talk, Mr McReady. Just relax."

Hell, yes. He was forgetting that. Must relax. Take it easy. Save up until he had squared up with Bill. Should have done it long ago. But that would have been no good. He couldn't see the way then. But now the way was clear.

What a night! Thank the Lord it was over. Things didn't seem so bad once daylight came.

Nine o'clock, and instead of old Bill Amity, his partner, Wilkins, walked in.

No, Ben thought, he didn't walk in, he crept in, because Wilkins was a creepy sort of bloke. He crept around the office, sidling in one door and out the other like a blasted carpet snake, and when you spoke to him his eyes sort of flickered at you and away again. A carpet snake used his tongue that way, but Wilkins kept his tongue tucked inside his prim little mouth and flickered with his eyes. When he answered you he pursed his little mouth up like a rosebud. He didn't drink, he didn't smoke, and he didn't swear. Bill said he was married but had no kids. Of course you *could* say that didn't actually prove anything.

Ben had once asked Bill why he had taken Wilkins into the firm, and Bill had smiled and said, "I'll admit he's not very convincing in the courtroom, but he's a wizard on law."

Turning his head to greet Wilkins now, Ben asked, "Bill crook?"

"No, Mr McReady." The prim little mouth pursed up. "He had to appear in court this morning, so he asked me to come. Didn't Miss Arnedale tell you?"

"No. She had other things on her mind. But it doesn't matter."

No, it didn't matter in the least now. He was no longer in need of Bill's sage advice; he knew what to do and he only wanted some one to put it down on paper and wrap it up legally. Thank heaven the pain had eased until it was quite bearable, and he no longer had to pause and gasp for breath. Why, he'd romp through this interview in a canter.

"Drag yourself up a chair. I want to alter my will, bring it up to date."

"Yes, Mr McReady. We anticipated that. Will it be a very complicated one?"

"It won't be complicated at all. It'll be short and straight-out. I'll tell you what I want and you can get it all set out legally and bring it back here for me to sign. And don't waste too much time over it because there mightn't *be* too much time."

"If I might make a suggestion, Mr McReady; I'll take it down in longhand now, read it back to you, and you can sign the rough draft straight away. I'll then have it properly set out and typed at the office. If anything should—er—happen before we have the typed copy prepared this one would be legally binding."

"That's a brain-wave. Better shove those things off the table and write there." Ben waited until Wilkins was ready and then said slowly, "All the horses I have in training and all the horses set aside for training go to my trainer, Charlie Turner."

"Pardon me, Mr McReady, but does that include the colt you purchased in Sydney recently, for the sum of—er—five thousand guineas?"

"Of course it does."

"That makes it an extremely generous legacy."

"You think so? Let me tell you that if it hadn't been for Charlie I wouldn't have lived to buy that colt. He risked his life for me once. Don't you reckon that's worth a few lousy bloody horses? You just write down what I say and we'll argue the toss about it later if we have to."

Wilkins turned to his writing. He wrote rapidly, without once looking up, but when he finished he pursed his lips and let his eyes flicker from the will to Ben's face and back again.

"Before I read this back to you," he said ponderously, "I feel it my duty to point out that it contains several—er—anomalies." He had been warned that his client was dangerously ill, but now he feared that his mind was afflicted as well. "I mention this in case you wish to make some adjustments or alterations before you sign."

"Go ahead."

"I hope you won't feel annoyed if I display a rather, shall I say, intimate knowledge of your family affairs. One gets to hear these things, you know."

Ben snorted and said, "Oh, for God's sake, get on with it. I don't give a damn what you know about my family affairs."

"Very well." The flicker rested long enough to convey the impression of pained dignity. "You have never been on very friendly terms with your daughter, yet you leave practically the whole of your money to her, unconditionally."

"'To do what she bloody well likes with,' was what I said and that's what I meant. I don't give two hoots what she does with it."

"You make no mention whatever of your son-in-law."

"I never meant to. This will ain't a bookmakers' benefit fund."

"Nor your grandson."

"He'll cadge enough from his mother. No need for me to add to it."

"Now we come to your granddaughter, Jane Arnedale. She has always been your favourite yet you bequeath her a mere fifty pounds! Has she done something to displease you?"

"She's never displeased me in her life."

"Then why——"

"Because I don't believe it's a good thing for a woman to have more money than her husband. The bloke Jane is gunna marry has only got ninety-odd quid, so he'll have a good lead on her."

"The point may be contested."

"You mean Jane might hire some smart lawyer to prove I'm of unsound mind? That's what you're tryin' to do now, ain't it? Find out if I'm off me bloody rocker. Well, you can forget about both ideas. Jane won't contest the will and I'm as sane as you are. Doc Stuart is due along shortly and we'll get him to sign a certificate to prove it if you like."

"Mr McReady! I was only trying——"

"Righto. Skip it. What's your next point?"

"You leave Wavering Downs, complete with stock and everything else on it, to your overseer, Reid Calder. I presume you have a very high regard for this young man, otherwise you would not be treating him so handsomely."

"I have."

"Has he money of his own?"

"Reid? He's never been able to save more than a few quid in his life."

"Then I feel that I should point out that you are leaving him with no working capital whatsoever. He will find himself with a large property and yet be in a position where he is even unable to pay his stockmen the wages due to them when he takes over."

Ben sighed and screwed up his face in pain. This business was taking longer than he had anticipated. It was tiring him, and he couldn't afford to let it tire him—yet.

"When I started on Wavering Downs," he explained patiently, "I was a long way behind where this lad'll kick off. There wasn't a decent fence or yard on the place and I had a wallopin' great overdraft a buck kangaroo couldn't jump over. I had to sell more than half the stock before the bank manager stopped snappin' at me heels like a hungry bloody cattle-dog. Reid won't have to sell half his herd but he'll have to crawl to a bank manager for an overdraft because this year's fat bullocks have been sold. He's probably closing the deal at this minute. That means he'll have to sell a fair few breeders to satisfy the bank. Do him good. Teach him the tough way, the way I learned."

"Thank you, Mr McReady. I see your points, with the exception of Jane Arnedale's legacy. But no doubt your mind is made up."

"It is. And it's sound. Jane's marrying Reid Calder."

"Oh, I see." The rosebud primness of his little mouth made it clear that Wilkins saw but did not altogether approve. "If I might make a suggestion. Your object in leaving the station to young Calder is to ensure the happiness of your grand-daughter. Then why not add some rider to the clause? Something to the effect that if the marriage fails the property will revert to her?"

"Like hell! You may know a lot about law, Wilkins, but you don't know much about the facts of life. Start dishin' out presents with strings attached to 'em and you'll end up comin' a big gutser with the strings tangled around your own legs. With me it's all or nothin'. I'll admit it's a bit of a risk, but the man who never took a risk never got anywhere."

★ 25 ★

NEVER having taken a risk Wilkins failed to see Ben's point. He read the will aloud, and when Ben nodded his approval he said:

"It only remains to get two witnesses and your signature. If you'll excuse me I'll see if I can get two of the staff."

In the hallway he found Bishop Coudrey earnestly explaining to Matron and Dr Stuart that he only wanted to see Ben McReady for two minutes and he most certainly would not tire him.

As Ben had said, the Bishop was a very hard man to keep out.

"Witness his signature?" he said. "Certainly, Mr Wilkins. That is, with Dr Stuart's and Matron's permissions."

Dr Stuart laughed. "You'll get through the pearly gates, Bishop. I'd like to see the gatekeepers try to stop you." He turned to Matron. "Come along Matron. We'll take him in and you can be the second witness."

Painfully Ben scrawled his signature. He watched Matron and Bishop Coudrey add theirs and he closed his eyes. Thank God that was over. He'd made it! He'd lasted the distance, but with nothing up his sleeve. God! This pain coming back! This bloody stabbing pain. And this airless gasping. But it didn't matter now. He was past the post.

From a far-off world voices came floating down.

"Oxygen, Matron. . . ." Deft fingers at his nose, forcing the tube into his nostril. . . . "Yes, morphia please, Matron. . . ." "Thank you, Bishop, if you wouldn't mind. . . ." The faint stab of a needle in his arm. Or was it some one else's arm. . . ? Drifting. Floating. Where was he? Up in a plane with Ken flying it? No, that couldn't be. There was brigalow all around him. Christ, the scrub was thick. . . ! "I've rung the house, Doctor. Mrs Arnedale is out but her daughter is on her way now. . . ." Janie! No, not Janie! Don't let her in here. The kid's had enough, hasn't she? First Biddy and now. . . .

Aaahh! That's better. He knew where he was now, knew where he was going, too. The scrub was opening up to show the white cliffs. He and Biddy were at the foot of the Jump-up. They'd lead their horses up, Biddy taking the lead while he followed. And at the top they'd find Anne, a radiant Anne with Dan standing on one side of her and Ken on the other.

Voices, more voices. Jane's impassioned voice. . . . "Do something, Doctor! Do something! Don't just stand there. Can't you do something? That's what doctors are for, isn't it?" Saying the things he'd wanted to say, but couldn't, years ago. . . . "Everything we can, Jane, dear. . . . Nothing more . . . not in any pain . . . not really conscious."

Wasn't he, be Jesus? He could see Jane, feel her soft curls against his cheek, hear her pleading, "Bossy, Bossy, don't you leave me, too."

"Janie," he whispered. "You and Reid. All fixed. 'Member what . . . what Spargo said? She'll be jake. . . . It's . . . it's in the bag."